The Orange Dragon Bowl

by

Betty P. Notzon

Copyright © 2016 and 2020 by Betty P. Notzon
All Rights Reserved
The Orange Dragon Bowl is a work of fiction. Except for public personae familiar to everyone, all other characters are entirely the author's creation and any resemblance to anyone living now or in the past is entirely coincidental.

To my Mom and Dad

PREFACE

The Orange Dragon Bowl is basically a house that Jack built, with "wings" added on where they seemed needed. The same for "guest quarters," "sleeping porches," "an attic," "a family room," and "extra storage space." But, like any house, the more I wrote the book, the more it seemed like a "home." Not to carry this house analogy too far, the more I wrote the book, the more it seemed like a real story about the trials and tribulations of a young teenager who faces a difficult year. Perhaps I should have used "challenging" and not "difficult" to describe Julie Tyler's year, but that would suggest that Julie is in some kind of contest that she intends to win. Real life, of course, isn't like that. Just surviving a difficult year can be triumphal.

There are many things that I didn't need to make up, but that worked as perfect twists and embellishments to the story. I had a schoolmate who did sew different buttons on her blouse to make it seem that she had more than one blouse. Shopping for a Christmas tree with my dad was waged exactly as Julie and her father went at it. The administration building at Ainsworth Country Day School (Ainsworth for short) is modeled after Deepwood Hall at Bay Path College, now University, and Woodland Hills is a vague approximation of Longmeadow, Massachusetts, where Bay Path is located.

I used my Aunt Betty as the model for Julie's Aunt Babs. Julie's Aunt Babs has the same looks and sense of humor as my aunt, who also died of breast cancer.

The humor that shows up repeatedly in the Tyler family even at the most unexpected times is not made up. The same was true of my family, thanks especially to the two stand-up comedians in my family, my dad and my twin brother Bruce. We may have been poor, but most of the time we were laughing too hard to notice.

Smitty's is modeled after the unparalleled-in-care-and-research University of Texas M. D. Anderson Cancer Center where I was so fortunate to work for twelve years. Leverett Sumner Smith was my great great grandfather. He owned a livery business in Springfield, Massachusetts, in the mid-1800s, and would probably have never imagined a cancer center being named after him, real or imaginary. But, then, the same might be said of M. D. Anderson who was in the cotton trade in Houston. Marilyn with the purse the size of Ohio is named after my sister in law, who would never carry such a large purse. Dr. Drescher is named for my great grandmother on my father's side. Her full name was Otillie Drescher, but I've spared Dr. Drescher the Otillie. Amalie seemed more considerate.

The award for similitude goes to Julie's mother, who is modeled on my mom. My mom, like Mona, had a knack for seeing things in a very clear light and never hesitating to say so. My mom considered herself very plain, like Mona. And, sadly, the story of the trick played on Julie's mother by the neighbor isn't made up. The same was done exactly as I describe it to my mother when she was a very little girl, and it left a deep emotional scar. It was one of the few things mom was never philosophical about. It was *grand* being able to record this account as a kind of payback to the woman who did such a despicable thing to a, yes, plain little girl.

Aside from the use of the above trove of memories, Julie's story is very much her own. It is *not* autobiographical!

B.P.N.

TABLE OF CONTENTS

CHAPTER 1 – The Start of a 100-Hour Day
CHAPTER 2 – Pressure Cooker
CHAPTER 3 – NASCAR Moment
CHAPTER 4 – Orange Dragon Bean Salad
CHAPTER 5 – Broken Tooth, etc.
CHAPTER 6 – Praline Cookie Triumph
CHAPTER 7 – Dance Disaster
CHAPTER 8 – The Real Star of the Show
CHAPTER 9 – Good Samaritans, Chapter 1
CHAPTER 10 – The Lowest Level of Hell
CHAPTER 11 – The Ninetieth Hour
CHAPTER 12 – A Regrettable Revelation
CHAPTER 13 – Bad Beginnings, Worse Endings
CHAPTER 14 – Battle Scars
CHAPTER 15 – The Curtain Closes
CHAPTER 16 – What It Must Feel Like To Be Alexander the Great
CHAPTER 17 – Nutcracker Sunday
CHAPTER 18 – Christmas Tree Saturday
CHAPTER 19 – The Sinking of the Titanic
CHAPTER 20 – An Unwanted Early Christmas Gift
CHAPTER 21 – Pizza Cure
CHAPTER 22 – A Blue Monday
CHAPTER 23 – Hurry Up And Wait
CHAPTER 24 – A Family Secret
CHAPTER 25 – Bad News
CHAPTER 26 – Monsieur Pierre to the Rescue
CHAPTER 27 – Father Desseau to the Rescue
CHAPTER 28 – Double Mastectomy Monday
CHAPTER 29 – Nemesis
CHAPTER 30 – All Things Considered
CHAPTER 31 – Cancer Woes
CHAPTER 32 – A Second Summons to Dr. Drescher's Office
CHAPTER 33 – Now What?!
CHAPTER 34 – A Wronged Man

CHAPTER 35 – Another Shattered Orange Dragon Bowl of Sorts
CHAPTER 36 – A Snowy Haven
CHAPTER 37 – Facing the Music
CHAPTER 38 – The Honest Truth
CHAPTER 39 – Another Scare
CHAPTER 40 – Good Samaritans, Chapter 2
CHAPTER 41 – Great Day in the Morning
CHAPTER 42 – More Cancer Fallout
CHAPTER 43 – Algebra Again . . .
CHAPTER 44 – Birthday Day
CHAPTER 45 – Good Samaritans, Chapter 3
CHAPTER 46 – Glacier National Park, finally
CHAPTER 47 – Enter Richard the Lionheart
CHAPTER 48 – Another Great Day to be Alive
CHAPTER 49 – Climb Every Mountain
CHAPTER 50 – Condolences and Consolations
CHAPTER 51 – The Second Annual Mother–Daughter Dinner

CHAPTER 1

The Start of a 100-Hour Day

Julie's eyes cracked open to splinters of sunlight stabbing through the branches of the tree outside her window. Birdsong wormed its way into her ears. Sunshine? Bird song?! What happened to the blizzard, hurricane, freezing rain, *any* catastrophic event (meteor shower, volcanic eruption, invasion of the body snatchers, anything including PG only) that was supposed to paralyze the city that day, force the cancelation of every social event that night? Clearly her ardent wishes had been callously ignored. The only dark cloud presaging bad weather that morning was the one inside her.

"Ohhhhhhh . . ." she groaned as she rolled over onto her side and clamped the pillow over her head, thereby hoping to suffocate herself by mistake, thus not, strictly speaking, committing suicide, which the Catholic church firmly frowned upon. The ridiculous thing was that it was such a stupid, *silly* thing to be in a stew about. *Really*. But it was beyond her 15-year-old mental prowess to put a stop to it.

"Julie, are you okay?" her mother called anxiously from just outside her door.

"I'm fine, Mom!" Julie called back, cracking the pillow just enough to make sure a healthy, hearty reply reached her mother's concerned ears. Good. Her inner Meryl Streep had come to the fore. Her voice carried not a hint of the angst (that interior dark cloud feeling) that was weighing heavily on her that morning. Since she'd turned fifteen, "angst" (German for 'increased anxiety, dread') was proving to be a very handy word, one she'd learned from reading a John Grisham book, of all things.

Today's angst had to do with the first ever mother–daughter dinner to be held at school that night. Some of the mothers had come up with the nifty (not!) idea as a way to raise money for scholarships to Ainsworth Country Day School, Ainsworth for short. Julie had no problem with that. With her mother a homemaker and her father an assistant D.A., the $10,000 a year for tuition was a lot for *her* parents. No, being a Bolshevik at heart, she believed no girl should be barred from getting the excellent education offered by Ainsworth for reasons of money alone.

Forgetting her plan to mistakenly suffocate herself, she threw back her pillow, rolled onto her back, and stared at the ceiling (the cool air with its healthy oxygen level felt good), and for, like, the *zillionth* time in the past two weeks, she thought about what had her in such a tizzy that morning. In a word, her mother. In three, her plain, unfashionable mother. So *many* of the daughters had *very* attractive, *very* (make that *très*) fashionable mothers. Hers was neither.

For example, there was Alexis Cowper, who looked like Princess Grace the younger, and *her* mother, who looked like Princess Grace the older. Then there was Angelina Baker with her long sleek black hair and peaches-and-cream complexion, who could be heard almost every Monday morning telling the Alexis crowd about the blue ribbons she and her mother had won at dressage competitions that weekend, all the while tossing her glorious glossy head of hair about like a horse's mane. Make that its tail, a place anatomically closer to the horse's hind quarters. Yes, that was the better place for Angelina given her snotty disdain of anyone who wasn't at least half Anglo-Saxon with preferably some relation who still lived in a castle in England. And then not the least of the mother–daughter duos was Dawn Dawson and her mother.

Dawn was the star (make that supernova) performer at any event that involved a stage and an audience. She could sing. She could dance—ballet, tap, modern, the troika—you name it. She could do it. She could also act. "She's born to the stage,"

Julie'd overheard Mr. Flouncy (that couldn't be his real name), the drama teacher, say once. And hadn't she cut her lovely long auburn hair short when she'd played the lead character, Nellie Forbush, in *South Pacific?* Short hair was, I mean, *much* more practical than long hair, she pointed out to, like, *everyone*, when one was "washing that man right out of my hair." She was a walking, talking talent show, and why shouldn't she be? She was, after all, the daughter of Billie Barr, an ex–Broadway star who'd given up her stage career to marry a very wealthy plastic surgeon and bear future generations of Broadway stars, all with perfect noses.

Then there were the fashions these *très* attractive women sported! Alexis's mother was pure Gucci. Angelina's was dyed-in-the-wool Savile Row, London. And Dawn's was OTT haute couture. (Julie knew because there was almost always a photo of the trendy threesome in the Ainsworth Social Committee section of the *Ainsworth Voice*, in which they were *always* wearing a *très* fashionable *ensemble*, pronounced *ahn-sahm-bleh,* the *bleh* breathed more than spoken.)

Then there was *her* mother, a plain Jane if there ever was one. Even her name was plain—Mona. But, no! She wasn't so callous as to think such a thought without feeling like a total crumb. In fact, when such thoughts about her mother drifted unbidden into her head, she always felt a well-deserved self-inflicted stab to her chest. Now, this morning of the day of the mother-daughter dinner, with this war of selfish concerns versus self-loathing raging inside her, she felt suddenly overwhelmed, sweaty, nauseated, faint—her fight-or-flight response totally disabled.

She groaned, rolled over onto her side, and crammed the pillow over her head again. (Just how long did it take to suffocate one's self?!) Her thoughts then crazily traced the same route they'd taken like a hundred maybe even a thousand times over the past couple weeks. First there was the fact that her mother was happily and unashamedly plain. Her light brown, corkscrew hair she always wore short in a blunt cut, held back with a very worn tortoise shell headband—so worn that it had a strange opaque, milky look to it. Beyond the tight grip of the headband, her hair bushed out in a mad corona of curls. As to her facial features, her eyes were small and brown. Her lips, not very visible when shut. Her nose small, but straight. Cheekbones, none. Chin? She definitely had one. It had become particularly evident when she turned 13, when she and her mother didn't always see eye to eye re: what a young teenage girl could and could not do. Otherwise, it was an okay chin. No mole on it with black hairs sprouting out of it, for example.

Her mother's figure? It was hard to tell. During the week her standard outfit was a denim jumper, under which she wore a variety of tops. In summer it doubled as a sundress. Only on Sundays and other special occasions did her mother dress up, always in the same simple peacock blue, crepe skimmer dress that buttoned down the front. Oh yes, on Sundays and special days she also doffed her navy blue espadrilles and wore low-heeled black pumps. As for makeup, she only wore lipstick, and only that on the same days she wore her black pumps. Jewelry? Besides her wedding band she only ever wore her watch and small pearl earrings, though on *very* special occasions she would don a strand of pearls. And, as already noted, even her mother's name was plain.

It wasn't that her mother didn't like clothes. It was just that they puzzled her . . . . It had something to do, Julie was sure, with the fact that she'd quit college when her mother was killed in a car crash and she came home to be a mother to her three younger siblings, two boys and one girl, the oldest only fourteen at the time. Then, her father, who was a fireman, died at a fire a year later, which made her the lone parent and provider. She'd gone to work as a secretary/legal assistant for the DA's office. That was where she'd met Julie's father, Robert Tyler, one of the assistant DAs. She'd worked for him, and according to him, had a natural legal brain. She could see through every argument, comb through mountains of court proceedings and find the right precedent to prosecute a case, and often convinced him, heatedly, when he was going at a prosecution the wrong way.

The story went that he'd finally fallen in love with her over a matter of buttons. Like many men, he didn't take much note of women's clothes. But, over the course of several months, he'd begun to realize that her mother seemed to always wear the same skirt and blouse to work. But what threw him off was that the buttons seemed to change from day-to-day, or maybe it was from week-to-week.

Anyway, one day, he asked her, in his usual blunt prosecutorial way, "Miss Burch, is your blouse always the same and the buttons change? Or is it the same kind of blouse with different buttons?"

Laughingly, she told him it was the former. She had only the one blouse, and when she got tired of one set of buttons, she sewed on different ones. She then proudly announced that she had four sets of buttons, including some rhinestone ones she wore on dressy occasions.

That last admission had been a challenge to her father to "ascertain whether she was perjuring herself with regard to the alleged rhinestone buttons." So he asked her out to dinner at a nice restaurant. She'd taken him up on the challenge, and she'd proved herself right. She did have rhinestone buttons! She also proved to be a delightful conversationalist, have a sharp wit, and have very definite ideas about just about everything, and willing to talk about her ideas (duke it out even) until the cows came home, though in their case that night it was until the restaurant closed.

And, *then* he'd discovered that she was a wonderful cook *and* a wonderful mother to her orphaned brothers and sister, all of whom were growing up "to be model citizens," his words. Until then, her mother hadn't talked much about her circumstances at home, i.e., the heavy load of responsibility and care she was carrying there. The combination of her humor, intelligence, selflessness, and cooking skills tumbled him, head over heels, in love with her.

Soon, not only did he become a regular guest at the Burch family table (he was batching it in those days), but he also "asked" if he might become a regular member of the family (i.e., by her marrying him). The family had a meeting, with her father present to defend himself, decided he'd pass muster as a *pro tem* dad, and he and her mother married. Julie was born soon after they married, and then that was it. Despite *trying* (Why did her mother always have to say that?), she never got pregnant again. Julie was all they got for children. But then, if you thought about it, her mother had pretty much discharged her parenting obligations by bringing up her three siblings, the last of whom went off to college when she, Julie, was only a toddler. (The two brothers were priests, one at the Vatican, the other somewhere in the Sudan—a very dangerous posting, but then the brother who was at the Vatican claimed that the Curia, the behind-the-scenes crew who ran the show in Rome, could be as dangerous as any enemy Sudani tribesman. Her Aunt Louise, her mother's younger sister, lived with her family in San Diego. She was a half-time homemaker married to a marine biologist and worked half-time as a laboratory assistant at the Scripps Institute.) So Julie had only vague recollections of being anything other than an only child. But she wasn't spoiled! Not with the father and mother she had! No way.

Anyway, the years when most girls are preoccupied with fashions and looks, her mother spent being a mother and provider. That part of her brain never got activated.

Julie veered sharply away from her mother. She loved clothes, jewelry, perfume, makeup—the works! Unfortunately, right now, she had to wear a uniform to school, thereby thwarting her fashionista leanings. Because of the rampant teen sex, and other non-academically conducive conditions, at the local public, Julie always mentally made that "pubic," high school, her parents were sending her to Ainsworth.

IN HER DEFENSE, until the day when she'd sat reading the flyer the teacher had passed out announcing the mother-daughter dinner, she'd never really given her mother's looks all that much thought. Really. As far as *her* own looks went, true, she was always inwardly pleased when people would remark on her close resemblance to her Aunt Babs, her father's sister, with her head of soft, dark-brown curls, her rosebud lips, her large gray eyes, and her adorable figure. But *that* thought and concerns about her mother's looks had *never* been thought in conjunction with each other!

BUT, when her large gray eyes snagged on the words "mother-daughter dinner" at the top of the announcement that had been passed out at the end of school two weeks ago, it was like a window shade snapped up in her brain that jarred loose a surprising landslide of panic about her mother and the impression she might make on the other girls at school, and their mothers.

Yes, yes, yes. It was stupid to give a darn about things like social status and money and looks. But tell that to her stupid, addled adolescent brain that had a "mind," ha, ha, of its own. Also of concern, and this was *something* to her credit, she didn't want her mother to be an outcast in the crowd of high-style, affluent women she expected would be at the dinner.

When she'd handed her mother the announcement about the dinner, she expected (hoped!) that her mother would be lukewarm about going. She'd avoided, so far, all the mothers' teas, luncheons, and other get-togethers, but those hadn't been big fundraisers. Julie was surprised, also dismayed, by her mother's enthusiasm for the dinner. She thought it a "wonderful" idea, sounding just like Grace Kelly in *High Society* when she said the word. What a perfect way to raise money for the school's scholarship fund! How "wonderful" it would be for the mothers and daughters to be gathered all in one place!

"I think I'll make my praline cookies—*if* I can find the recipe," she ended by saying, before sailing down the hallway to the kitchen, the announcement held aloft like a small sail, leaving Julie standing and feeling *very* alone in the dark hallway trying to figure out what had just happened and why she was suddenly feeling so alone in the world.

Her mother's praline cookies were at least one ray of sunshine. (It was also fortunate that their name fell into the *r*-to-*z* group of mothers–daughters who were supposed to bring a dessert.) Her mother's praline cookies were the hit of every Tyler family gathering. Even her dour Uncle John, your basic taciturn priest, the one at the Vatican, had once called them manna from heaven. Yes, there was some consolation in the fact that her mother wouldn't bring shame on her in the dessert department.

"Julie, get up!" her mother shouted from the bottom of the stairs. "Why are you being such a slugabed this morning? You're going to make all the girls in the carpool late!"

"I'm getting up, Mom!" Julie shouted.

Satisfied by the bony thumps of Julie's heels on the floor above her head, her mother went back to the kitchen. Not for the first time did Julie think that her mother hadn't needed a college degree. She'd gotten an advanced, or maybe it was honorary, degree in mothering by the time she was born.

CHAPTER 2

Pressure Cooker

There were two words that best sized up the day that followed—*pressure* and *cooker*. It was a no-brainer. Every St. Patrick's Day, her mother would haul out the old pressure cooker that had been *her* mother's and make corned beef and cabbage. When the meal was done, *done*, DONE, the valve on the top of the lid would be screaming like a veritable banshee, begorrah!

Julie was able to pay adequate attention in class, take notes, answer correctly all questions put to her, from naming Pericles as the leader of Athens during the Peloponnesian War to correctly naming all the steps in the Krebs cycle. But, while this didactic stuff was going on, there was a steady scream of steam issuing from the valve on the top of her pressure-cooker head that couldn't be ignored. In that regard it bore a striking resemblance to a mosquito that used one's face for take-off and landing practice when one was trying to get to sleep at night.

The wonderful butter-and–brown sugar aroma of the freshly baked praline cookies that greeted her just inside the door when she got home from school was something of a balm to her spirit, but it only temporarily silenced the "scream."

"I'm up here, honey!" her mother called from upstairs, putting on the-same-tired-blue-skimmer-dress-she'd-been-wearing-for-special-occasions-for-the-past-five-years, Julie thought glumly as she mounted the stairs one-word-per-step, wondering if the ache in her side presaged appendicitis, which would be an excellent excuse not to go to the dinner.

But the ache ceased the moment she espied the person emerging from her parents' bedroom. Who *was* this dazzling woman coming out of her parents' bedroom? Betty Davis?

Joan Fontaine? Vanna White? The woman sounded just like her mother. But the beauteous, smashing, chic stranger she beheld when she got to the second floor? The one who was saying that someone named Babs had taken her shopping for a new dress that day? Babs! It could only be her Aunt Babs, or was it her fairy god mother Babs? Was that a gilt pumpkin-shaped carriage she heard creakily pulling up in front of the house, come to fetch her mother to the ball? No, it was just Tilda Stein, their next-door neighbor, wheeling the recycling bin up her driveway. But, still, a kind of magical spell had been cast, and Julie was feeling appropriately bedazzled.

"Julie, goodness, what's gotten into you? You look like you've seen a ghost, Honey! Are you okay?" the woman with her mother's voice was saying, hugging her, enveloping her in a delicate cloud of *L'air du Temps,* trying to "bring her to . . . ."

Finally managing to haul her bottom lip up from where it dangled over her chest, Julie was able to mouth in a wondrous voice: "Mom, you look FAB-U-LOUS!" She sliced the syllables in three, exactly like Billy Crystal did.

Yes - *she* - *did*, as Cary Grant would have added. Specifically: her mother was attired in a silver gray knit dress with a silver serpentine belt. Around her neck was a heavy silk scarf in shades of gray and green and teal. She wore the usual pearl earrings and the same black pumps. She also had a little eye makeup on, besides her usual lipstick. It was amazing what a little mascara and eye shadow could do! And then there was her mother's hair! *Gone* were the bushy corkscrew curls, replaced with soft, shiny , *insouciant* curls. And gone was the headband that yanked her hair back like a sumo wrestler's. Instead the soft bouncy curls were caught up saucily on either side and held in place with shiny new tortoiseshell combs wrapped with golden wires.

"Your aunt has been pestering me for years to do something different with my hair. Goodness, I never thought this thing called a styling paddle could do anything with my awful hair," Julie's mother was now saying, as Julie's eyes and mouth vied with each other for the largest circumference.

"So, what's your *final*, final take?" her mother said, sashaying around the second-floor landing, finishing with a perfect Paris model pirouette in front of Julie.

"Mom, you look beautiful . . . ." There was just no other word for it.

Then an awful thought struck her. *Might* her mother have guessed the selfish, stupid, silly concerns about her plain looks she'd been having for the past two weeks? Had she talked in her sleep? Doodled something on the message pad by the phone while talking to a friend? Spent too much time poring over the magic-makeover sections in fashion magazines? Was her praise now a little OTT?

"Can I borrow the scarf, Mom?" she asked. It *was* a gorgeous scarf, and she would *love* to wear it. But it wasn't the scarf she wanted. She wanted to sidetrack any suspicions her mother might be having about her daughter's a little-too-enthusiastic take on the success of her Aunt Babs' handiwork.

"No!" her mother practically shouted. "The scarf isn't mine. Your aunt only lent it to me. She wants it back. Now, Julie, you need to get dressed yourself or we're going to be more than fashionably late to the dinner."

Her mother was right. She did a quick about-face into her bedroom and five minutes (tops!) later emerged attired in her green velveteen, long-sleeved, V-neck dress that stopped three inches above her knee. For shoes she wore soft black leather boots with chunky three-inch heels she'd gotten for Christmas the previous year and, on her legs, black textured opaque stockings.

As she clattered down the stairs, trying to convince herself that she and Sarah Jessica Parker were a match when it came to running in shoes with stilts for heels, as her father observed every time she wore them, she made the wondrous discovery that the dread that she'd been lugging around for the past two weeks was totally gone. Alexis Cowper's mother might look like Princess Grace but hers now looked like Jackie Kennedy!

She could hear her mother rushing around the kitchen, and when she went to see why, she discovered that her mother had as yet to stack the praline cookies onto a cake plate. This should have been done already, but per her mother as she was rushing about, the miracle makeover had made her late getting started on the cookies, which took a lot of time because there were so many steps in their making.

First one had to bake the cookies and let them cool. Then one made the praline topping, which had to be carefully ladled over a small mound of pecan pieces carefully arranged atop each cookie. Then one had to wait until the praline topping cooled and hardened, which it just now was. Then one had to arrange the oh-so-delicate and temperamental cookies very carefully on the plate so as not to disturb the scrumptious praline topping. Even with the two of them it took forever before they found a safe perch for the final cookie. Then they had to fasten long spans of sandwich wrap over the veritable mountain of cookies (her mother always made a double batch) to protect them during the jolting stop-and-go trip to the school. Both Julie's and her mother's hands were shaking by the time they were done. One just couldn't hurry praline cookies.

It was 6:15 when they were finally ready to leave. The standup reception began at 6:30. There would be wine for the mothers, non-inebriating punch for the daughters. (The wine dispensing was to be closely overseen by the physical education teacher, a woman with a passion for tai chi and weight-lifting. Drats.) The dinner proper began at 7:15. *However*, the school was on the other side of town. They had to make their way through an infinitude of fiendish commuter traffic. And then there was her mother's driving. To say that she drove like an elderly snail was *not* an exaggeration. Her mother had actually, once, gotten a traffic ticket for *going too slow* on the freeway. (Her mother's death in a car accident had made Mrs. Tyler phobic about highways and speed.) Now her mother didn't do highways, only city streets.

And then, just as they were maneuvering themselves, and

the cake plate with its praline cookie massif, out the door, Julie's father arrived home from work. Upon beholding his wife's smashing looks, he went down on one knee and passionately proposed marriage to her, to which her mother replied: "You're already married, Bob Tyler. Just be glad your wife is an understanding woman." It *was* funny, and they all laughed uproariously, but that was more time lost.

CHAPTER 3

NASCAR Moment

Maybe it was the swanky dress and the new hairdo, but to Julie's astonishment, her mother began driving more aggressively than usual, as in she became one with the pack of road hogs, maniacs, cretins, morons, and people on steroids making driving a contact sport that night. She blithely cut in and out of lanes, tailgated cars that had the temerity to get in front of her, went through yellow lights that were really more red than yellow (summer sunset would be about the right name for the color), and even honked at a car that didn't move for two seconds after a light turned green.

Sooner than Julie could have imagined possible, they were in the very affluent part of town where her school was. This part of town was distinguished by the posh name Woodland Hills. There were now no traffic jams and stoplights to hold them up; those were for lesser mortals who needed to be treated like herds of cattle. Now there was just the occasional dignified stop sign to genteelly remind them that they were still on public roads. And since there were large, lavish stretches of wooded land between the houses, well, mansions really, that nestled into the elegant sloping terrain of Woodland Hills, the roads were artfully curvy and relatively clear of traffic. As the road swept majestically before them, and the clock on the dashboard crept steadily toward 7 o'clock, her mother began to gun it on every clear stretch.

The tires squealed breathily around curves. Every stop at every stop sign was a polite nod, like ballerinas do when they acknowledge applause. Then another curious sound was layered onto the squealing of the tires, a funny high-pitched whine, a mosquito-like sound. But as the sound came closer, it morphed into a very clear law enforcement sound. Her mother seemed not to notice it, just continued merrily, blithely, on her way, seeming to enjoy how the various curves and pauses at stop signs "played" with her new-found curls. And, then, from out of the dark night, there suddenly tore up from behind them a monster as if from hell raking them all over with enraged flashing lights. And, then, came a *voice*. It was the same voice, Julie was sure, as the one that barked at Charlton Heston, playing Moses, to take off his sandals on the top of Mount Sinai since he was treading on holy ground.

"I want the person in the gray Volvo to pull over to the side of the road, come to a complete stop, and turn off the engine."

Julie's mother looked over at her, her face contorting itself into all the various expressions of surprise and shock. 'Who me?' it seemed to say.

"Mom, I think he means you," Julie said, trying to break the news to her mother as gently as she could.

"Oh no, oh my gosh, oh dear Lord, oh my word," her mother squealed frantically as she wrenched the steering wheel hard to the right, then to the left, then to the right. Only now did Julie appreciate what it must have been like for the helpless little plastic people in her toy car as she'd driven it crazily up and over every piece of furniture, ending with an off-road maneuver up and over the rump and then down the snout of their old dog Patches, who just wanted to snooze until he died.

Her mother finally managed to bring the car over to the side of the road, put the car in park, and turn off the engine, per Officer God's instructions. Then she peered panic-stricken into the rearview mirror. Was she now supposed to take off her shoes and hide behind a rock so as to see only God's back? A lot was at stake here. And, just like God, when it came to omniscience, this policeman had it in spades. He now called over the loud speaker that he wanted Julie and her mother to get out of the car and stand facing the vehicle, pronounced ve-hick-al, with their hands placed on the roof. They were to "remain in that position until I approach the vehicle and am able to make an ascertainment of the situation."

Julie was a little confused. What were they supposed to do? If she raised her hand, would he mind repeating the instructions? She didn't think he'd said anything about taking off their shoes lest they tread on holy ground, but should she just to be on the safe side?

This got her, of all the most stupid, imbecilic things she could pick to do right then, *laughing—uncontrollably*. She couldn't help it. Worse, it was laughter that spilled out of her, made it almost impossible to breathe, to say nothing of get out of the car, place her hands on the roof, and keep them there until the policeman could "ascertain the situation."

Her mother, meanwhile, had also gotten herself standing with her hands on the roof of the car, her dressy purse dangling at a frantic angle from her wrist. First, she glared at her daughter, who seemed suddenly to be bereft of all reason, worse, had abandoned her in a moment of great need, then she looked over meekly at the huge bulky form of the policemen as it approached the car.

Outlined by the bright flashing headlights of the squad car, it was the trademark policeman shape as it sauntered toward them. Officer God's cop form stopped next to her mother, who was now looking up at him with a frightened-small-animal look. Once at their car, the policeman sidled around until he stood with his feet apart facing her mother, the gravel growling under his heavy boots, his shoulders and head thrust back, his hands on the bulky belt that had to, Julie realized, include a loaded pistol. That got her attention. *That* throttled the last of her addled laughter.

In an appropriately stony voice, the policeman barked "I clocked your speed at 45 in a 30 mile per hour zone, and the last three of your stops were rolling stops. Name?" he asked, not missing a beat.

"Mona—Mona Tyler," her mother responded in a small,

contrite voice.

The policeman made a robot-like nod, as he seemingly carved her mother's name on the top ticket of a pad of tickets he had drawn deftly from the back of his belt like Gary Cooper pulling his Colt 45 from his holster in *High Noon*.

"Address?" the policeman barked next.

Her mother answered in the same small, contrite voice.

Once the officer had etched that information on the ticket, he grabbed a flashlight from his belt. In the same motion, he clicked it on, shone it on Julie's mother's stricken face and then on Julie's tear-stained face.

He made a small grunt and then deftly shone the flashlight into the front of the car. He scoured the seats, the dashboard, the console, and the floor with the light.

He made a louder grunt, as though he were surprised, and maybe a little disappointed, not to find a Zip-lock bag bulging with cocaine crammed into the cup-holder.

With another deft movement, he shone the light into the back of the car, including the rear compartment. The light roamed insensitively over the spare tire and an assemblage of summer-related objects that would probably stay there until Christmas, when they'd have to make room for the Christmas tree.

He finished his inspection of the car interior by shining the flashlight first on the backseat and then on the floor. He brought the light to a sudden halt when it fell on the plate of praline cookies covered with plastic wrap. The floor of the rear seat had seemed the best place to put it. Also a perfect place to hide a mountain of marijuana-laced cookies.

"What is that?" the policeman asked, scribbling the light over the cookies "concealed" in the back.

"Cookies," her mother answered simply.

"What *kind* of cookies?" he demanded with appropriate-to-the-occasion, professional-law-enforcement annoyance in his voice.

'Oh no—,' thought Julie, 'he thinks we've got Alice B. Toklas cookies.'

"Praline cookies" her mother replied. "Would you like to take a couple to have during your supper break?" she asked in her best hostess voice.

Julie put her head down and *willed* herself not to shriek with laughter.

"No thanks," the policeman said gruffly and shifted uncomfortably as he stood in place. He was clearly more at home with hardened criminals than with the likes of Mrs. Tyler.

"To whom is the car registered?" the man now barked in a gruff voice that would restore the proper law enforcement tone to the setting.

"Tweedledum," her mother answered simply, directly, honestly.

Julie wanted to disappear, dissolve into laughter, die! Tweedledum was her mother's affectionate nickname for her father. His for her was Tweedledee. It had to do with some costumes they'd worn to a party when she was too young to remember, for which she should probably be grateful. But she needed to get serious, her mother was clearly losing her composure and her silliness probably wasn't helping.

The officer, too, seemed to be losing his composure. Worse, he seemed to have been thrown totally for a loop. There'd been nothing in any of his officers' training or policemen retreats and encounter groups to prepare him for such an eventuality.

"Tweedledum is your husband's name?" he asked in an incredulous, almost human, voice.

"Oh, dear, no—" her mother laughed to cover up her silly goof. "That's my nickname for him. I'm so flustered my brain isn't functioning. His name is Bob, I mean Robert, Robert Tyler," she said.

Back to his humanoid self, the man jotted Mr. Tyler's name down on the ticket.

"Is he the Bob Tyler who's the assistant DA?" the policeman asked, looking up mid-chisel stroke.

"Why, yes, he's my husband," her mother answered.

"Best man in the DA's office," he barked. "He gets convictions that stick on the first go. Makes our jobs a lot easier because we don't have to keep rounding up crooks for the same crimes, or worse." At this he paused and thought for a moment. "I'll tell you what, given you're Bob Tyler's wife, we'll forget this ticket." True to his word, he tore the ticket off the pad and tore it up. "Tell your husband this ticket is on me. *But*," he said firmly, back into his tough policeman persona, "No more speeding. And when you see one of those funny little red octagonal signs with the letters S-T-O-P on it, I want you to put your right foot on the little pedal to the left of the gas pedal, and push down *very* hard on it. That will make the car stop. Will you do that for me?" he said in his best Mr. Rogers' voice.

"Oh, yes, officer. I certainly will," her mother answered dutifully.

"Tell your husband that Bill Ward said hello. And," here he paused and said very softly, very sweetly, "I'm sorry I made your daughter cry."

CHAPTER 4

Orange Dragon Bean Salad

Back in the car and on their way to Julie's school, Julie and her mother lapsed into silence. Julie didn't know what was going on in her mother's brain, but *she* was busy basking in thoughts of Officer Ward's praise for her father and also in his tender (fatherly? – he might be someone's father.) words of apology for being the cause of her tears. True, her tears weren't from crying but from laughing, which *could* have been funny. But, right then, she just wanted to privately savor his kind words until they'd lost their warmth.

After that, Julie's mother diligently did everything Officer Ward/God/Mr. Rogers had told her to do, and when they got to the school and parked the car, made it across the parking lot with the awkward plate of cookies, made it through the double doors into the school, and down the hall toward the dining room where the mother–daughter dinner was clearly already in full swing.

To Julie's utter amazement, the dining room had been transformed from its usual din of high-pitched, high-spirited, hyena-like young female voices to a place of hushed, sane, civil voices having calm, pleasant, polite conversations. Likewise, the room had been transformed from a place of harsh fluorescent light that only encouraged hysteria to a serene place lit mainly by candlelight. The tables had been covered with heavy white damask tablecloths, and each had a glass vase full of roses of varying colors and kinds—obviously the last roses of summer harvested from someone's rose garden.

The soft velvet-like darkness and the gentle sheen of candlelight on all the female faces made Julie feel as though she were entering a special realm—a place apart from the hectic pandemonium of the world. A temporary haven from terrorist bombs, bloody coups, earthquakes, global warming, volcanic eruptions, moon-sized meteors headed directly for Earth, pandemics (Ebola, SARS, Black Death, obesity, etc.), and all the other megadisasters that threatened to destroy life any day now.

Not surprisingly, everyone was well into eating their dinner. They rushed over to the long table against the wall where the food was arrayed. A kitchen employee helped them find a place for the plate of cookies at the end of the long table where other desserts had been set.

A quick scan of the other desserts told Julie that her mother's praline cookies had some tough competition, including some delectable-looking lemon bars and what looked like chocolate-peanut butter brownies. She wasn't worried, though. No one could beat her mother's praline cookies in either the delectable-looking or -eating competition.

Before getting any food, they decided to find places to sit. But the combination of the dimly lighted room and the animation of all its occupants blurred details. It was impossible, without infrared goggles, to spot two places together at any table no matter how much they craned their necks.

"Here, let me help you find a place to sit," the same lunchroom employee who'd helped them find a place for the cookies had come over and was now guiding each of them with a hand on the small of their backs.

She led them to a table in the center of the room. "There—right there," she said in a loud whisper, and pointed to two places at a table. Julie and her mother quickly went over, put their dressy purses on the two vacant chairs, and then went to get their food. Julie saw that the person to her immediate left was Jane Webb, one of her oldest friends at school. Jane and Julie exchanged enthusiastic greetings just before she and her mother went back to the food table.

They discovered when they got there, much to their dismay, that most of the obviously more popular dishes were cleaned of their contents and what remained was not very choice.

Starting with the salads, among the empty and almost empty bowls, there was only one with enough salad to make a helping for each of them. It was a bean salad—black beans, red beans, lima beans, chickpeas, and maybe a speckle of chopped chive, all glistening with a coating of, what looked like, Italian dressing straight out of a bottle. It didn't surprise Julie that people wouldn't be too taken with a bean salad. The reason could be summed up in two words "unappetizing" and "flatulent." They each helped themselves to a small spoonful of the salad.

"Oh my word," her mother gasped as she took her helping of the salad, "that bowl has got to be worth at least a thousand dollars. It's the Orange Dragon pattern made by Shreveport—one of the most expensive chinas, and one of the most expensive Shreveport patterns."

Her mother should know. Hadn't she worked every summer in high school in the fine china department at Ashcroft's, the store where every bride worth her salt registered?

"Who would bring such a valuable bowl to such a gathering," her mother wondered aloud. Clothes her mother could skip, but china was a different story. She loved it. There wasn't a movie with a dinner scene in it that her mother didn't have her nose pressed against the screen trying to identify the china pattern.

Julie couldn't for the life of her comprehend why anyone would spend a thousand dollars on such a bowl. She thought it was a pretty ugly pattern and had visions of being at some very formal dinner and shrieking when the head of a gilt orange dragon suddenly emerged between the peas and mashed potatoes.

They finished selecting their food and hurried back to their places. Julie and Jane introduced their mothers to each other. Then Julie's mother turned to the woman on her right, held out her hand, and said brightly: "Hello, my name is Mona Tyler—Julie Tyler's mother."

This was followed by—silence, a stony, impenetrable, inexplicable silence. What Julie saw wasn't so much a face as a facial expression, one that sent a chill down her spine. It was a terrifying ancient Greek drama mask—the Medusa one with her writhing snake hair. That wasn't her being funny. It was the best description of the "face" she could come up with.

Julie felt her heart and throat constrict. How could anyone so dislike her mother at a first meeting? A sort-of explanation was supplied by the person on the other side of the woman—Alexis Cowper. That would make her Alexis's mother, and her Princess-Grace-the-older features confirmed it. After casting (raking!) her eyes first down and then up her mother's form, Mrs. Cowper swiveled her head (raptor bird–like) toward Alexis and, next to her, Dawn Dawson and her mother. Julie wanted to reach out, grab Mrs. Cowper by her Gucci scarf, and twist it until she coughed up a pleasant hello to her mother. But this really wasn't the place for such playground behavior. Alexis did her usual look-right-through-Julie-as-if-she-didn't-exist snub. Julie could handle that, but what gave with her mother and *her* mother?

Mrs. Webb amply made up for Mrs. Cowper's strange hostility, and the four, Jane, her mother, Julie, and her mother, were soon engaged in a lively, pleasant conversation. Julie could see Dawn Dawson and her mother having an equally lively conversation with the Cowper duo. Fine.

CHAPTER 5

Broken Tooth, etc.

Distracted by the conversation, dizzily gabbing away, Julie paid no attention to what she was putting in her mouth, until suddenly she bit down on a rock, something hard, maybe a small meteor. Pain engulfed her jaw, fanned down her neck, and slammed into her collarbone.

She wanted to scream, to shriek, to cry out in agony. But, once again, the civility, the calm dignity, the etiquette proper to the occasion quashed that. Instead, she, as unnoticed as she could, fished the offending object out of her mouth. An olive pit! The bean salad in the Orange Dragon bowl had been laced with unpitted black olives that looked just like black beans.... Who would do such a crummy thing? Was this someone's idea of a joke?

And then she heard another rocklike crunch come from her mother's direction. "Oh my word," her mother cried out in a low, likewise decorous, voice. "An olive pit!" she whispered incredulously as she stared at the thing she'd just fished from her mouth. "Who would be so benighted as to put small unpitted black olives into a bean salad meant to be eaten in a candle-lit room?" her mother asked of Julie in a harsh whisper that became harsher with each word. Julie just opened her eyes wide, shrugged, and said "I dunno, Mom. Beats me. I got one, too." With that, she showed her mother the pit she'd just extracted from her mouth. It all confirmed her suspicion that nothing good could come out of a bowl decorated with writhing, fire-breathing orange dragons.

In the midst of the lively conversation they resumed with the Webbs, Julie saw Dawn Dawson and her mother stand up, make some hurried explanations to the two Cowper women, and then rush off as if on pressing business.

That left Alexis and her mother by themselves—alone, exposed, uncomfortable, and exiled from the happy, friendly conversation that had sprung up between the Tylers and Webbs.

In fact, happy, light-hearted female chatter that ebbed and flowed like playful surf cavorting along a shoreline filled the candle-lit room—at least that's what it seemed like to Julie. The Webbs and Tylers would gladly have included the Cowpers in their conversation, but the two immediately made it *quite* clear that they preferred their own company atop their rocky exposed perch on Mt. Olympus. This they communicated by straightening their backs, turning toward each other, and conversing in low, sibilant voices, their eyes flickering snakelike around the room, and then always, ultimately, fastening on Julie and her mother, especially her mother . . . . Julie hoped an albatross with filled-to-capacity bowels would soon fly over them on their rocky promontory.

Then Julie saw the two places vacated by Dawn Dawson and her mother being taken by a black girl a couple years ahead of her named Gloria Jackson and a small, make that tiny, woman who couldn't possibly be her mother. She was too old. Might she even be Gloria's great grandmother? Where Gloria glowed with life and vigor and vitality, the woman with her was small and stooped and gray all over, from her hat (a strange thing that looked like a stack of pancakes), to her hair (knotted in a bun at the nape of her neck), to her simple gray flannel suit with a large cameo pinned at the nape of her neck. In stark contrast, Gloria wore a short, black, felt, flared skirt, black stockings, clunky heeled black shoes, an orange mohair sweater with flecks of gold in it, and large gold hoop earrings. Gloria was, Julie knew, one of the scholarship recipients, so by being there, they were, in effect, helping pay for the scholarship that paid for her schooling. Julie hardly knew Gloria, but she did know that she was universally popular at school. It was like she had some kind of magnetic pull. Gloria had flocks of friends, even down to the first graders and the Black and Hispanic workers at the school.

Maybe it was just IT.

Gloria, in her beautiful lush, ebony voice introduced the small, delicate woman as her grandmother, Martha Jackson. Jackson was a common enough name among Blacks, Julie thought. Could that mean that Gloria's mother wasn't married when.... Julie left the end of the thought unspoken in her head. Gloria's parentage was none of her business.

And then something happened that Julie didn't think could happen anymore in modern civilized society. As Gloria and her grandmother introduced themselves to all at the table, she distinctly heard Mrs. Cowper oath the "n" word to Alexis, who laughed back smartly at her mother's remark. (Her mother was later to confirm that she had heard, and seen, it, too.) Nonetheless, Mrs. Cowper's acknowledgment of Mrs. Jackson's introduction was less chilly than the reception she'd given to her mother. Most curious.

As Martha Jackson greeted all at the table, she said something like "so pleased to meet you" and "so pleased to make your acquaintance" to each person, accompanied by a slight gracious nod of her head, her hands folded against her waist in a pose of ultimate refinement.

Gloria and her grandmother then went to the food table and returned with plates of food. The Tyler and Webb women welcomed the Jacksons to their conversation. Alexis Cowper and her mother maintained their haughty distain from atop Mt. Olympus. (Julie was just then studying Greek history, so Greek mythology was influencing a lot of her mental imagery.) Apparently the albatross had yet to dump the contents of its bowels on them. It could wait. She was a patient person.

It was hard to hear everything that Gloria and her grandmother were saying, but Julie *was* able to make out Mrs. Jackson saying that they were late because she didn't get done with her housekeeper duties at a nearby mansion in Woodland Hills until 7:00 in the evening. Julie was immediately cowed. The woman had been unapologetically forthright about being late because of her housekeeper duties—as if she'd been late because her last brain surgery of the day had been more complicated than expected!

Gloria, who, during all this, was looking at her grandmother with eyes full of love and devotion, was also clearly not discomfited by her grandmother's lowly (i.e., servile) work or her plainness. *That* got Julie feeling like a total worm, the kind that comes out after a heavy rain, is run over by a car, and then lies there flattened until it dries up and blows away.... Hadn't she, for the past two weeks, been hoping for violent weather, any act of God, inadvertent suffocation, *appendicitis* rather than attend the mother–daughter dinner with her plain mother? But, then, there *had* been Alexis's mother's rudeness to her mother, which had been exactly, maybe even worse than, what she'd dreaded might happen. All right, she was still a worm, maybe just not one run over by a car....

Right then a hollow cracking sound reverberated around the table that by now was quite familiar to Julie. The orange dragon bean salad had just claimed its third victim. Confirming this, Martha Jackson's face crumpled in a pain that no amount of gentility could mask.

"Granny, are you okay?" Gloria said, grabbing her grandmother's arm, leaning over to look into the old woman's face. The alarm on Gloria's face and anxiety in her voice made it clear that her grandmother was everything to her, that anything that harmed her could throw everything in her life out of kilter, like what an earthquake would do to the city that sat over it.

Slowly, very slowly, the look of pain ebbed from Mrs. Jackson's face and was replaced with a quiet, contained dignity as the woman very discreetly removed what was clearly an olive pit and part of a molar from her mouth.

"Granny, you broke a tooth on an olive pit in a bean salad with black beans that look just like black olives!" Gloria exclaimed in a voice that increased in outrage and volume.

Julie and her mother looked at each other with stricken eyes. They should have paid attention to what the Jacksons had on their plates, warned them to stay clear of the landmine bean salad. They bore some of the blame.

"It's okay, dear," Mrs. Jackson was saying to her granddaughter, and she patted her granddaughter's arm reassuringly. "A broken tooth is nothing to make an issue of." And that was that as far as Mrs. Jackson was concerned.

But Gloria was of a different stripe from her grandmother. "Granny, spiking a bean salad with unpitted black olives is—is—a criminal offense," she said in a, this time, very loud and enraged voice. Gloria wasn't about to be a pansy to protocol and correct form when her beloved grandmother had been "criminally" assaulted by a bean salad. (Julie was later to learn that Gloria wanted to become a public defender. It was clear that night that she was already honing her courtroom persona.)

"Whoever made that salad should at least pay for your dentist bill," Gloria said more indignantly, more loudly.

"Gloria, *enough*," her grandmother said in a stern whisper, taking no more sass from her granddaughter. "It's *not* worth making a scene about. Now hush up—"

"Yes, Granny," Gloria murmured. But when she looked up and out, she had this look of a periscope scanning the room, looking for the guilty party, so she could at least fire a torpedo-like glare at the reprobate. In the meantime, Gloria's grandmother had very discreetly wrapped the tooth fragment in a delicate white lace–edged handkerchief, which she then stowed in a little black crepe purse with a rhinestone clasp. That done, and the purse snapped close, Mrs. Jackson turned and continued talking amiably away with the Tylers and the Webbs as if she'd only had to interrupt the conversation to delicately dab a speck of bean salad off her lip.

CHAPTER 6
Praline Cookie Triumph

The genteel hum of conversation and musical clinking of silverware on china gradually transitioned to a loud murmuring as, with an added harsh scraping of chairs, the mothers and daughters who'd finished their main course began to process to the dessert table. Everyone returning seemed to already be having a sugar high. There was certainly a lot of laughter and semi-remorseful banter.

"Well, it looks as though tomorrow is going to be a salad day for me" and "I'm going to have to call that 1-800 number I saw on a billboard advertising a free consult for liposuction" and "I think I just outgrew my dress" were just a few of the merry comments that reached Julie's ears. Best of all, she could see that, among the rich, sugary, calorie-laden delights heaped on each woman's dessert plate, was at least one of her mother's praline cookies. That tickled her to no end. It was like a vote cast in favor of her mother's cookies.

Curiously, the Cowpers returned with nary one of her mother's cookies. What did that mean? Also, what had the Cowpers brought? Since their name began with C, it had to be an appetizer, or maybe it was a salad, she wasn't sure, hadn't paid attention to anything other than what the Ts had to bring.

Twenty minutes later, Julie and her mother were done with their meals. Now it was their turn to process to the dessert table.

She noticed right off that only a small mound of her mother's praline cookies remained, but she didn't take one. She'd leave them for others to enjoy. This wasn't her being thoughtful so much as just wanting her mother to win more votes in the dessert popularity contest. There was really no such thing planned for the evening, but it was okay to pretend there was.

As with the main meal selections, what was left of the desserts was pretty meager, pretty unappetizing, depressing even. All the lemon bars and chocolate-peanut butter brownies, of which there hadn't been many, were gone. There was a pudding that could be a chocolate trifle, or maybe it was turkey innards. Something that looked like sea kelp bars. Oatmeal cookies that looked to be made out of wood chips with dead house flies for raisins.

Julie and her mother ended up cutting slices of a store-bought coconut cream pie. It was the only thing that looked safe to eat. They'd had enough food trauma for the night. It didn't matter. What did was that her mother's cookies had proved to be delicious enough looking to garner lots of attention.

And then, as if on cue, just as Julie turned to go back to her table, she heard someone say, clear as day: "Oh my goodness, this is the *most* delicious cookie I've ever eaten!" Julie knew without even looking that the cookie being praised, raised!, to the heavens was one of her mother's famous, fabled praline cookies. She hadn't been wrong! There *was* a dessert popularity contest of sorts. And it was soon obvious that her mother was the winner hands down. Words of praise arose from the crowd of women like a flock of songbirds taking flight. "Out of this world," "delectable," "divine." These were just a sampling of the praise that reached Julie's ears. Her dour uncle, the priest at The Vatican, had got it right when he'd dubbed them manna from heaven. The cookies certainly belonged in some spiritual realm.

"I'm going back for another cookie before they're all gone." "Me, too." "Me, three!" someone shouted with a laugh. Julie could hear at least a dozen chairs being pushed back as others had the same idea.

"It's a good thing I doubled the recipe," Julie's mother

whispered to Julie as they found themselves having to edge around a small crowd of women and their daughters racing to the dessert table to score more of her mother's Mount Olympus praline cookies.

Gone was the quiet dignity, the arch propriety, the civilized demeanor of the dinner. It was every woman and girl for herself. In the midst of the uproar, someone who must have grown up in a family of fifteen shouted: "There should be only one cookie per person!"

"Yes—that's only fair!" someone laughed in response. Julie couldn't believe the fun her mother's cookies had sparked.

That, in turn, sparked in Julie an unexpected serious, almost sad, thought. In another hour or so, the dinner would be over. All of them would have to reenter the dark, dank, still fall night and the dining room would be empty, dark, and silent, too. Would there remain any trace of the laughter and happy conversation of the evening except in her memory? It seemed a shame for all that joy to be lost forever. Maybe the glow of the candle-lit room, the merry laughter, and the bright faces of the crowd would enter space and keep on going until it reached a dark, lonely planet a trillion miles away and made it bloom into a star. It was a silly thought, but, still, one worth thinking and storing away for other such occasions.

CHAPTER 7

Dance Disaster

Mrs. Tyler remained nonchalantly silent as the praise for her cookies finally, like diminutive birds, resumed their quiet perches. Julie understood the reason for her mother's desire not to be known as the bringer of the praline cookies. Her mother was staunchly opposed to blowing one's horn.

As to the coconut cream pie they were eating, her mother had to agree with her—that it tasted like "unscented shaving cream."

Then, out of the blue, came a bark, not of a dog but of someone who was mightily incensed. "These cookies sure make up for that deadly bean salad!" the outraged voice said. It was either Joan Rivers or Phyllis Diller, but that couldn't be because they were both dead. But, then their kind of sarcasm would assuredly extend from the grave.

That loosed a veritable landslide of similar remarks. Gone were the songbirds. Crows now seemed to be cawing from the rafters. "Abject stupidity!" "Criminal assault!" "An injury lawyer would have a field day wherever that salad was served!" These were the comments that reached Julie's ears, anyway.

Julie and her mother said nothing, and neither did Mrs. Jackson and Gloria, though Gloria obviously had a store of nasty verbiage she would have gladly spat out. It didn't become a room-wide thing like the praise of her mother's cookies had been. But, somehow, the general jollity of the room was affected, reduced a fraction. The star of the night was dimmed a bit.

That got Julie to thinking. *Was* the person who'd brought the salad just plain stupid? Maybe it didn't occur to them that black beans and black olives look an awful lot alike, especially in a room lit mostly by candles(?) Or had the person added the unpitted olives to the salad with malicious intent—thought they'd have a little fun? See how many broken molars they could score? She knew, from listening to her father talk about the various cases he prosecuted, that human depravity knew no bounds.

She also knew that, if *she* were the idiot who'd brought the salad, and she were Japanese, she'd be crawling under the table right now and committing hari-kari with her dinner knife.

Further such thoughts were interrupted by the loud crackling sound of a microphone being turned on, followed by the very familiar voice of Dr. Drescher, the executive director of the school calling out "Ladies—" in her slight German accent. Long used to bringing roomfuls of slightly crazed girls to attention, she called out in a louder, firmer, but still patient, voice "Ladies?!"

Some of the girls didn't like her and called her "the Fuehrer," but Julie felt otherwise. Besides a doctorate in education, she also had a PhD in history and taught history on top of keeping everything running smoothly at the school. It was she who was teaching the ancient Greek history course Julie was taking, the one that was decorating all her mental imagery with Grecian touches. Julie'd also heard she could be very supportive when some student was going through some kind of trouble, as she was to discover soon enough.

Julie could just make out the woman standing in a small patch of light cast by an overhead bank of fluorescent lights. Behind her bobbed white and black balloons that had been taped onto the wall, along with silver stars shimmering with a coating of glitter. There was a pleased gasp from all present. They were all now like gleeful children suddenly happening upon another fun romp, having now gorged themselves on her mother's praline cookies and having thoroughly shamed the bringer of the bean salad.

Once the room had reached some semblance of silence,

Dr. Drescher welcomed everyone, thanked them all for coming and for contributing both food and money to the occasion. "I am most pleased to announce that the total amount of money raised has come to $20,543!" This drew a loud round of applause. "So we have enough money to pay for two years of one more deserving girl's schooling at Ainsworth Country Day School," she finished midst the continued clapping. She noticed Gloria Jackson and her grandmother clapping particularly enthusiastically.

During all this, Julie's abjectly silly alter ego was wondering who the heck would pay an amount that ended with three dollars. The tickets were 20 dollars each. Everything else was by check or cash?!

"Now," uttered Dr. Drescher, breathlessly, as if she were too excited for words, "we have some wonderful entertainment for you. One of our very talented students, Dawn Dawson, whom I know many of you already know." There was a round of applause to affirm this fact. (Julie didn't clap. She couldn't bring herself to cheer on people who were in close cahoots with the Cowper women. She hoped Alexis and her mother noticed.) "Dawn is joined by her mother, the one-time Billie Barr, whose Broadway credits are legendary," Dr. Drescher needed to raise her voice here to be heard above the enthusiasm with which the entertainment was greeted. "They have generously offered to give us their very special song-and-dance rendition of 'Top Hat' by the one and only Irving Berlin!"

Everyone (except for Julie) clapped in thrilled expectation of the performance, as Dr. Drescher moved herself and the microphone out of the limelight cast by the overhead fluorescent lights. Then there came from just outside and to the right of the blackness that rimmed the patch of bright light the rhythmic tapping of tap shoes. Julie was immediately caught up by the throbbing tapping of the shoes transmitted across the floor and right up her legs. It could have been *her* in the spotlight tap-dancing into the blue-white brightness of the lights as the music swelled over the sound system in the dining room, with

Fred Astaire, himself, singing the lyrics.

Both Dawson women wore a slinky, strapless, black satin costume with a tuxedo front. Their legs were encased in black net stockings. The legs of the costumes were cut high, almost to the waist. Each wore the requisite top hat, black bowtie, and white cuffs with glittering rhinestone cufflinks, and each carried a silver-headed cane.

The bust line was cut daringly low. On Dawn, it revealed beautiful, high, well-shaped breasts. On her mother, it revealed a disturbing amount of old, sloppy breast tissue. A further look suggested Mrs. Dawson's costume had to have hailed from her younger, slimmer, Broadway days. She'd clearly gained a few pounds in the interim, most of them emerging out from under some edge of the costume.

It also soon became painfully apparent that her famed Broadway talent was, like the light of dying stars, now a pitiful, feeble light just now reaching earth from a trillion miles away. Her "star" was dead. While her daughter sailed along doing a very talented job of translating the Irving Berlin number into movement and sound that would have made Fred Astaire go hip-hip-hooray, her mother heavily and awkwardly plowed through the routine, clomping her steps and weaving her arms about gorilla-like. Worse, the more she did so, the more her breasts began to emerge from the top of her costume. All Julie could think of was rising bread dough. But there was nothing funny about what they were witnessing. It was just plain awful. In fact, Mrs. Dawson's performance was so bad she ended up stealing the show from her very own daughter. It was all one could pay attention to.

Finally, the "entertainment" came to a merciful end, and the room exploded with applause, the kind airplane passengers erupt into when a plane finally hits the runway after descending through a heaving maelstrom of turbulence and are glad to still be alive and safely on solid ground... Julie clapped wildly, too.

There were two expressions on Mrs. Dawson's face during the hearty applause. One was a glow of pride as she looked adoringly at her daughter. But when she looked out at the audience, at the roomful of mothers and their daughters, her face just went *plop,* much like her breast tissue had been doing five minutes before.

Word later got around the school that Dawn had talked her mother into performing the number with her, much against her will. When Julie told her mother what she'd heard, her mother said "Oh, really—" And then after a short, thoughtful, pause, she added "someone bred to stardom and fame would also be well trained in the art of damage control." Her mother said no more and went back to what she was doing, leaving Julie to 'get it,' which she did.

The joyous dinner, the praline cookie jubilee, the bean salad uproar, the "entertainment" disaster now over, the overhead lights came on fully, and the mothers and their daughters hurriedly began to stir. It was late, almost 9 o'clock, and the girls all had school the next day. The mothers had their full days ahead as well. As the mothers and daughters finished conversations and bid their farewells, Julie didn't hear one person say anything, good or bad, about the "entertainment," and also nothing more about the bean salad. But everyone did look very tired.

CHAPTER 8

The Real Star of the Show

Julie and her mother said their goodbyes to Mrs. Jackson and Gloria and Mrs. Webb and Jane. The Cowpers left without saying a word to any of them. It was okay. No one was offended. No one missed them! By then they'd become like ghosts at the table, kind of like the Haunted House ride at Disney World where, as one passes sideways along mirrors in one's little rollicking car, one can see a ghost sitting squarely between you and the car's other passenger. That's what they reminded Julie of, with an inward cackle.

When Julie and her mother went to collect the cake plate, they found that it had been cleaned of every speck of praline cookie. Even a forensics expert would have had a hard time identifying what food had been on the plate, Julie thought delightedly.

By then, much of the crowd was either heading toward the double doors to the hallway or had just entered the hallway.

"Oh, *meine Güte!*" Dr. Drescher shouted suddenly, reverting, inexplicably, to her native German. Everyone who wasn't within earshot (the man, or was that the woman, on the moon?) stopped, turned, and swarmed back into the dining room? What *meine Güte* thing had just happened!? The question was on all their stricken faces.

"*You* are the person who made those, those *wunderbar* cookies," Dr. Drescher exclaimed to Julie's mother, resorting to yet another German word to express her feelings.

"Y-yes," Julie's mother admitted, looking stricken. Had she broken some important school rule by making them? Would she be getting detention??

But that wasn't the case at all, as borne out by the hordes of women, among them Dr. Drescher, who soon surrounded her, all of them clamoring for her recipe for the cookies, handing her all kinds of slips of paper (envelope flaps, an upcoming dentist appointment card for a root canal..., even an old boarding pass for a Continental Airlines flight to Tampa dating from 1996) with e-mail addresses scribbled somewhere on them. Wonderful, wunderbar...the cookies were delicious in any language.

Her mother the movie star being swarmed by fans asking for autographs, Julie found herself thrust, banished!, to the margins of the crowd, holding the plate which her mother had handed her when she started getting swamped with the bits of paper. But Julie didn't mind. She was pleased as punch. Hadn't her mother turned out to be the real star of the evening?!

It took some time for Julie and her mother to neaten and then stow all the slips of paper in their small dressy purses. By the time they left, everyone, except for kitchen help making hollow-banging-stainless-steel noises in the kitchen, was gone. Someone had turned off the lights in the hallway, a janitor maybe or a night watchman. The only light shining was in the entryway at the end of the hall. The rest was all in shadows.

Just as they stepped into the hallway, they saw, strangely, halfway down, two heads poke out of the ladies' room—like worms out of an apple. The two heads then looked up and down the hallway, as if to see whether the coast was clear(?)

Because the behavior of these two beings was so strange, Julie and her mother hung back, standing silently just inside the dining room doorway until they heard the sound of feet clattering down the hallway, making a run for it to the parking lot door. At that point, Julie and her mother emerged from the dining room doorway. What the heck was going on? Then they got the shock of their lives. The strange prowlers in Ainsworth's darkened hallway were none other than Alexis Cowper and her mother, as the bright overhead light in the entranceway made unmistakably clear. Then came an even greater shock. As Mrs. Cowper backed her way out of the door, Julie saw that she clasped in her arms none other than the Orange Dragon bowl. Julie and her mother gasped. Mrs. Cowper was the lunatic, sadist, or was she just the nincompoop, who'd brought the landmine bean salad to the dinner.

Julie's mother grabbed her arm and pulled her back into the doorway. "Let's give them plenty of time to get to their car and on their way," she said in a low voice. "I don't want them to know that someone saw them with the bowl."

Julie didn't know whether that was her mother being considerate or sensing that it would be best to let the woman think she'd made a clean escape. Otherwise there might be serious consequences. It had to be the latter. There was something about Alexis and her mother that scared her, something that after two hours around them said they were people not to be crossed.

Once the door to the parking lot clanked shut, they figured it was safe to come out of hiding. Now they could make their own clattering way down the darkened hallway. They cracked the outside door to make sure it was safe to leave without being seen.

A car was just then making its way out of the lot. It could only be the Cowpers. Wait, shouldn't they be driving a broom?

"That must be the Cowturds," her mother observed as they hurried toward their car.

Julie couldn't believe what her mother'd just said. She burst out laughing, even jumped up and down from the force of the laughter coming out of her. Her mother, who never said anything even remotely crude, had been the innocent victim of the proverbial Freudian slip. She'd given the demon duo the family name they justly deserved.

"Julie, what on earth is so funny?" her mother demanded, put out by her daughter's sudden bout of inanity, or maybe it was insanity. It was late, she was tired, and she wasn't in the mood for silliness of any sort.

"Mom, you called the Cowpers the Cowturds," Julie finally managed to get out.

"I did not, Julie. I would *never* say something crude like that," her mother replied fiercely.

It was true. Her mother never even said shucks. But that made what she'd said even funnier.

"I *know*, Mom. But it's what you *said*. You called the Cowpers the name they deserved, especially now that we know that they were the ones who brought that tooth-decimating salad," Julie said. She wanted to erupt in further peals of laughter, but she could tell by the look on her mother's face, even in the dim light of the parking lot, that she'd better pipe down or risk a Martha Jackson–type reproof.

But, then, her mother did laugh, did find her Freudian slip funny, not uproariously as Julie had, but enough to show that she saw the humor in what she'd said and was enjoying it quite a bit.

Then came another slip of sorts. They'd resumed walking to their car and had made it about ten feet when they found themselves standing in a strange slippery, slurpy substance that, even more strangely, *clinked*.

"What on earth," Mrs. Tyler murmured and looked down at her feet. Julie, too.

"Oh, no—" they both wailed as they beheld their feet sinking into a glistening quagmire of bean salad slashed with the shards of what had been a thousand-dollar Orange Dragon bowl. In her probable haste to get the damning bowl with its lethal contents into the car, Mrs. Cowper must have dropped the bowl.

They immediately stepped out of the disgusting substance and gave their shoes a good scrape on the pavement like one would any outdoor ground substance of a suspicious nature. Cowturds was now a *very* fit name for the Cowpers.

"How awful," Julie's mother said.

Also offal, thought Julie. Once again she found herself trying to figure out the Cowpers' behavior. Why were they so rude to her mother? Why call the Jacksons the "n" word? Why did they bring the awful/offal salad to the first-ever mother-daughter dinner at Ainsworth?

Well, she thought as she buckled her seatbelt while her mother started up the car, at least tonight had proved that there was *some* justice in the world. The Cowpers thoroughly shamed. The Dawsons' fame in tatters. Her mother? The clear winner of the dessert contest at the first-ever mother-daughter dinner at Ainsworth. As they drove out of the parking lot, both Julie and her mother were quiet, each, it would stand to reason, trying to make sense of the Cowpers' strange behavior.

Mrs. Tyler voiced her thoughts first. "Julie, under no circumstances, do I want you to tell *anyone* what we saw tonight."

Julie had to think about that for a second. What difference would it make if word got around about the person who'd made the salad? Didn't they deserve it?

"Julie? I'm expecting a 'yes' from you," (She'd clearly picked up some pointers from Martha Jackson that night.)

"Yes, Mom. I mean *no*, I won't tell anyone," Julie said contritely, when, actually, what she most wanted to do was, that night before going to bed, tweet the identity of the bean salad culprit to the entire Ainsworth student body.

CHAPTER 9

Good Samaritans, Chapter 1

As Julie and her mother headed down Woodland Hills Boulevard, the artfully curvy road they'd taken to get to Ainsworth, they spotted two figures, one tall, one small, hurrying along the side of the road. It was unlikely for two people to be walking at such a fast pace along the side of such a road so late on a weekday night. Someone walking a dog would be more, like, ambling, *and* wouldn't be dressed in skirts and heels.

As they drew alongside the two people, Julie gasped. "Mom, it's Gloria Jackson and her grandmother."

"Goodness, it's not safe for them, even in this neighborhood, to be out on such a lonely road at this hour of the night. I wonder if they need a ride."

She stopped the car, put it in reverse, and backed it up until they were alongside the hurrying women, who now showed some panic in their steps at the prospect of a strange car approaching them out of the night. Julie quickly rolled down her window and hollered "Gloria! It's me Julie Tyler. "Do you need a ride somewhere?!"

"Oh, yes, that would be wonderful," she could hear Gloria's rich, relieved, voice gushing out of the darkness. "We're trying to get to the bus terminal where Woodland Hills Boulevard meets the beltway. The last cross-town bus for the day leaves in seven minutes."

"We'll be glad to take you," Julie's mother called across the front seat and pressed the button that unlocked the rear doors.

Gloria and her grandmother scrambled into the back seat, uttering profuse thanks as they did so, and they were, once again, on their way—at an arthritic snail's pace—or so it seemed, now that time had become the enemy for a second time that night.

"What time does your bus leave the terminal?" Mrs. Tyler called cheerily to the two in the backseat, glancing down at the clock on the dashboard as she did so.

"9:30," Gloria answered tensely, tersely.

The clock showed an unnerving 9:24.

With that, Woodland Hills Boulevard became 100 miles long. At every curve and rise in the road, there was just more wood-lined roadway and no hint of a beltway in the distance. It was as if they'd entered a fairytale about a witch who added miles to a road just out of spite, because she got her kicks out of seeing people miss their buses. And, of course, her mother had to keep the car at a steady 30 mph. Officer Ward could still be prowling the neighborhood looking for speeders and rolling stoppers, and this time he might not be so forgiving.

Soon the car clock showed a fiendish 9:29. And then, wonderfully, the horizon became bright with halogen lighting. They'd reached the public-transportation heavenly Jerusalem —the beltway and the bus terminal! Hallelujah!!

But their collective joy was short-lived. Just as her mother pulled into the terminal, a bus was pulling out onto the feeder road to the beltway. Seeing it, Gloria and her grandmother wailed. "There goes our bus!" Gloria added. The witch had won.

For a moment, everything in the car became absolutely still. (What was that thing she'd learned in science about the inertia of rest? Had they just disproved the theory that there was no such thing as *absolute* rest?)

"Well," Julie's mother said briskly, the first to brave the now very unsettled waters of their situation. "We'll just follow the bus to the next stop and you can catch it there."

From the far reaches of the back seat came Mrs. Jackson's mournful voice: "I'm afraid that won't work, Mona. The bus goes directly up onto the beltway and doesn't stop until it gets to our side of town."

"Oh," Julie's mother said in a small voice, her simple solution foiled. The bus was, sure enough, Julie could see, roaring hungrily up the ramp onto the beltway like some monstrous beast, a dragon perhaps, hell bent on devouring every last bit of concrete and steel of which the highway was constructed.

"Well, then," her mother said simply, "I'll drive you home, Martha. We can't just go off and leave you here. It won't be an imposition."

After a short silence, Mrs. Jackson replied in an even more mournful voice. "I can't let you do that, Mona."

"Martha, it's no inconvenience. I'd be delighted to do it," Julie's mother insisted brightly. Julie had detected a warning in Mrs. Jackson's voice that her mother didn't seem to have picked up on.

"Mona, I can't put you in such a position," Mrs. Jackson responded in a firm voice pitched lower than her usual voice, "We can call a taxicab. I've got my cell phone and the phone number of the cab company we use in my address book."

With that she rummaged around in her dressy black crepe purse with its rhinestone clasp, which its maker back in the 1950s(?) had probably never expected would contain a phone, especially considering that phones at that time, according to all the movies Julie'd watched, were huge black clunky things with *dials* to call a person's number.

In the backseat, Mrs. Jackson had reached the cab company but seemed to be having some kind of unsatisfactory conversation with the dispatcher.

"But this is the company we always use. I don't understand why you no longer provide service to the MLK Boulevard area."

A further pause during which more reasons for denying service were obviously being given.

"I understand your new policy. But, as this is a weekday night and it is not yet 10 o'clock, I would think that there would be no problem with conveying my granddaughter and me to our home on A Street. We're at the bus terminal now and it's only 15 minutes to our house. I—"

The dispatcher must have hung up on Mrs. Jackson (The jerk! Hadn't anyone taught him, or her, manners?) because she now said, in a very mournful voice, "Mona, I'm afraid we will need to take you up on your kind offer to drive us home, though I most regret the need to do so."

Such formal language. Also unnerving.

Mrs. Tyler, like a St. Bernard on its first rescue mission, said in a gung ho peppy voice that was clearly artificial (she'd picked up on the minor key Mrs. Jackson's words had been said in) that she would be glad to drive the Jacksons home. Yessirree.

There was one problem with her mother's scheme, Julie realized immediately. Her mother didn't do freeways, highways, beltways—anything with posted speeds over 65 and only on and off ramps, not side streets you could pull into in a pinch —something her mother was now lamely explaining to Mrs. Jackson and Gloria, who, of course, as any normal person would, had just directed her onto the freeway to get them to their home on A Street.

After Mrs. Tyler's admission, everyone fell silent (another inertia of rest moment). Finally Gloria murmured in a voice that now seemed to come from Mars: "Well, the best way to get to our house on surface roads is to continue down this feeder road until we get to Merdor. We'll need to take a left on it and continue until we get to a rotary. MLK Boulevard, which connects with it, takes us right to A Street, where our house is."

It all sounded so simple. Go straight, take a left on Merdor, take MLK Boulevard off the rotary, take a right onto A St. But what was that about a street called Merdor? It wasn't making her jump and down happily, inside her head, that the name of the street they needed to find sounded an awful lot like "murder," something that, really, she could give a miss to that night and not feel as though she'd led a deprived life.

What happened in the next half hour gave Julie an excellent opportunity to ponder Jesus's parable of The Good Samaritan (something their priest was always referring to as a teaching moment). Yes, yes, she'd heard homily after homily on it her entire life. But, tonight, it was to take on an entirely different meaning. First off, she always thought it'd taken place in some barren desert place where the sun beat down pitilessly on the injured traveler. The desert they were about to enter was a barren place of sorts, but one that she thought maybe even a hardy Samaritan wouldn't venture into.

First they went through what appeared to be a factory district where everything was boarded up, looked not to have been occupied since the turn of the century, the 19th one. Julie even saw a faded sign advertising celluloid collars and another "fine leather grips for the discriminating traveller." She wasn't sure what celluloid collars and grips were, but then, probably, no one her age, even her mother's age, would know what they were.

A couple more blocks worth of the factory ghost town, and Gloria shouted, this time from right behind Julie's left ear: "This is Merdor. Take a left here!" Julie could feel Gloria's hot breath on the back of her neck. It told her how anxious the girl was.

Finding Merdor was not, as the name suggested, anything to cheer about. Anything but. The place they were now entering made a desert, any desert, seem a hearty, welcoming place. Julie found herself gazing out at something like a horrible sore encrusted with barely livable-looking buildings. The only sign of life was an occasional feeble, frightened light peeking out through a barely visible window. She couldn't imagine living in such a place. For sure she'd live longer in a desert than she would here. In a desert, without water, she'd maybe live for a couple days. Here, she'd die of fright in a matter of minutes.

Julie looked over at her mother. When she was, like, three years old her mother might have been able to look over at her in her little car seat and give her a quick smile that said: "don't worry, honey, mommy's got everything under control." Now that Julie was in her teens, her mother had long ceased to have power over every ill. In fact, it seemed to Julie that it was her mother who needed the heartening. She could tell by the way her mother was gripping the steering wheel that it had become a kind of lifesaver, the one thing that gave her some control of their current situation. Which it was, in fact.

Julie began to see on every vertical surface—the sides of buildings, billboards, even the risers of steps—curious meaningless words that looked like dead people outlines. Gang signs! The words sounded in Julie's head like a scream in the night. They were now in that part of the city that was always in the news because of gang violence. At the end of every local newscast the announcer could be heard droning in an ever-more-weary voice: "And there was more gang violence in the West End last night, resulting in [fill in the blank] deaths." The number of the dead was the only thing that varied from day to day. Here also dwelt the worst denizens of the ghetto, the drug dealers, pimps, and prostitutes. This was, she was sure, the fabled lowest level of hell.

Then, straight ahead was a rotary, *the* rotary.

"This is the rotary I was talking about!" Gloria shouted, still right behind Julie's ear, but that was okay. "Just take the second street off the rotary. It's MLK Boulevard. After about four blocks it intersects with A Street. We live at number 32."

Gloria sounded relieved, happy. Thus Julie felt safe feeling the same, but she'd jumped the gun. The rotary had been only a temporary oasis of normalcy. Once on MLK Boulevard, they plunged into an even worse place, an abyss, a biblical valley of the shadow of death. Julie didn't look to her left or right. She couldn't. Her neck was locked rigid by fright.

Ahead, lit by the Volvo's headlights, was a street consisting of cracked concrete, black patches of macadam that looked cancerous, manhole covers with a slimy sheen, trash, garbage, and she didn't want to know what else creating a grimy ruffle in the gutters. Two, three blocks and Gloria said, still right behind her: "Right here. Take a right. This is A Street."

****

After the hell hole they'd been in for the past hour—it was now almost 10:30—the house at 32 A Street came as a total surprise. Julie now knew how Red Riding Hood felt when she finally found her grandmother's house—but *before* she discovered the wolf had eaten her grandmother and taken her place. Julie remembered the second half of the story only afterward.

Painted a light color, that proved in the daytime to be a pale yellow, the house had delicate, lace-like latticework on a porch that encircled the front and side of the house. Dark shutters neatly bracketed each window. The house was further encircled by a prim white picket fence and, just inside that, dark clumps of gnarled rosebushes still bedecked with blossoms that looked white in the dark of night.

In the backseat Mrs. Jackson was saying, as her mother made a U-turn in the street and brought the car to a stop in front of the house, "I was born, raised, married, and raised my daughter in this house. And now I'm raising my granddaughter in it." She said the last bit triumphantly as if Gloria was at the pinnacle of the house's lineage. Julie couldn't help but notice that she offered few details about her daughter, Gloria's mother. Only that she'd been raised there.

What Mrs. Jackson was really telling them, and Julie knew this right off, was that the ghetto had been a bona fide neighborhood at one time. That at one time (the time when the house was built) it had been a place where you could amble about the streets day or night, have friendly chats with neighbors, play badminton in the street, all without fear of getting stabbed or shot. One could also get a taxi to it any time of the day or night.

As Gloria and her grandmother climbed out of the car uttering profuse thanks for driving them home, Gloria told them how to get to the freeway, which was the quickest (also safest) way home. That, of course, wasn't taking into account her mother's silly hang-up about driving on freeways, which Gloria must have forgotten. Somehow they'd make it.

Julie and her mother were grimly silent as they watched the two women make their way up the sidewalk to the house, climb the steps to the porch with all its fussy Victorian finery, and give them a farewell wave that looked ominously final.

"Okay," her mother said with a fortifying intake of breath as she put the car in drive and pulled away from the curb. "Here we go—" She sounded like a paratrooper about to parachute into a war zone. And it wasn't?

CHAPTER 10

The Lowest Level of Hell

As Julie and her mother returned to MLK Boulevard and the fear- and violence-crazed world of the ghetto, which this was, Julie got to thinking about Martin Luther King. The things that he had lived for and died for. The things that he had so passionately, so possibly, proclaimed in his "I Have a Dream" speech. *This* place was no dream. It was a nightmare writ large in senseless gang slogans. Julie wondered, as she let her eyes rove uneasily from left to right and back again, taking in just the bare minimum of what she could handle, whether the bullet that had killed Dr. King might have done him a favor. This place would have broken his heart. It wouldn't have been his blood, but his tears, that would have trickled into the gutters lined with condoms and hypodermic needles and the blood that spurted from gang violence and just flowed like waste into the sewers. It would have been a long, lingering death.

The unhappy buildings they found themselves passing between as they began their timid way down MLK Boulevard were so plastered with rotting boards and graffiti that it was impossible to guess their reason for being built, for existing. No traces remained of what that had been, something that probably only a good medical examiner could detect.

Julie could see ahead of them, four blocks down, the halogen glow of the rotary. It was so simple, so doable. Four blocks, you hit the rotary, you go another three blocks, and you're at the beltway. Those had been Gloria's instructions.

However, because her eyes were now so fixed, riveted, on the brightly lit rotary, she didn't see, on both sides of the street, that where there should have been sharp right angles where the buildings met the pavement, there were dark clumps and strange forms that she couldn't have figured out the nature of anyway. Then, suddenly, like some evil craft project come to life—one where small sponges turn into full-size dinosaurs when wet—the figures began to move and wriggle, take on bodily form. It was still only when the figures burst forth with monstrous shrieks, shouts, strangled cries, and with what her innocent mind took as someone firing caps, that some DNA in her that went back to an early Stone Age ancestor explained to her what was happening. She'd been right about the reptiles, just wrong about the eon. These were two reptilian monsters of the early 21st century coming at each other ready to fight to the death. Julie could hear the bodies of the gang members writhing and working their way snakelike along the sides of their car, trying to get at each other.

Julie and her mother both screamed. There was no other way to express their terror. They were now, Julie realized hopelessly, in the death-grip of two rival street gangs.

On the left, the gang members wore black sweatshirts with hoods pulled up over their heads. These hid their features, made them faceless. All had obscenely large pacifiers hanging from a cord around their necks. The other gang, surging from the right, likewise wore black hooded sweatshirts. But their hoods weren't pulled so far forward as the rival gang's so that their "battle regalia," a blood-red do-rag, could be seen. Nonetheless, their features were also hidden. They too were faceless.

Then, amazingly, she saw, almost like an apparition, a strip of pavement open up between the closing ranks of the two gangs. It was exactly a car's width. It wasn't paved with yellow bricks, but it would do.

"Gun it, Mom!" Julie shrieked at her mother. They could, in that split second, escape the closing grip of the two gangs.

But Julie's mother was frozen—petrified—by fright. Or maybe she just was acting like a normal, considerate human being who didn't want to chance hitting and hurting someone. So, instead of gunning it, she came to a complete halt right in the narrow bit of street that was still left to them, and was soon gone.

At that point, the car was slammed even more violently by the seething mass of dark angry bodies as the rival gang members joined battle. The gang members threw themselves over, around, behind, and in front of their car. Did they even know it was there? The bodies, the voices, the knees and feet and elbows of the gang members on the hood and roof of their car—all became blunt weapons pounding, punching, and ramming every bit of the car, the air in the car punched by the sound made her eardrums hurt.

Then came more popping sounds and more shrieks. This wasn't just some reality show that they could skip over on a channel search. They were in a for-real war zone, where real ammunition was being fired and real lives were probably being lost. The side and back windows of the car and the windshield were now clogged with bodies. An odd thought struck Julie. Each gang member believed that he stood, that night, to die a hero's death. But this was no lofty cause being fought for. Didn't they understand this? This was a silly game that should be fought with wooden swords.

For a silly reason that could only be an impulse, Julie's mother turned on the windshield wipers, as if they could wipe the windshield clean of the bodies. But, of course, the wipers were immobilized by the press of the gang members heaped up on the hood. And, then, for another even sillier reason, she began frantically to push the windshield washer lever, uttering funny little cries with each push. Amazingly, to Julie's and her mother's combined disbelief, this had some effect.

Whether it was because the gang members were bewildered by the sudden appearance of the cold, soapy substance that *couldn't*, in their vast experience, be blood, or whether the fluid made the windshield too slimy for good traction, the gang members just began to slip off the windshield. *And*, in their wake, the gang members on the hood and those in front and behind them also began to slither away from the car like the reptiles they were.

And then, *wonderfully, clearly*, she heard the clarion call—the trumpets of Heaven sounding—shriek of police sirens blaring, coming closer and closer.

This was all that was needed to drive the gang members back into the dens and holes, *not* the breastworks of brave soldiers, they'd emerged from. They slunk away from their battlefield and hid like cowards in the shadows. There wasn't a brave heart to be had in the whole stinking lot of them.

Then, much to Julie's amazement, because she didn't think her mother had it in her, her mother rammed her foot down on the gas pedal, the car went tearing down the street, and before she could even *think* "Jack Sprat," let alone say it, they were entering the rotary. On their way, a whole fleet of squad cars was coming from the opposite direction, heading, it had to be, to the gang fight. Their sirens blaring and their lights flashing, they had also assumed monster-like proportions. Well, but, one had to fight fire with fire.

It was speed limits be damned as her mother continued to tear down the mostly deserted MLK Boulevard. And when they reached the beltway, incredibly, her mother sped up the ramp like a seasoned commuter and kept it at a steady 65 miles an hour until they reached the exit for their neighborhood—a place where the greatest danger was getting conked on the head by an acorn being gnawed by a bumbling squirrel.

Hardly slowing down, Julie's mother drove the car right into the garage, turned off the motor, and placed her hands in her lap, their "boat" brought to a safe anchorage. They were home, safe and sound, and now they had only to get out of the car and into the house. But neither made a move to do so. It was like they were bolted in place by left-over fear. They were still in battle readiness, or something like that, Julie thought.

"Come on, sweetheart," Mrs. Tyler said, reaching over and stroking Julie's cheek, her hand clearly shaking. "We'd better get going. Your father will be wondering where we are."

As she opened the door and climbed stiffly out of the car,

as if she'd been sitting there for hours, Julie discovered that the edge of the cake plate, which she'd taken into her lap when the Jacksons got in, had etched deep creases into the palms of her hands where she'd been gripping it. The next day there were bruises where the creases had been.

CHAPTER 11

The Ninetieth Hour

In the house, in the quiet calm of the kitchen, in which a vague praline cookie aroma hung in the air, they met a different kind of man ready to wage war—her father.

"Where have you been?" he shouted, his large dark form blocking the doorway into the lit hallway. Julie had never seen this side of her father. Anger? Worry? Exasperation? What was it that was making him stand like that, his shoulders hunched up, his hands held out from his hips like Gary Cooper in *High Noon*?

"We gave one of Julie's friends and her mother, well, her grandmother, really, a ride home," her mother said simply, obviously not wanting to go into detail about their hour-plus sojourn in hell.

"Where do they live? Moscow?" her father asked, not satisfied with Mrs. Tyler's answer.

"No, no—just the other side of town," her mother tossed off as airily as she could.

"I tried calling you on your cell phone," her father continued his interrogation, off on another tack, "but, guess what, it rang in the bedroom, and *you* didn't answer it because, well, how could you, you didn't have it with you! And why did we get you that phone, despite your protests? In case you got into some kind of trouble!"

So *this*, Julie thought, was the man who so effectively prosecuted cases, *fought* to protect innocent people from murderers, rapists, pederasts, con artists, thieves, and crooks of every ilk. Oh yes, and street gang members. How could she forget....

"I've been frantic with worry about you, Mona," her

father continued, still on the warpath. "When it got to be 10 o'clock, I tried calling the school, but there was no answer. So I drove over to it. All I found was the night-time security guard, who said the dinner had been over for more than an hour. No one was there but him. He had no idea where you two might be. I was just getting ready to call the police!"

"Actually, Dad—" Julie said, with a burble of laughter, "the police are busy breaking up the gang fight we were in . . . ." The words just came tumbling out of her mouth like little hare-brained children. And then she saw her mother looking at her with a look that said "How can you be letting me down like this. I thought we were friends."

"A gang fight?!" her father bellowed in a voice that was now more stunned than stern.

Julie's mother, after taking a deep, reluctant, breath, and giving Julie another glare at her "betrayal," went on to patiently explain in a quiet, measured voice how they'd ended up *having* to drive Gloria and her grandmother home, which turned out to be on the west side of town. How they'd gotten lost on the way to the Jacksons because of her phobia about driving on superhighways. But what else could she have done? She couldn't go off and leave Martha Jackson and her granddaughter in the middle of nowhere . . . . And then, she described the gang fight they'd narrowly escaped in the barest, least worrisome, detail.

Julie decided it was okay to go ahead and describe the regalia of each gang—the gigantic pacifiers of the left-hand gang and the blood-red do-rags of the other. Per her father, they were the Scars and the Black Lilies, the most-feared gangs in the city. (And, yes, on the next day's news, they were to learn that one of them had been killed and five badly wounded "in the gang violence that once more shattered the night in the west side of town." So those popping sounds had definitely been guns, and the one person who'd been killed might have lain just to the rear of their bumper as they sped away. She decided her father didn't need to know about the gunshots they'd heard.

Then, suddenly, her father went from raging to reaching

out and gathering his "two favorite gals" into his arms. "Goodness, you two. What am I going to do with you?" He held them both tight. He'd been very worried, and with good reason.

(Later her mother told him of the little scrape she'd had with the law and that Officer Ward sent his greetings. And, oh by the way, she had inadvertently revealed her nickname for him, Tweedledum. He'd growled somewhat at that, knowing that by midnight it had been tweeted, texted, e-mailed, and radioed to every cop, detective, lawyer, and judge in the city. From now until he retired he could count on being called Tweedledum, or maybe Tweedle for short.)

As Julie drifted off to sleep that night, she had one, no make that two, thoughts. The first was about Officer Ward. He could very well, probably was, in one of the police cruisers rushing to the scene of the gang fight. This was Officer Ward's daily fare. It would explain his steely presence. But she'd also seen the policeman's soft side, his apology for upsetting Julie, thinking he'd made her cry. And then she thought of Gloria and her grandmother who didn't wear belts hung with all kinds of armament. Gloria and Mrs. Jackson's only weapons, from what she could tell, were their rosebushes, their picket fence, and the long hatpin in Mrs. Jackson's funny hat. But somehow they hadn't come across as being any less invincible than Officer Ward.

As sleep finally closed over her tired brain, she could hear the funny rocking sound and the little calls and other noises that frequently emanated from her parents' bedroom just on the other side of the wall. She knew exactly what was going on on the other side of the wall, *barely* three feet from her head! And, no, this wasn't the first time it occurred to her that she'd gotten her start in life just three feet from where she lay.

CHAPTER 12

A Regrettable Revelation

The next day at school, Julie was headed to her algebra class, her least favorite subject. She was convinced that algebra had been devised by the devil. Why else all those fiendish Xs, Ys, and Zs circling around like buzzards waiting to fly down and feast on one's innards after one'd succumbed to total despair at ever finding the identity of Z and decided to fall on one's sharpened No. 2 pencil.

"Hey, girl!" she heard Gloria calling from right behind her, like they were best friends—even sisters. Considering what they'd been through the night before, it seemed as though some kind of blood tie had formed between them.

"Did you and your mother get home all right last night? Right after you left, we heard all these police sirens. It sounded like there must have been some kind of gang violence. It's a pretty common thing in our part of town." With that Gloria had leveled her dark brown eyes on Julie's gray ones with a look that said "I expect you to be honest with me," which Julie'd swear was said in Mrs. Jackson's voice.

"Well," Julie began hesitantly, not wanting to tell all the gory details, "we did find ourselves sort of in the middle of a gang fight. But we were able to get away from it just in time." She zipped through the last sentence like her mother had sped away from the scene of the gang fight, hoping Gloria would leave it at that. She didn't want the girl, whom she'd come to really like in the matter of, what?, twelve hours, to get the idea that the difference between their neighborhoods, and other things, put the kibosh on a friendship.

And then she did something very stupid. She spilled the

beans. That is, she told Gloria who, and how she knew, brought the bean salad. And she didn't leave out any details. She even got down to minutiae, such as the pathetic sight the Cowpers had made when they scurried like rats down the hallway with the incriminating Orange Dragon bowl in plain sight. How they'd found themselves treading in bean salad ooze spangled with the glittering shards of the Orange Dragon bowl, etc., etc., etc. She told herself afterwards that she'd only done it to change the topic, get away from further talk of the gang fight. What other reason could there be? Would she, to be precise, need to go to confession for spreading salacious gossip?

When, however, Gloria got an outraged, indignant look on her face just as she was finishing the telling of her tale, the word 'darn!' sounded in her head. But it really needed to be 'dam!,' as in something that would have stopped her mindless flow of words. But it was too late. The beans had been spilt.

"Those bi . . . " Gloria started to say. But she didn't get to finish the word, because the bell indicating the start of classes cut her off. They should now be sitting at their desks in their next classes.

They said quick goodbyes and then sped off in different directions, each into her own orbit at school and at home as well.

At home that night, Julie told her mother about meeting up with Gloria, how Gloria'd sought her out to make sure they'd gotten home all right that night.

"What a considerate thing to do," her mother mused, before saying, in no uncertain words: "Julie, I hope you didn't tell her anything about our seeing the Cowpers leaving the school with that Orange Dragon bowl."

The words 'too late' and 'double dam' sounded in her head. "I don't think I did, Mom. There wouldn't have been much time. It was right after lunch, and everyone was rushing to class." She let her words drift out into a lengthy ellipsis, tried to sound vague, amnesic even, anything so as to keep her denial from being an out-and-out lie. Her mother did give her one of her "oh, really" looks, which said she hadn't entirely bought what she'd just said.

* * * *

A couple weeks later, long after Julie and her mother had filled her father in on all the other more benign aspects of the mother–daughter dinner—the praline cookie triumph, the land-mine bean salad, Mrs. Jackson's resulting broken tooth, the failed top hat number, the smashed Orange Dragon bowl—Julie was at school. It'd been a worse than usual day so far. She'd started her period at 4 o'clock that morning, and she'd had killer cramps ever since. But she'd made it through lunch, and there was some cause for jubilation that there were only three more periods, no pun intended, and the day would be "ovah," as Arnold Schwarzenegger would put it.

It was right after lunch and everyone was rushing to get to their next class. She was, however, in a state of such abject menstrual misery that she wasn't paying any attention to the usual semi-hysterical cacophony of female voices that made the hallway into a kind of chamber of horrors, one which she was usually an enthusiastic participant in. It could have been due to her estrogen-sodden state, but the noise seemed louder, higher on the shriek scale. She was just glad that her next class was a study period in the school library. There she could huddle down behind the vertical files, lean her head on her hand with her nose pointing in the general direction of her open history book, and snooze.

Oh, but, besides her period, there'd been a sudden cold snap that day. It was early December, and neither the school's nor her heating system had started to take much effect. It was freezing in the library, colder even than the classrooms that morning, and sitting still, in the cold, by the window in the library, it seemed like her cramps were twisting and torquing her into an abstract sculpture titled "Woman in Eternal Hormonal Hell." She tried to solace herself with the sure knowledge that there were now only two and a half more hours in the day. She'd soon be home, where she could curl up under the mohair throw, on the couch, in the living room, in her warm flannel nightgown with nary a waistband or other constricting thing to compound her menstrual misery. . It was her carrot on a string, though she'd prefer a hot cup of tea to a cold carrot on that bitterly cold day.

CHAPTER 13

Bad Beginnings, Worse Endings

Those comforting thoughts proved fleeting. The day was not yet done—not by a long shot.

The further woe took the form of a summons to go immediately to Dr. Drescher's office, delivered by one of the pages who did various tasks for the faculty and staff. Pages weren't flunkies. To be a page was a special honor, a hallowed station in life! The pages formed an elite cadre of girls who were mostly tall, attractive in ways that suggested some distant Greek god ancestry, were members of the senior class, and, oh yes, were able to strike an archly aloof pose when the occasion warranted, as it apparently had in Julie's case.

The piece of paper the page had just thrust under her nose had, printed on the top, "From the desk of Dr. Amalie Drescher" and, in the white space below it, "Miss Tyler— Please come to my office *immediately*. A serious matter has arisen that requires your involvement," written in, what must have been, Dr. Drescher's bold black-ink handwriting. Julie's cramps crescendoed as she gathered up her books and backpack and scrambled after the page, who, her mission done, was already far down the hallway striding as swiftly away from Julie, the common miscreant, as correct form allowed.

A serious matter? She wondered frantically as she scurried down the hallway. What matter had she been involved in that was, could be, serious? What could she possibly have done to attract the attention of the Fuehrer? Thumbing through all the possibilities in her head, she came up . . . empty handed, also empty headed. The only students summoned in such manner to see Dr. Drescher were ones who had done something very seriously wrong, like stolen something, destroyed or damaged school property, cheated on a test, or—what else—had sex in the basement with the school maintenance man? She wasn't making that last one up. According to school lore, the latter had supposedly happened. The student and the maintenance man had been long gone by the time Julie started at Ainsworth, but the incident was still a hot topic of conversation.

Getting to Dr. Drescher's office required that she go outside and follow a covered walkway that connected the classroom building with the administration building. Winter, having that day cast off the shackles of autumn, was now celebrating its hard-won freedom. It was bitterly cold. And the winter wind was having a jolly "go" at *whooshing* through the open space between the two buildings, bending low in howling abandon, and swooping everything up—trees, shrubs, the American flag on the flagpole, Julie's hair. Nothing was spared its *joie de vivre!*

Meanwhile, ripples of menstrual pain were fanning out in Julie's torso and even up into her chest and armpits, where they didn't belong. Her teeth chattered with cold and anxiety and dread. And then the wind, which was having such a jolly time, had a deliriously fun time making the heavy door of the administration building almost impossible to open. Julie had to yank it hard to open it, in the process losing her grip on the history book stuffed with papers she was holding in the crook of her arm. And *then*, when she leaned forward to pick up the book and its contents, didn't her backpack, heavy with other books and other large sharp objects (a crowbar?, a tire iron?, a battle hatchet?), swing off her shoulder, slam into the side of her leg, and then slide to the ground giving her leg a nice bruise and an artfully done scrape. So, while propping the door open with her right leg and buttock, she leaned down into the frigid swirling air and somehow managed to gather up all her belongings and history papers, which had begun to cavort about like butterflies on some kind of recreational drug.

Finally she got herself and all her belongings indoors. The

quiet and warmth of the building that greeted her once the outside door was closed were a temporary balm to her sore, aching spirit. The administration building had been a mansion back in its heyday, the late 19th century. It had been the home of a very wealthy family whose wealth had come from the manufacture of ice skates, a business, like so many in the city, that was now long gone. The upper floor of the administration building was where, appropriately, the highest tier of administrative staff had their offices—the deans of this and that, the treasurer, the assistant executive director. *Everyone* knew where Dr. Drescher's office was. It was a no-brainer. From early morning to sometimes late in the evening, Dr. Drescher's form could be seen bent intently over her desk in front of the large, decorative, arched window right over the entrance, well, the portico really, to the mansion. Julie knew exactly where to go.

As the physiological and mental hubbub that had been interrupted by the front door fiasco resumed its merciless course, Julie was only dimly aware of walking across the polished parquet floor of the entrance hall and climbing the grand curving stairway that led to the second floor where Dr. Drescher had her office. The rooms on the ground floor had pretty much retained their original uses. A dining room, a library, a spacious parlor, all fitted out with appropriately elegant furniture (actually, furnishings left by the ice skate family), were used for special school functions—meetings of the board of trustees, the annual new student "tea," receptions for visiting dignitaries, the induction of students into the Keystone Honor Society, of which Julie was already a member, and other occasions of similar merit.

Catching a glimpse of herself in a large mirror at the top of the stairs, she discovered the wind had given her a wild, Phyllis Diller hairdo. She slapped her miscreant curls into place. Misbehavior seemed to be the order of the day.

When Julie was ushered into Dr. Drescher's office by her secretary, who had the cold, uncaring comportment of an SS officer, Julie suddenly "knew" why she'd been summoned. She'd somehow overlooked one serious matter that might require her "involvement."

There in complete leaden silence sat Dr. Drescher, behind her desk, with the very sullen forms of Gloria Jackson and Alexis Cowper sitting across from her. Dr. Drescher looked up when Julie came in and motioned for Julie to take the unoccupied chair *between* Gloria and Alexis. Julie's heart was now beating like a kettledrum in her chest, vying with her menstrual cramps for mastery of her body. She was also keenly aware that there was, like, some kind of seething storm raging in the space between the two girls, the space she had been instructed to occupy.

Dr. Drescher spoke first.

"I'm sorry to have," the *have* came out more like "haff" because of her German accent "to have summoned you here, Julie. I know you're an excellent—a *model*—student," she said. At this, Julie's heartbeat slowed a bit. Nothing too disturbing so far.

"*However*," Dr. Drescher said sharply. Julie's heart resumed its frantic beating.

With that, Dr. Drescher went on to relate, to Julie's increasing horror, how Gloria had confronted Alexis in the very crowded hallway, after lunch that day, with the dentist's bill for fixing Mrs. Jackson's broken tooth, with the expectation that the Cowpers foot the bill . . . (Julie found out later that the dentist's bill had amounted to a whopping two thousand dollars.)

"Gloria alleges that Mrs. Cowper brought the bean salad with the unpitted olives her grandmother broke her tooth on, but has admitted that she learned this second-hand from you—that you and your mother were the ones who apparently saw Mrs. Cowper leaving the school building carrying the bowl the salad came in."

Something about the word *alleges* made Julie go limp inside. It was explained by what Dr. Drescher said next. When confronted with the bill, Alexis had flat out denied that her mother'd brought the salad and that, therefore, her mother shouldn't be responsible for paying it. Then, apparently, Gloria had insisted that Alexis's mother *had* made the salad and Alexis said she *hadn't*. So, as Gloria later told her later, after a succession of had's and hadn't's that had escalated in ferocity and velocity, a couple of male faculty, who'd been passing through the hallways, had grabbed the two girls by their arms and hauled them over to Dr. Drescher's office, where Gloria and Alexis had continued their battle of the had's and hadn't's. (That would explain the increase in the noise level of the voices in the corridor after lunch, Julie realized. Had she failed to notice that she was also feeling depressed that day?)

"So, I've had to ask you to come here to verify Gloria's . . . ." Here Dr. Drescher paused to find the right, the least offensive, least litigious . . . , word for what she, and her mother, had seen. "Claims" was the word she finally chose, but it came out lamely—more like a wimpy dash than a word.

This was followed by a looming, cavernous silence.

It took Dr. Drescher and Gloria staring, and Alexis glaring, at Julie to make her realize that this was her cue. This silence was where she was supposed to tell the three of them what she and her mother had seen the night of the dinner. Or was it to puke? Suddenly the second became the more likely of the two. Mustering up her courage, and forcing the contents of her stomach back where they belonged, she began talking, in a, surprising even to her, fairly steady, you might even call it courageous, voice.

"We, my mother and I," she began, "got held up leaving so that we could get all the pieces of paper into our purses." A puzzled expression appeared on Dr. Drescher's face. "The slips of paper the different moms had written their e-mail addresses on so my mother could send them her recipe for the praline cookies—" she explained. Dr. Drescher got a brief reminiscent smile on her face at the mention of the *wunderbar* cookies, a word she was likely not going to be using that afternoon. She gave Julie a knowing nod, followed by a curt nod that said "please continue," which Julie dutifully did.

"As we were leaving the lunchroom, we saw Alexis and

her mother come out of the ladies' room and run down the hallway to the outside door." (Something about the unflattering description of the Cowpers' scurrilous behavior gave her more courage, because it was *oh so true*.)

"When Alexis's mother turned to open the door, we could see, *because there's a bright light there*." (Julie underscored those words, too. Good lighting would be a critical factor in her description, based on her reading of all of Elizabeth George's Inspector Lynley books.) "That she was carrying the bowl decorated with orange dragons, the one that had the bean salad with the unpitted black olives in it. I *know* because both my mother and I had some of the salad, and *both* of us," she said with a totally justified amount of venom, "were *surprised* to find that it had unpitted black olives that you couldn't tell from the black beans especially in a candlelit room—"

The rafters didn't exactly resound with her words. But there was a clear note of triumph in them. (She didn't say anything about the broken bowl in the parking lot. That seemed like overkill.) Her feeling of exultation was short-lived.

"That's *completely* untrue. You're lying!!!" Alexis screamed. Worse, she'd leaned over so that her mouth was barely three inches from Julie's ear. Julie felt the words ricochet around inside her head. It was like something Tweety-bird would do to Felix the Cat, but nobody was laughing.

"Mother and I *did* go to the ladies' room as we were leaving, Dr. Drescher," Alexis had now turned and was saying oh-so-politely to Dr. Drescher, "but the rest is a <u>fat lie</u>. YOU'RE LYING, JULIE TYLER!!!!" Alexis had turned (like a gun turret) and exploded this accusation into Julie's ear, which was still recovering from her earlier salvo.

Julie could never have guessed that a name, hers in this case, could be used as a weapon—a dagger. Julie experienced each of the four syllables of her name as a deep jab into her chest. And, come to think of it, which she did later, weren't these, ironically, the very first words Alexis had ever actually uttered to her?

But, then, something arose in Julie's chest. It was a righteous, glorious, St.-George-slaying-the-(orange?)-dragon anger. No one had ever accused her of lying. She was not lying now, would *never* make up such a hideous lie, and she would *not* accept the wicked girl's accusation lying down.

CHAPTER 14
Battle Scars

In a firm, quiet, resolute voice, that took Julie by surprise, she said, not looking at anyone, but nonetheless, expecting *everyone*, including the dignified stillness of Dr. Drescher's office, to listen: "I know what my mother and I *both* saw, which was Alexis and her mother leaving the school carrying the valuable bowl the bean salad was in, the one with the pitted olives in it that caused Mrs. Jackson's tooth to break." (There was just nothing like having truth on her side.)

Julie heard the beginning of a small *yelp* from Alexis, but Dr. Drescher cut her off. "Are you sure, Julie, that the bowl Mrs. Cowper was carrying was the same one the salad came in?"

"Yes." Julie answered simply, looking directly at Dr. Drescher. "In fact, when my mother was in college, she had a part-time job which involved selling fine china. She immediately recognized the bowl."

And then Alexis, this time successfully, cut Julie off. "That's all got to be totally made up, Dr. Drescher. My mother brought bread!!"

"I know what we saw, Dr. Drescher," Julie said simply and firmly, managing with the sharp edge of her voice to cut Alexis off, but also wishing desperately for the megavolcano at Yellowstone National Park to erupt—anything to end this awful conversation. But Alexis was having none of anything Julie said. She'd argue until she was blue in the face or until the cows came home, whichever came last.

"Don't believe her, Dr. Drescher! Julie and her mother have a very good reason to be making up lies about me and my mother." They were ugly words said in an ugly voice. Julie was stunned, also mystified. What "very good reason" would she and her mother have to lie about the bringer of this stupid bean salad that was still managing to cause harm—like the increase in her menstrual cramps wasn't an indication of?

Sensing that the discussion was getting way out of hand, indeed veering into treacherous uncharted waters, Dr. Drescher shouted, commanded!, "Enuff. Enuff—There's no need for further talk. Gloria, if you'll give me your grandmother's dentist's bill, I'll have my secretary submit a claim. The school has insurance to cover injuries sustained on school property, which should cover your grandmother's dentist's bill. You're entirely right in your belief that your family shouldn't have to bear the costs. Now, let us get on with each of our busy days."

With that, Dr. Drescher stood up. The meeting?, discussion?, battle? was over, and it hadn't required the Yellowstone volcano to blow its lid. A truce, of sorts, had been declared. Gloria left the battlefield satisfied that her demands had been met. Alexis, and by extension her mother, left the battlefield undefeated, her and her mother's reputation quite intact. And Julie? She followed up the rear dragging her backpack like a defeated soldier dragging his sword from a bloody field. (And wasn't she, fittingly, beginning to feel the beginning trickle of warm blood in her underpants that said she'd better change her tampon *soon*.) She'd not been cleared of being a liar. *And* she and her mother had been "accused" of having a reason to lie. She was sick. She was frightened. She was numb with unhappiness.

"Julie," Dr. Drescher called softly just as Julie got to the doorway leading out of her office, her heart dropping into her shoes at being held up for one more second. "Just a moment. I want to say something to you in private before you leave." She walked quickly across the room, reached around Julie, and pushed the door close.

Julie stopped but didn't turn toward Dr. Drescher. That would have enabled Dr. Drescher to see the tears of hurt in her eyes and the red splotches of anger on her cheeks, both of which, for her, were a private matter. However, she couldn't *not* stop.

She was, after all, in the presence of the executive director, the head honcho, of the school. So she stopped, her head hanging down in obvious defeat. Dr. Drescher, respectfully, stood behind her, and addressed her words to Julie's back.

"I'm really very sorry to haff involved you, Julie," Dr. Drescher said in a totally un–Dr. Drescher, almost motherly, voice. "I would understand if you feel angry about the way things ended," as in being called a liar and not being cleared of the accusation, Julie thought bitterly. "But," here the school's head director seemed to be struggling for the right words, in *English*, to say to Julie. "I know how unjustly treated you must be feeling. I wish I could haff ended things today more satisfactorily—more to *everyone's* benefit. *That* was my aim. But," and Julie heard her breathe out a long, discouraged sigh, "Today no one was the clear victor, Julie, if that's any solace to you. But I want to tell you that I was most impressed with the way you conducted yourself today. You were wronged, and I could have understood if you'd reacted differently—viciously even. But, instead, you maintained your composure and dignity, and in that your honor, and," she added in almost a whisper, "Gloria's honor as well." Dr. Drescher left it at that. Comments about Alexis's conduct were conspicuously lacking, or were they?

Dr. Drescher reached around Julie, opened the door, and Julie drifted wordlessly out the door, through the secretary's office, down the elegant stairway, and then back out into the winter winds from hell.

Back to where she'd been sitting in the library, via the bathroom to change her tampon, Julie found herself just staring out the window at the greenery being pummeled by the wind. Feeling similarly pummeled, she tried to make sense of what had just happened. Whatever it was, it was like trying to grab ahold of something on the top shelf of a cupboard but, not only could you not get ahold of it, you couldn't even tell what it was, and the more your fingers touched it, the more it got pushed beyond reach.

CHAPTER 15

The Curtain Closes

When Julie got home, enough time had elapsed after the incident in Dr. Drescher's office for her to decide not to tell her mother anything about it. For one thing, she was still trying to process, assemble into some kind of recognizable form, the craziness of the experience. For another, her menstrual cramps were still wreaking havoc with the lower half of her body. She wasn't having much luck dealing with either. It did help, though, that soon she was in her flannel nightgown, under the mohair throw, cup of tea in hand. After supper, back in her manufactured cocoon, Greek history book in hand, the phone rang. No big deal there. It did that a lot in her household.

Her mother answered it. She could tell by the tone of her mother's voice that it wasn't someone really familiar like her Aunt Babs. But it also wasn't someone her mother minded talking to. One word, "Martha," told her all she needed to know. It was Martha Jackson calling, as it turned out, to apologize for her granddaughter's "unpardonable behavior," not only for involving Julie in her dispute with Alexis, but then putting Julie into the position of having to clear her name. Mrs. Jackson talked for a bit longer, off on other less toxic subjects than Alexis Cowper and her sadistic mother. With promises to have lunch some day after Christmas, Mrs. Tyler got off the phone.

Her mother didn't immediately get up, just looked down into her lap seeming to ponder something very deeply. Finally she got up and, not surprisingly, came over to where Julie was perched on the couch. The closer her mother got, the more she had this awful feeling that, period or no period, she was about to get a stern lecture for telling Gloria that it was the Cowpers who'd brought the dratted orange dragon bean salad. She even pulled her knees up for protection against her mother's verbal onslaught.

As her mother sat at the end of the couch just vacated by her cowardly legs, Julie decided it'd be best to get the jump on her mother.

"I know, Mom, I know," she said, "I shouldn't have told Gloria about what we saw. It just came out the day after the dinner when she tracked me down to find out if we'd gotten home okay." (She knew, once those words had fled her mouth, that her mother could have justifiably taken her to task for denying telling Gloria about their sighting of the Cowpers with the damning bowl. But, if her mother noted it, she kept quiet about it now.) Having cleared that tricky little hurdle, and because she knew her mother expected it, Julie began to tell her mother her version of what had happened that afternoon. As she did so, for some weird reason, she found herself mentally stitching a gold thread that linked one figure in the carpet to the next, giving the carpet a forlorn gildedness.

Everything was going along fine until she got to the part where Alexis accused her of being a liar. First her voice started to wobble, then tears began to well up from her lower lids, and, then, didn't she finally dissolve into body-wracking sobs. Estrogen had to be behind that last thing. She never cried like that. But, her head now buried in her hands, she did feel, most wonderfully, her mother's arms wrapping themselves around her and giving her a good heartening, healing hug. Maybe her mother could still right all the wrongs in her life. Would her mother mind going and sitting in the rocking chair so that she could sit in her lap and be rocked as she hadn't been since she was five

"Oh, Julie—dearest, sweetest Julie," her mother crooned into her daughter's mass of now very tangled curly hair. "Welcome to the adult world of slander, spite, and meanness of spirit."

But her mother wasn't done with her words of worldly

wisdom. She proceeded, by way of a further lesson in the meanness of the world, to tell her about something that had happened to her a long time ago at church, of all places. Someone, starting with the Altar Guild, of which she'd been a long-time member, and was no longer, had begun to spread a completely false rumor that she and Julie's father had *had* to get married, that she was pregnant when she married her father.

Julie immediately understood how the rumor *could* have started. She had, in fact, been born exactly *seven and a half* months after her parents' wedding day. But she'd been a preemie, and her mother had pictures of her little three-pound self lying curled up like a little caterpillar in an incubator as proof. The point her mother was making to her now, which Julie understood loud and clear, was that the rumor (this one completely untrue) had caused her mother an inordinate amount of trouble. And hadn't she, likewise, had an inordinate amount of trouble at school that day for spreading a *true* rumor, one that truly deserved to be spread if you asked her?

"Suddenly, people I'd known for years started shunning me," her mother was saying. "It was your Aunt Babs who finally got wind of the gossip that was circulating around the church, that explained the snubbing I was getting. But the thing that hurt the most, sweetheart, besides the fact that people I'd thought of as friends had turned against me, was that there were people at church who believed, probably some who still do, that you started off illegitimate."

'*Ouch*,' thought Julie. Now she was really getting her mother's message. The false rumor about her start in life had caused her mother, her father, *her*, great hurt. The same went for her! Hadn't she set in motion the inside scoop on the bean salad that, something told her, wasn't going to reach the inertia of rest for a long time. It didn't matter even that *her* gossip was true....

"Hey, what are you two ladies having a tête-à-tête about?" It was her father who'd walked (stalked?!) silently in on his stocking feet and was now peering down at his two favorite girls. It was clear to his lawyerly eye that something was amiss.

"Julie had a rather unpleasant experience at school today," her mother said but didn't elaborate. Her father'd had a bad day at work, having lost a case against a very clever defense lawyer who'd managed to get a trial dismissed on the basis of a completely hokum technicality. That way of "losing" a case always made him angry. He could cope with losing a case in a fair court battle, but getting something dismissed on a technicality was, in his mind, tantamount to cheating.

After her father went back to his newspaper and her mother went back to the kitchen, and Julie was left alone on the couch, she found herself back to reaching for, trying to grasp, that unknown object on the top shelf of a closet. What did Alexis mean when she accused Julie and her mother of having some kind of motive for telling a "lie" about the Cowpers? And there was another niggling concern. What was behind the Cowpers bringing the orange dragon bean salad? That is, was it just stupid, or was there something more diabolical about it? And then there was her mother's story of the gossip that had been circulated about her at church. Could the Cowpers have somehow been responsible for the rumor? But, no, that was silliness talking. Alexis had started at Ainsworth only that fall. The Cowpers were new to the city as far as she knew. She knew nothing about where she'd come from. Maybe a dumpster, a gypsy camp, a deep chasm in the earth which belched forth sulfurous fumes.

CHAPTER 16

What It Must Feel Like To Be Alexander the Great

That night Julie got a good night's sleep. She awoke refreshed and cheerful. Today was a different world from yesterday's. As per her mood, the sun was duly shining, the sky couldn't have been bluer, and the wind had tired of its mad romp, "winded" most likely. Mercifully, also, a truce had been called in her abdomen. Of course, the guerilla warfare of the menstrual cramps (i.e., cramps encamped in the long, low hills of her abdominal muscles, the sudden bursts of shooting pains across her abdomen, merciless hours of waiting until the "enemy" fell silent) would resume next month and every month thereafter for a very long time, until such time as she became pregnant or menopausal, neither of which, she'd heard, was a total joyride.

Julie hopped happily out of the car at school and chirruped a happy goodbye to her mother. Her mother'd driven her to school, even though another mother was carpooling that week. Her mother'd said it was because she needed to do some Christmas shopping, and mornings were always better for that. But her mother couldn't fool her. Julie knew it was really because her mother wanted to make sure that her little unhappy chick of the night before got a good dose of motherly nurturing before she left the nest and embarked on another day at school fraught with the angst any day can dish out. Yesterday being a perfect example of that. Truth be told, as she made her way into the school, Julie felt much like how Alexander the Great must have felt when he strode gleefully into yet another kingdom to conquer.

As it turned out, however, like most good moods, it didn't

last long, just up until lunchtime. It was Gloria's doing, or undoing, as the case may be.

"Julie!" Julie heard her name called out just as she emerged from the bathroom on her way to fourth period after lunch. It was Gloria, wearing a sorry, sadder-but-wiser, look. "I really need to apologize to you about yesterday."

"It's okay, Gloria," Julie said as Gloria came and stood next to her, close enough for a confidential conversation, though the halls were now ricocheting with the usual din of female voices, putting normal voices on a par with, like, sign language. "Honestly, it was really my fault to begin with. I should have known better than tell you about the Cowpers bringing the salad."

"Don't blame yourself, Julie," Gloria said emphatically. "Don't you see? If you hadn't told me who brought the salad, my Granny would have had to find some way to pay the $2,000 dentist's bill. That's like two million dollars for us. It wouldn't have occurred to me that the school would have insurance that would pay for it. I only thought that Alexis's family should be responsible since it was her mother who brought the salad. And it really *should* have just ended there, *not* in Dr. Drescher's office. It shouldn't be the insurance company that has to foot the bill. They're not the ones who brought the salad!" Gloria was now, Julie thought, re-re-*re*-experiencing the outrage she'd felt first the night of the mother–daughter dinner.

Julie had to vent a little laugh at this point. Yes, she was glad the dentist's bill would be paid, albeit by the insurance company, but she could have done without the drama that had unfolded the day before in Dr. Drescher's office.

Gloria, hearing Julie's laugh, laughed, too. "Yeah, I know. I could have picked a much better way to find out about the insurance . . . ." Here she paused, crossed her arms over her chest, and got a very odd look on her face. "Julie," she said tentatively, "I don't mean to pry, but what was that all about, that bit about you and your mother lying—of having a reason to lie about them bringing the salad . . . . Have your family and the Cowpers crossed swords or something?"

Julie shook her head no, feeling a chill go down her spine as she did so. So, in the midst of all the pandemonium in Dr. Drescher's office the day before, Gloria had also noticed Alexis's strange accusation. All she could say was: "Gloria, I haven't got a clue what that was all about. My Dad's an assistant DA, and he crosses swords with people every day, but there's nothing personal between us and the Cowpers that I know of. Alexis is just this girl who's acted like I don't exist since she started school here this year. My Mom certainly doesn't know either Alexis or her mother—though the way she treated my mother at the dinner, you'd think she was some kind of arch-enemy."

"Hmm, I didn't notice that," Gloria said, "But, then, I was too busy dealing with Mrs. Cowper saying the 'n' word in a stage whisper when we sat down." So Julie and her mother had both heard right. Worse, the Jacksons had heard, too.

Here Gloria paused as she brought her renewed anger at the racial slur under control, so she could tell Julie more of the saga of yesterday's nutty experience.

"What you also need to know, Julie, because it's the real reason why Dr. Drescher ended up summoning you, is that Alexis accused me of making the story up. She accused me of noticing that she and her mother were of the 'moneyed class.' Yes," Gloria said in a voice ridged with fury, "those were here exact words. And, so, that made me and my grandmother 'gold-diggers,' *also* Alexis's word."

Julie felt her mouth hang open. She knew, of course, because of what Dr. Drescher had said to her before she'd left the office, that she'd been summoned to clear Gloria's name. She hadn't known just how nasty things had gotten. Alexis Cowper's behavior was abominable, deplorable, there was no adequate word for it. Maybe she'd need to make one up, something like gograstruqlergugical.

"Julie, I am really sorry about that," Gloria said, seeing the distress on Julie's face. "I never expected that things would go so haywire. But, girl, are you *sure* you and the Cowpers haven't crossed swords?"

All Julie could do was shake her head 'no,' feeling as she did so as if gravity was suddenly exerting a stronger pull on all of her innards.

And then, off on another tack, Gloria, the defense lawyer in the making, had further disquieting observations to impart. "Think of it, Julie, Alexis and her mother were both at the table when Granny broke her tooth. Granny was sitting right next to Alexis. They *had* to notice that my grandmother'd broken her tooth on an unpitted olive in the salad they'd brought. You and your mother did, and you were sitting across from us. They should have, if they were decent people, said something before the dinner was over—at least apologized, made some kind of amends. Instead they just sat there like those stupid statues on Easter Island staring off into thin air."

Julie had a good laugh at that. Yes, that was a perfect description of the demon duo from the beginning to the end of the dinner. But what Gloria was saying was disturbing. Mrs. Cowper and her daughter had sat in total (stony!) oblivious silence all while three people at their table had been nastily surprised by the unpitted olives in the bean salad *they* had brought. They couldn't have missed all three incidents, and certainly not the third one when Mrs. Jackson broke her tooth. The sound of it had reverberated around the table.

But, then—there being *some* justice in the world—there'd been all the umbrage about the land-mined bean salad voiced by quite a few people in the room— "flushed out" by her mother's cookies as it happened. Maybe Alexis and her mother didn't know about the unpitted olives in the salad. *Maybe* a cook, a maid, some hireling had made it. Still, Alexis and her mother had chosen to sneak out of the building with the damning bowl rather than acknowledge any guilt. That was certainly incriminating behavior of the first order.

Once more Julie found herself feeling emotionally ravaged by the Cowpers. There was something about the brand of anger they kept stoking up in her that didn't seem good for her health.

Before they could talk more, the bell announcing the beginning of afternoon classes rang. They had to run to get to class before getting marked down as late. It was when, out of breath, she sat down in her next class that she discovered she'd lost her wonderful Alexander the Great mood. Flown the coop. Gone. She now, no longer, felt like conquering India.

CHAPTER 17

Nutcracker Sunday

Three weeks later, Julie had pretty much put the orange dragon bean salad incident out of her head. This was helped along by the fact that the countdown to Christmas was approaching its juggernaut phase. It had now become like a huge snowball rolling out-of-control down a hill, gobbling up every happy holiday-maker in its path. Julie gloried in this phase of the season. She *knew*, because she'd heard it every one of the four Sundays in Advent for as far back as she could remember, that this was *supposed* to be a time of preparation for, and meditation on, the coming of the light of Christ into a very dark world, *not* the time for abandoned merrymaking.

But Father Desseau, on that second Sunday in Advent, knew he was wasting his breath. One could tell from the look of tired resignation in his old eyes as he painfully mounted the steps to the pulpit that, except maybe for the three old nuns in complete habits who always sat in the first pew, he was essentially talking to a church full of four-year-olds whose thoughts were completely tangled up in either tinsel or strands of Christmas lights.

The men would be trying to decide whether their wives would prefer a new iron or a new food processor for Christmas, and also, did their wives need, like, the model number *and* the bar code of the drills they wanted? Otherwise, they'd be sure to get the wrong one. They only hoped it wasn't a bathrobe. *Please,* not another bathrobe. Others would be girding their loins to get through the complete Christmas card list that afternoon. Some were reminding themselves to remember to get from, or give to, *whomever* that fabulous scallop casserole recipe. Many of the women were wondering *what* to wear to the work Christmas party that none of their co-workers would have remembered seeing on them for the past five years. Many of the men would be thinking about the Christmas lights that still needed to be put up, so the kids would stop their pestering. Et cetera.

On this second Sunday in Advent, Julie's brain was completely given over to thoughts of the coming afternoon. It was the afternoon she, her mother, and her Aunt Babs traditionally went to see *The Nutcracker* performed by the Boston Ballet.

And it wasn't just the ballet. The day also included a late-afternoon champagne luncheon at The Yorkshire Hotel across the street from Jarvis Hall where the ballet was performed. After the final bow, and after Clara wakes up one more year in a row and discovers that the broken Nutcracker Prince nutcracker wasn't broken after all, or was it?, Julie, her mother, and her Aunt Babs then processed across the street to the city's oldest and grandest hotel, The Yorkshire. This was also the time when, after two and a half hours of watching lithe ballet bodies perfectly leap, plié, pirouette, arabesque, fouetté, and perfectly execute every other ballet move in the book, Julie felt like she had a turnip body and logs for legs. *Thump, thump, thump* her legs went as they clumped across the street to the hotel with her aunt and mother in tow, who also were not looking too graceful. But who could wearing winter boots?

However, as soon as she entered the gilded glory of The Yorkshire, she doffed her turnip awkwardness and donned, for a total of about two hours, what it must have felt like to be a Vanderbilt or an Astor at the turn of the century (the nineteenth one).

Her father and Uncle Pete, Babs' husband? First of all, they didn't "do" men in tights and women in tutus, though it seemed to Julie that tights were pretty much what football players were wearing these days. Regardless, this was the zenith time of the pro football season. About the time Julie's mother and her Aunt Babs were taking their first sips of champagne, and Julie her first sip of 7-Up, in a champagne glass (her Aunt Babs' idea), her father and uncle would be refilling their pilsner glasses with beer and ordering out for a pepperoni pizza. They wouldn't be doing this until halftime, though, so as not to miss any of the important plays. They didn't "do" halftimes either, which they scorned about as much as ballet.

That Sunday was ended on a particularly glorious note. Warmed by the food, the conversation, the champagne, and the gilded glory of The Yorkshire's formal dining room, they discovered, when they emerged from the hotel into the dark winter chill, that tutu-like flakes of snow were pirouetting to the ground—the kind that usually presaged a serious snowstorm.

All three of them, not just Julie, became 5-year-olds. They laughed and giggled as they flung their arms out to greet the snow. They arched their heads back so that the snowflakes could settle and melt with tiny stings of cold on their warm faces.

And then they did what is, like, *genetically encoded* in people to do at the season's first snowfall. They stuck out their tongues so that some of the flakes bowed low onto their warm tongues—so that they could contain within them these angelic bits of joy that had descended through thousands of feet of thin air (from heaven!) to their waiting tongues.

Unfortunately, though, only about seven inches of snow fell that night, not enough to cancel school the next day. Drats, Julie thought when she turned on her laptop while getting dressed and saw from the local morning newscast that it was going to be a business-as-usual day. Nothing was canceled.

CHAPTER 18

Christmas Tree Saturday

    Another Christmas tradition in the Tyler family was the annual expedition to get a Christmas tree on the Saturday just before Christmas, so it wouldn't be shedding a blitzkrieg of needles by Christmas day. It was an outing that included only Julie and her father. Her mother stayed home and did a thorough cleaning of the house, which she much preferred to watching Julie and her father's annual bloodless battle as they tried to sway the decision toward each other's camp. (Julie always accused her mother of being Swiss on this day, since she always remained staunchly neutral as to the type, height, breadth, fullness, *and*, most cowardly, cost of the tree.) Julie's father always held fast for a tree that wasn't too expensive. Five bucks was a good price, and he refused to take inflation into account. Julie fought for a tree that had enough branches for at least five ornaments. Actually, what she *really* wanted was a tree fit for the White House but knew that would never happen, not with Scrooge Tyler for a father.

    The day always began with Julie and her father clearing a space in the living room where there were corner windows visible from the street. (Christmas is all about *sharing*, after all.) This involved moving a two-tiered knickknack table bedecked with Henredon porcelain objects out into the hallway next to the bench that usually stood alone in the hallway. In strict accordance with tradition, when Julie and her father began to execute the knickknack table maneuver, her mother would be standing at the kitchen end of the hallway with her hands clapped anxiously to her cheeks and uttering mouse-like squeals and shrieks until the table was safely placed in its temporary hallway home.

"Your mother sure has this thing about china bibelots," her father would always grumble under his breath as the little china objects did their annual holiday spin on the slick surface of the table. (Julie knew for a fact, because her father said it every year as soon as they were in the front seat of the car and backing out of the driveway, that he loved her mother very much *but* he'd be just as happy with plastic molded chairs and end tables made out of cinderblocks. "Things you could just hose down," he always added for the sake of clarity. Julie, on cue, would always laugh. But the treasonous truth was that the older she got, the more she was tending toward porcelain than plastic things.)

The space for the tree cleared, and her mother restoring all her traumatized china darlings to their correct places on the table, Julie and her father would hop into her mother's car, since you couldn't get a Christmas tree in the trunk of her Dad's small Toyota, and be on their way.

Lunch always came next, at The Lido, the oldest Italian restaurant in town. The Lido was not known for its cuisine. In that regard, it couldn't hold a candle-stuffed-into-a-chianti bottle to the newer, swankier, more *Italian* Italian restaurants in town. But it did have atmosphere that you couldn't beat. Where else was there a restaurant still run by the same family (the *fifth* generation of Brunellis) that had opened it in the 1920s? Where else in town could you find original (vintage!) red plastic–upholstered booths, badly worn testaments to the heft of hundreds of hungry diners' bodies over the past hundred years. Where else could you still find wall-mounted jukeboxes with *Al Di La*, *O Sole Mio*, and *Volare* (and that still played one song for a dime or three for a quarter!)? Where else were there walls plastered with framed photos (including some of Mafioso-looking types, one actually carrying a violin case, and lots of boxers, the pugilists not the dogs) that went back, probably, to the day the first Brunelli set foot on Ellis Island, or snuck ashore, whichever.

And where else could you walk into a place with the accumulated smell, almost a 100 years' worth, of garlic, tomato sauce, meatballs, sausage, and pepperoni. And, oh yes, The Lido only did the basic pastas—spaghetti, ravioli, penne, ziti, and lasagna, combined with some variation on tomato sauce. The waiters gave the hairy eyeball to anyone who had the temerity to ask for cappelletti, farfalle, rotini, cavatelli, orecchiette, or any other snobby kind of pasta, because it was like insulting the don. There were no green foods at The Lido, unless you counted the pale green chunks of iceberg lettuce floating in vinegar and oil that constituted the "house salad." The Lido was also famous for its garlic bread—bread saturated with a garlic-olive oil mixture, topped with a quarter-inch of parmesan, then melted down and toasted under the broiler. Yum!

After eating their usual meatballs and spaghetti (Julie's father) and spaghetti and meat sauce (Julie), they set off for Harper's Christmas tree lot, at most times of the year a sadly unnoticed vacant lot next to an unhappy-looking laundromat. Christmas was the only time of year the lot got any attention, making it better off than most of the other vacant lots in town.

Fortified by their Italian meal, and breathing clouds of garlic-laden steam, Julie and her father got out of the car at the Christmas tree lot, metaphorically hitching on their "helmets," "body armor," and "M16 rifles" in readiness for this year's battle of the Christmas trees. There'd been a dusting of snow the night before, so all the trees, even the pathetic ones with only five branches, were looking their festive best.

Per tradition, they first did a quick tour of the trees for sale, the reconnaissance phase. This involved looking without stopping to inspect the more than a hundred trees tied pertly to upright poles. It always seemed like looking for a dog at the SPCA. Each one seemed to be yipping and yapping and saying "please take me home," "please take me home."

After that, they'd get down to the serious business of reaching some truce on a tree that came within reach of both of their criteria, i.e., cheap versus White House-perfect. This year, however, something unexpected happened. Not a pleasant surprise. One that ruined the day for Julie, perhaps forever.

Just as they were finishing up their quick reconnoiter of the trees on display, they bumped into, literally, Alexis Cowper and her mother.

Julie's first response was a quick sucking in of breath—shock. Alexis's, too, for that matter. The two hadn't really seen each other since the incident in Dr. Drescher's office, not that Alexis had ever actually "seen" her in anything but the strict physiologic sense.

Then came an even greater shock.

"Well, Bob Tyler, how *are* you?" Mrs. Cowper, like, gushed when she saw Julie's father.

"I'm doing well, Alexandra. How are you?" Mr. Tyler said in a tight voice Julie'd never heard her father use before.

"Why, I'm doing marvelously. I didn't know you lived here— And what happened to your calling me Lex—that's what you always called me," she cooed as she looked up at him from under her long (were they real or the expensive woven-in kind?) eyelashes.

This was not the same woman who'd mauled her mother with unfriendliness at the mother–daughter dinner. Just the opposite. This was a woman who was now sultry, seductive, sexy, and snake-y. (All those sibilant, hissing *s*'s were so satisfyingly reptilian in reference to this woman who'd acted like a Gila monster toward her mother.) She was wearing black leggings tucked into fur-lined boots. She had beautiful legs, all the way up to her crotch, which the leggings seemed to have been worn precisely to reveal. Her short jacket looked to be mink. The gorgeous silk scarf that had been artfully swept around her neck was, of course, from the house of Gucci. Her blonde hair (very expertly dyed, Julie had to say) sprang with life and curls and insouciance, or was it insolence?, as she found an infinite number of ways and reasons to toss and shake it so that it could correctly reflect in gold and bronze highlights the winter afternoon sun.

About this point, Julie realized that neither she, nor Alexis for that matter, "existed" in this conversation. They were small moons circling in very distant orbits the "planet" Alexis's mother and Julie's father were on.

"I've always lived here, Alexandra." Her father's words were delivered tersely, tensely. Julie could see that Mrs. Cowper hadn't missed this *slight* slight. Her expression had gone from saccharine to sour before you could hear the "period" at the end of his sentence. But she recovered fast like all reptiles.

"Of course, how silly of me. I'd forgotten that. It's been so many years—since our senior year in college . . . ." Here her words just trailed off into a barren, bleak place, which, in Julie's mind, no one would want to make into a National Park. And then Mrs. Cowper looked up at her father and actually fluttered her eyelashes at him. Julie felt anew the desire to grab the woman by her Gucci scarf and twist it until she coughed up a truly contrite "sorry."

Her father, wonderfully, was clearly not keen on reminiscing or renewing old acquaintances and his eyes were very much averted from Mrs. Cowper's.

"I came back here as soon as I finished law school, Alexandra," he said in a firm monotone in keeping with his other responses to the woman. "I've been working in the D.A.'s office ever since I got my law degree and passed the bar. By the way, this is my daughter, Julie."

"Oh, and this is my daughter, Alexis," Alexandra (or was it Lex?) Cowper said, somewhat thrown off balance, as if she'd forgotten she even had a daughter, which, of course, she hadn't had back when her father and Alexis's mother had apparently been chums of some kind or other. Mrs. Cowper righted herself quickly. "But I believe our daughters know each other—from school," she said with an oh-so-charming, drooling smile at Julie's father.

Julie's father smiled and said hello to Alexis, who made a swift "curtsey" of a smile, before resuming her regulation hostility.

"Gosh, Bob—I can't tell you how thrilled I am to see you.

How could I have not remembered that you live here. I should have given you a call. I'm somewhat new in town. I came here after my divorce from Alexis's father. It just seemed a good idea to get away from all the unpleasantries that involved and make a new start in a new city."

At this news, Julie's father started, like actors "start" in movies when they get shot. Julie started, too, like one would do when the good guy gets shot out of nowhere.

"Well, Alexandra, I'm pretty tied up with my family life and job."

"Of course you are, Bob," Mrs. Cowper gushed again. "You're doing, after all, exactly what you wanted to do when you became a lawyer, and from what I hear, you're doing a very good job of being a public prosecutor . . . ." Here Mrs. Cowper's words drifted out, and she looked up at her father with an on-so-knowing smile. Then she had the nerve, of all things, to do a little pelvic thrust, *then* reach out and caress his sleeve, oh so affectionately, with a sleek, black leather–gloved hand. Julie hadn't blinked during all this. Her eyes were frozen open with some kind of fear.

What the heck is going, had gone, on between her father and Mrs. Cowper—in college, before her mother and father had met and married, before she was born, before he'd entered law school?

"Yes, Alexandra, I am doing *exactly* what I wanted to do in my work and in my life, and both have proved very full and very satisfying."

Her father's words, it was very apparent to Julie, had sent an unmistakable warning to this woman who'd seen fit to be forward toward her father in ways that *really* only her mother had a right to be. Suddenly surging up in her was the same righteous anger this woman, and her daughter, had now stoked for the third time.

"Bob," Mrs. Cowper then cooed oh-so-sultrily, "really, we must get together for lunch and catch up on old times."

At that, her father started again, sustaining another gun-shot-like wound to the chest. "Alexandra," he said in a voice so choked by some kind of strong emotion it was almost a whisper, "frankly, my family and work life keep me too busy for renewing old acquaintances. And some old friendships are best kept in the past." He then leveled his eyes at Mrs. Cowper with a look of, not hatred, not disgust, just pity.

"Well, then," Mrs. Cowper said in a low growl of a voice, narrowing her eyes like a cat, and letting her eyes "stray" all over her father, "I'll leave you with my best wishes for the holiday, *and* for the rest of your life." With that, she turned on her heel and walked away. The cheeks of her tiny bottom did a smart *rat-a-tat-tat* as she marched toward the parking lot. Alexis followed up the 'rear,' Julie noted viciously. This small witticism didn't, though, put a dent in her, now, totally unnerved state. Soon the BMW they'd gotten into sped out of the parking lot, without a Christmas tree.... But a Christmas tree couldn't have fit into the small, sporty, fast series 3 BMW, well maybe one with enough branches for five ornaments.

Julie and her father resumed their search for a tree. But the sky had fallen in on their day. Her father was clearly distracted, and Julie felt as though her heart, her world, her love for her mother and father had been ravaged by an evil force, the *Cow-turds*!, again.

They selected a tree, but there was no time-honored friendly tussle. They pretty much just turned and took the first tree, the first balsam tree, they saw. It just happened that it was White House perfect. But it was an empty victory for Julie. It had been hard-won for all the wrong reasons.

CHAPTER 19

The Sinking of the Titanic

The weather in the car was like the weather outside—chilly. Maybe chillier. And tense with some kind of looming danger.

Julie felt as though something like an iceberg had wedged itself between her and her father following the encounter with the Cowpers. This brought to mind that other iceberg, the one that had lurked in the dark and lacerated the hull of the *Titanic*. It seemed as mammoth and dangerous.

So, Gloria had been right, it suddenly hit her. There was some kind of history with the Cowpers, some reason maybe for the Cowpers to have it in for them, the Tylers.

She could hear the bristling and almost silky rustling of the fit-for-the-White-House balsam tree in the back as it settled its silken "flounces" grandly into place, in the process filling the interior of the car with its magnificent fragrance. But Julie was too unhappy right then to care. It *was* fitting that it felt as if there were thousands of needles prickling her skin. She was that scared by what had just happened in the Christmas tree lot.

"Julie," her father said softly, quietly, stiffly.

She couldn't look at her father. It made her too uncomfortable. She didn't want to see the expression on his face left over from seeing Mrs. Cowper—Lex, discover the effect of it on him. The glove compartment was the safest bet for now.

"I need to explain to you something about Alexandra Cowper and how I knew her, especially after what you witnessed today," he said in a quiet voice that scared her all the more.

Julie didn't know what her father was about to tell her,

but her gut reaction was to shout "no, don't!" It didn't matter. Like it or not, she had to listen, learn what there was between them and the Cowpers that had now gone from a basically silly (benign) incident at school to a *malignant* force that seemed to want to disrupt their lives in any way it could.

Her father began his story of Mrs. Cowper in a very solemn way.

"I didn't know your friend's mother as Alexandra Cowper," he said.

Julie had to interrupt her father there, set him straight, that Alexis was no friend, had been the girl who'd accused her of lying, been behind the incident that had landed her in Dr. Drescher's office a little over three weeks ago.

"Ah," her father said, throwing his head back a little when he heard that. "Why am I not surprised," he said more to himself than her. "Another case of the apple not falling far from the tree. That probably makes it even more important for you to hear my story." He said this looking directly over at Julie, as if trying to decide whether she was ready to hear the X-rated version or maybe only the PG version of his long-ago relationship with Alexandra Cowper.

Julie had to force herself to detach her eyes from the glovebox and look over at her father. She could feel her eyes squinting shut like they would do on a windy day in March when there was all kinds of grit in the air. It was the only defense she had. She could see her father's eyes looking steadily, honestly at her but she couldn't see the expression on his face. "Go ahead, Dad," she finally said in a shaky, scared voice.

For the next several minutes her eyes were back to staring fixedly at the glove compartment, while her brain maddeningly crisscrossed the four corners of the lid with some kind of dull wire, nothing golden or silver for sure.

Her father had known Alexandra Cowper as Alexandra Riley-Dolan. She'd been the captain of the cheerleading squad. He'd been the star quarterback of the football team. It was the classic all-American pairing of the most-attractive female on campus with the most-all-around-good-catch male. They'd dated for a couple months, mostly just going to parties together. They *hadn't* kissed *once*, her father emphasized fiercely at that point.

One night, totally out of the blue, as he was walking Alexandra to her sorority house after a late-night party on campus, she all of a sudden started talking about marriage, not in general, but *with him*. So serious was she about it, and so certain of his feelings in return, that she'd picked out a wedding gown and bridesmaid dresses, arranged for the reception at a local restaurant, ordered the flowers, and lined up her bridesmaids!!! All that remained to be done, her father growled, was "to get the marriage license and have the blood tests."

Julie wasn't holding up well at this point. She felt tangled up in some kind of web, one fashioned by a poisonous spider, and the spider was getting closer and closer. She could hear the crepitating (crispy and crackly) sounds of the spider's legs as it climbed toward her, but she couldn't see it yet and she couldn't move away from it either, the web held her so fast.

"Granted I hadn't had much experience with women, growing up in all-male Catholic schools," her father was now saying in a voice that was just plain bleak, like the moors described in *Jane Eyre*, was what went through Julie's mind. "But I had been around my two older sisters Babs and Bobbie a lot, and from all their chatter about things male and female, I knew this was not the way one went about settling on marriage. I also knew with complete certainty, the moment Alexandra brought up the idea of marriage, that she was not the woman I wanted to marry, share a life with, bear my children."

Julie was thrilled to hear him say that. Felt her chest fill with a loud cheer that would have exploded out of her, except that her father'd continued talking, telling her more of his long-ago thwarting of Alexandra Riley-Dolan Cowper's marriage plans, and from the tone of his voice, it was far too soon to cheer about anything.

"I had the good sense not to trample overly on Alexandra's feelings, break the news gently. I knew that being spurned in love was not an easy thing for anyone to accept, especially a young woman, *especially* one like Alexandra. So I mumbled a lot of kind and considerate things, told her I'd enjoyed her company, we'd had a lot of fun together, et cetera, et cetera, but, not only did I not want to marry until I was finished with law school, I was pretty certain she was not the right person for me. For one, I doubted she would be happy being the wife of a humble public prosecutor making a public prosecutor's wages. I told her that if I'd given her the wrong impression, I was very sorry about that, and that in the interest of not leading her on, it would be best for us to stop seeing each other."

In Julie's mind, the story should have ended there. If she'd been Alexandra, and she had to admit the woman had shown extremely good judgment in choosing her father as the man she wanted to be her husband, she was sure her father's rejection would have split her heart in two. She'd have gone back to her dorm room, wept the night through, skipped classes the next day, and probably worn black for at least a week, like the old Italian woman behind the cash register at The Lido always did. Alexandra's response had been the polar opposite, emphasis on *polar* (i.e., the climate in the car right then). Per her father, Alexandra proceeded to call him every rotten name in the book, including some he wouldn't expect a young woman to even know, and finished by telling him in an ugly voice that he'd regret not marrying her. She could've made him a very rich lawyer by just snapping her fingers, wherewith she'd snapped her fingers in his face, her father said. "As if I wanted to become a rich lawyer.... Well, of course, Alexandra had no notion of doing something for just the good of mankind. From there," her father took a deep breath in preparation for telling more of his story about the Orange Dragon woman, "she oathed, and, believe me, that isn't a word I use very often, she *oathed* that I'd pay for it, that she was not someone to be tossed away like a used tissue. She'd make my life absolute hell for jilting her. Yes, those were her exact words," her father said in a tired voice as if he'd had this conversation many times.

Here he took a deep, mournful breath, sat back in his seat, and looked out the windshield at the Christmas tree lot, which now had loads of happy, convivial people walking around looking for the perfect tree—kids, dogs, young couples, grandparents with canes with someone holding them by the other elbow to make sure they didn't trip over something on the uneven ground. Had that been them just a little while ago? No, that was someone else.

"Which she did," her father barked, as in Alexandra had proceeded to make life hell for him. "Alexandra went to her room in the sorority house that night and slashed her wrists with a dull Bic razor, a suicide attempt that seemed to have been done entirely for dramatic effect. She'd not needed much more than a couple bandages from what I heard," her father growled, "but still she insisted her sorority sisters take her to the infirmary where, of course, there'd be a handy little record of the visit and the why of it and the who of it—yes, especially *who* had driven her to do such a desperate act.

"A couple days later," he continued in a now outraged voice, "after a good dozen of her sorority sisters sought me out to tell me what Alexandra had done, and didn't I want to come over and see Alexandra, patch things up with her, she was such a sweetie, after all, and 'she just adores you,' more than one girl told me, during which time I didn't so much as send her a get-well card," he said angrily, "she betook herself to the dean of students and accused me of trying to rape her, and because she'd been so upset, she'd tried to slash her wrists even. See, she was still wearing the bandages, I'm sure she said to the man."

The wail that Julie let out at this shocking turn in her father's story was a mind-numbing concoction of horror, anger, hurt, anguish, outrage, and some others she couldn't name just then. The spider had sneaked up behind her unseen and driven its venom deep inside her. The seething maelstrom of emotions charging up and down every neuron in her body was the venom's deadly effect.

Seeing Julie's distress, her father reached over and wrapped his arms about her, pulling her toward him in the process. She was desperately needing both the comfort and warmth of his arms. She was shivering now from both cold *and* fright. He held her that way as he told her the rest of the story, leaning his chin into her mop of curls, giving her a good hug when he'd come to some particularly distressing place in his story.

The dean had called him in and told him what Alexandra had accused him of. At that, apparently, he'd broken down and wept pretty unabashedly. "It was not your basic macho reaction." Here he let out a small laugh at his immediate reaction. Here he gave Julie one of his first heartening hugs. "The dean then explained that, he was very sorry, but there would have to be a thorough investigation into the incident, that he knew it would be rough on me, but that was just the way it needed to be."

Strangely, here her father's voice went from a straightforward narration of events to one of bewilderment. "A day or so went by, and I'm expecting campus police to show up with their paddy wagon. Instead I got another summons to the dean's office. Thinking that this was it, this was when I'd learn about all the investigations, hearings, and the like lined up for me, the dean, when I was ushered into his office, couldn't have been more pleasant, kind even.

"Apparently, certain facts had come to light that shed complete doubt on Alexandra's allegations, and so there would be no further investigation. One curious thing the dean said, that made me realize why everyone thought so highly of him, was that he'd been particularly troubled by the fact that Alexandra claimed she'd attempted suicide because of the attempted rape. He went on to explain that in his twenty-year experience as the dean of students, he'd never known a student to attempt suicide after any kind of forced sexual act, even make just a *show* of it, as of course Alexandra had. Alexandra's actions *were* typical, however, in the dean's experience, of a young woman disappointed in love.

"In fact, before the dean did anything further with regard to an investigation involving me, he'd talked with the house mother of the sorority, who turned out to be well aware of the incident, and the woman said that, as far as she was aware, Alexandra had returned to the sorority house that night weeping because I had broken off with her. It wasn't until later that Alexandra came to her saying that I had tried to rape her. She told her that, in such an event, she would need to see the dean of students, which, of course, Alexandra did.

"The dean told me that second time I was called to his office that, because of what the house mother had said, and because he considered it unusual for a girl to attempt suicide (especially a faked one) after an attempted rape, he'd talked to a couple of Alexandra's sorority sisters, and *not* the girl who'd accompanied her to his office that morning. As he had expected, they all had the impression that Alexandra had returned that night in a state because I had broken off the engagement. And what was she going to do with the wedding dress she was already having altered and so on."

Here Julie had to lean back and say to her father: "Dad, it sounds as though this Alexandra Riley-Dolan was a complete nut case."

Mr. Tyler laughed. "Yes, I suppose that would be a good name for her in the vernacular. But, the final important thing that had made the dean reconsider who the real culprit in the matter was had to do with some additional evidence that had come to light from an unexpected source and that he wasn't free to discuss at all. This final evidence had provided the final proof that, as he suspected, Alexandra had not been the victim of a rape but had been jilted and she was now making false charges against an innocent man as an act of retribution, which was also a serious crime."

Hooray! Julie wanted to shout. But, when she sat back and took one look at her father, she realized from his grim expression that that would be jumping the gun. It would appear that good had as yet to triumph over evil.

Per her father, thwarted in her attempt to use official means to undo him, Alexandra began to spread rumors about his repeated attempts to rape her. It was a vicious smear campaign. "She told all of her sorority sisters, fellow cheerleaders, everyone on the football team, everyone in the debating society I belonged to, even managed to get things printed in the campus newspaper that didn't name me, but by then, she'd spread the story so far and wide that no one could be in any doubt as to who the perpetrator of the rapes was. Yes, I said *rapes*," he said fiercely. "No longer had I just *attempted* to rape her, I'd actually managed to do so more than once after I'd gotten her so drunk she didn't even know what was happening until it was too late...."

At that the interior of the car went sodden with gloom. The happy Christmas tree shoppers who continued to come and go like little plastic Fisher Price people, gleeful and *so enjoying* the ritual of buying that year's Christmas tree was even more at odds with the lack of cheer inside their car, as if they were now in some kind of dank vacuum and soon they'd be out of oxygen and they'd die. Even in the dark, with the sun almost down, the look of woe Julie saw on her father's face was enough to make her heart stop.

"To make an already too long story short," he said, starting up in a voice missing the authority and assurance it usually had, "I ended up quitting school at the end of the year. Alexandra just made it her job to make my life miserable. She spread her rape story around enough that no one wanted anything to do with me. You'd think I was the campus ax murderer or something. I had wanted to study law at Notre Dame, but could only do that if I got a football scholarship. But, somehow Alexandra saw to it that the football coach was forced to fire me from the team. I think her family or maybe the family of a friend were big donors to the football scholarship program, and she somehow got them to make that year's donation contingent on my being kicked off the team.

"So, as you already know, I ended up getting my undergraduate degree and law degree going to night school at the local state college, which had nowhere near the clout that a Notre Dame education would have had."

So, in a nutshell, Alexandra the nut case, had managed to get back at her father in spades for jilting her. What was that about a woman scorned—something from Shakespeare or maybe it was the Old Testament. Clearly Alexandra was one in a long line of women who would exact revenge until she'd wrung the last drop of blood out of her victim. And, of course, this raised the question: why had Alexandra and her equally loathsome daughter suddenly shown up in their hometown that year??

Feigning a punch at her chin by way of trying to get her to smile, lighten up the mood in the car, her father then started the car, and they were soon headed home with their fit-for-the-White-House tree in the back. Julie, nonetheless, was aware of only one real emotion—fear. Generalized fear. She might be only 15-years-old but she was enough of a female to know that people like Alexandra clung to their meanness and spite like a tick with a payload of some disease ten-times worse than Lyme disease. And hadn't she learned that lesson well from that little scene of her daughter's in Dr. Drescher's office a couple weeks ago.

That fear turned to downright panic when they got home. It was just the wrenching sight of her mother, as they were coming in the door with the Christmas tree, without any makeup, a faded yellow bandana tied around her head of frizzy curls, which was how she'd gone back to wearing her hair most days ("the styling paddles take too much time" was her excuse), and wearing old baggy sweatpants and an old tee-shirt of her father's. It was her customary apparel for cleaning the house on Christmas tree Saturday. But on this Christmas tree Saturday all Julie could think of when she beheld her ultra-plain mother in her ultra-ugly getup was the still-beautiful Mrs. Cowper in her archly fashionable attire and her little bottom doing its oh-so-alluring *rat-a-tat-tat* thing. Her mother was undeniably, scarily plain, even frumpy.

On a somewhat brighter note, she went on to spend a pleasant evening decorating the tree, with Handel's *Messiah*, broadcast over the local PBS station, playing in the background. She'd heard of the chorale and heard various parts of it, but never the whole thing. It really was glorious. But when the tenor sang a heart-rending aria describing Jesus as "a man of sorrows and acquainted with grief," she'd had to sit down, put her face in her hands, and have a good cry. (Her parents were upstairs in the sitting-room portion of their bedroom.) Of course, it was because, in her mind, it wasn't just Jesus who'd endured undeserved punishment. So had her father, as she'd learned fresh that day.

In bed, just as her brain was shutting down for the night, had drifted to the halfway point between wakefulness and sleep, a very distressing thought suddenly ripped through her brain, stunning her, getting her sitting bolt upright in bed. Her father'd said nothing to her mother, as far as she knew, about their encounter with Alexandra Riley-Dolan Cowper in the Christmas tree lot that afternoon. Why not?

CHAPTER 20

An Unwanted Early Christmas Gift

When the balsam scent hit Julie's nostrils the moment she walked in the door the afternoon of the last day of school before Christmas vacation, the long narrative of the previous Saturday did a fast trot through her brain as she threw her backpack, winter jacket, and scarf onto the bench in the hallway. Her brain was soon on a different trajectory. One directed at the kitchen and the mincemeat and pecan tarts, raspberry bars, rum balls, chocolate mint brownies, shortbread cookies, and, of course, praline cookies that should now be bedecking the kitchen counters. Today was the day her mother was going to do her annual day-long Christmas baking.

But the kitchen was strangely dark, there was no potpourri of butter and brown sugar and cinnamon and mince and raspberry and chocolate and mint intermingling with the balsam fragrance of the Christmas tree hanging in the air, and the house was oddly still.

It was then that she became aware of the dark form of her mother curled up on the couch, completely still and walled in by a box of Kleenex and a small mountain range of used tissues. Her mother seemed not there, as in, scarily, *Night of the Living Dead* not there. Her eyes were directed at the Christmas tree but not fastened on it. Her eyes were staring with fear at some kind of disturbance inside her head.

"Mom—" Julie cried out, ran over to her mother, and sat on the coffee table opposite her mother. (Her first thought was the Cowpers. What further mischief had they sown to bring her mother so low?) Her mother's eyes were swollen from weeping. But she never wept. Just an occasional light sprinkle of tears at weddings, funerals, and the end of sad movies.

"Hi, sweetheart," her mother said in a soft, wobbly voice. And hearing the question in Julie's one utterance, she proceeded to explain in a quiet, quavering voice what the "bad news" was. As she did so, the already dimly lit room darkened further as the winter sun slunk down behind the horizon, as if it were ashamed of what its light had illumined that day.

"Breast cancer." Those were the words that struck like a bolt of lightning from out of the inky blackness of her mother's labored story of her past week. She'd found a lump in her breast while showering the week before. She'd gone to see her gynecologist that day. He hadn't liked what he felt. He'd sent her for a mammogram and ultrasound the next day. He'd called her with the radiologist's report that morning. (She'd said nothing to Julie or her father about it because . . . she hoped she wouldn't have to. Simple.) Not so simple. The findings pointed to some kind of "potentially malignant mass" in her breast with possibly some disease in her lymph nodes. (What was that other recent brush she'd had with a cancer—oh, yes, her father's story about Alexandra Cowper's malignant behavior.)

After a short silence, to give the three words "potentially malignant mass" enough time, Julie thought, to smash themselves to smithereens in the darkest corner of the room, her mother told her the rest of the details. Dr. Chambers, her gynecologist, was concerned enough about the findings that he'd already gotten her an appointment at the Leverett Sumner Smith Memorial Cancer Center in town, known to all, simply, as Smitty's.

Suddenly, Julie hated this Dr. Chambers' guts. Couldn't he have waited until after Christmas before putting his "thoughtful" little "gift" under their tree?

Her mother must have read her mind, because she said next. "Dr. Chambers apologized for calling me with the bad news just before Christmas. He only did it, he said, because ordinarily it's very hard to get an appointment in the breast cancer clinic at Smitty's. Holidays are relatively quiet, I guess. Most patients, especially those from out of town, want to schedule treatments and other stuff around the holidays. My appointment is with someone with a name that must break a record for the number of syllables it has—Padma Ramachandran. I don't even know if it's a man or a woman," her mother said with a small attempt at a laugh.

With that, the two of them fell silent. Julie, for sure, didn't know what to say. All she knew was that between her and her mother, in the little intimate space that separated them, in the silence of the room, was an unwelcome lump, a mass, a tumor that was growing, invading, their lives.

She felt this sudden urge to do something, anything!, to somehow make things better.

"Cambric tea," she said, her index finger pointing toward the ceiling like an exclamation point. "Let's have some cambric tea." Tea that was half milk, half tea, sweetened with *a lot* of sugar, and that was the best remedy for any kind of woe, though it couldn't cure cancer.

"Yes. Cambric tea—that's what's called for," her mother said in an almost exultant voice.

Julie was halfway to the kitchen, when she suddenly stopped, spun around, dashed over to the Christmas tree, and plugged in the lights. The tree's lovely lit presence, the scent of balsam, which the warm lights further stoked, the two steaming cups of cambric tea— Soon, they were in a haven where, at least temporarily, they were beyond the reach of the enemy outside world. But, of course, they did have an enemy of sorts in their midst.

But their moment of calm didn't last long. A car pulling into the driveway and two small *toots* on the horn announced that her father was home, and early at that. They could hear him whistling "Deck the Halls with Boughs of Holly" as he got out of the car, let himself in the backdoor, and cross the kitchen. He seldom whistled. His work seldom left him jolly at the end of the day. Julie and her mother looked wretchedly at each other. His rare, well-deserved, jolly mood was about to be wrecked.

Julie's father must have guessed that something was wrong as soon as he entered the dark kitchen because he immediately stopped whistling the Christmas carol. He wasn't a caveman kind of man who expected supper to be on the table as soon as he walked in the door. But it was unusual for the kitchen to be dark at this time of the day. And he, too, was expecting to snatch a couple cookies before her mother's dread right hand slapped his away.

"Mona? Julie? What's going on?" he asked from the living room doorway. What he saw were two white faces turned toward him with a look of fright on a par with that depicted in the painting called *The Scream*. For reasons her parents couldn't fathom, Julie had a copy of it taped onto the back of her door. It depicted how she often felt, she'd tried to explain to them.

Anyway, at the sound of his deep voice, at the sight of his tall, strong figure in the doorway, Julie and Julie's mother both burst into tears.

Of the two women, Julie was the one best able to communicate the bad news, to explain what was going on, to her father. Her father sat on his haunches between the two of them, his hands clasped on their nearest shoulders, looking from one to the other with concerned eyes. He was keeping his emotions masterfully in check, not because he wanted to, Julie realized as she blinked at him through a thick film of tears that just wouldn't stop coming, but because he had to be their "fortress," their "place of refuge," at that moment.

CHAPTER 21

Pizza Cure

Their sobs almost under control, Julie's father reached out and gathered her mother, his wife, into his arms. He held her tight, as if he didn't want to ever let her go. Julie, as she was left to sniff and wipe away her tears on her own, could see that both of them had their eyes squeezed shut. It was a private moment, and she was just an onlooker.

But then, going from the sublime to the ridiculous, her father couldn't take any more of her mother's sniffing. He reached into his pocket, took out a large white handkerchief, dabbed at her mother's tears, and then put the handkerchief to her nose. With a certain amount of parental authority he said "Okay—now blow your nose, Tweedle," which her mother did, giggling at being an annoying little kid with a runny nose.

"Thanks, Tweedle," she said softly back to him.

Her mother then slumped back on the couch and emptied her lungs of air in one long sigh.

Then she looked at Julie and her father with a look of clear regret and said "I'm sorry, you two. I'm sorry to be putting you through all this."

Before either of them could protest that she didn't need to apologize for anything, that it was silly of her to even think that, she put up her hand and said "yes, yes, I know. It's not anyone's fault, *really*. It's just that, well, I can't help but feel as though it *is* my fault. I haven't had a mammogram for five years. I've been careless about doing breast exams. And my mother had breast cancer, so I should have been more vigilant, and I—just—stuck my head in the sand." At that she teared up again. "I *loathe* myself," she said in an ugly voice turned viciously on herself.

Julie and her father said nothing. They could only look at her mother and see her flaying herself alive for "being such a half-wit," the name she gave herself next. What happened to Tweedle, Julie wondered.

"Mona," her father said softly, after a bit, now seated opposite her on the coffee table. Julie'd scooted over closer to her mother so she could feel better the reassuring warmth of both her parents' bodies—'for as long as they're both alive.' The words crept through her brain like a night-time intruder . . . . It was an awful thought.

Her mother raised her red-rimmed eyes and looked at him. It was a look, Julie could see, that was pleading for forgiveness, also for help.

"How do you know, for sure, that a little extra vigilance, care, might have prevented the tumor, might have caught it earlier?" her father asked.

Mrs. Tyler said nothing, just looked at him sadly, as tears continued to slide down her cheeks and drip from her chin.

He waited for an answer.

Finally her mother said, with a small wag of her head, "I don't know anything for sure, Bob."

"And, if it'd been found three months ago, would you be feeling any better that night?"

Mrs. Tyler sighed and thought. "Probably not," she said gazing over at the Christmas tree. "I guess I'd be feeling as badly as I am tonight." She said with a sad laugh.

"And so would we, sweetheart," her father continued in a gentle prosecutor's voice. "So, there's no way, now, to set time back to when the tumor was, maybe, smaller, to the day before the first cancer cell formed even. And what if you'd been a good girl and had a mammogram on that particular day?"

He fell silent again, waiting for her mother to respond.

"The findings would have come back okay," she said quietly. "I probably would have still not found the tumor until last week, and it *is* small, about the size of a small marble. It was just easy to find, because it's up toward the top of my breast, near my breast bone."

"So," Julie's father said, summing up his argument, "would it make you feel better if I put you over my knee and spanked you?"

At that Mrs. Tyler laughed. "Yes," she said, laughing harder.

"Julie, how would you like to punish your mother?" Mr. Tyler asked, flourishing his hand at her mother magician-style and grinning at Julie.

"That's an easy one," she crowed. "Chewing and popping a whole pack of bubble gum, in the car, with the heater on high, with Mom driving so she can't slug me." (Her mother hated bubble gum.)

"Okay. Okay," her mother said laughing. "I'll gladly take my punishment."

****

That night they had an Al Capone pizza from The Lido for supper. (Her mother was understandably not up to cooking supper.) The name for the pizza, Julie figured, must have to do with its having all the toppings, even anchovies, plus the blood (tomato sauce), guts (green peppers), spent cartridge shells (*pitted* black olives), and other gory toppings for which Al Capone was famous.

They ate the pizza in the living room with the only light coming from the White House–perfect Christmas tree. Someone turned on the local PBS station, which was playing gorgeous high-brow Christmas music—excerpts from *The Messiah*, Handels' Christmas Oratorio, and lots of Bach and Purcell. Julie, though, would remain an ardent fan of "All I Want for Christmas Is My Two Front Teeth," "Here Comes Santa Claus," and "Christmas Time Is Here Again," sung by Alvin and the Chipmunks until she was at least in her mid-twenties.

Close to midnight they cleared up the pizza mess. As they

did so they made a pact. They would not tell anyone, family or friend, about her mother's breast tumor, until after Christmas, maybe not until after New Year. It was only partly for the *unselfish* reason that they wanted to spare the people they loved sorrow at this joyous time of year. Mostly it was because they wanted to, like little kids, pretend that it was just another jolly Christmas, until, that is, the following Monday morning and her mother's appointment at Smitty's with someone with the strange, Indian?, name of Padma Ramachandran.

    Then it dawned on Julie's mother as they were climbing the stairs to go to bed, that she *had* to show up with a load of baked goods at her Aunt Ellen's on Christmas day or the jig would be up. Questions would be asked and honest answers required. It was then that Julie heard someone say, someone with a voice just like hers, someone with flapping lips, "Don't worry, Mom. I'll bake everything tomorrow!"

    Which she did, along with her mother. They'd never teamed up like that before, and they had a jolly time of it. It helped that Julie didn't think about her mother's cancer for at least two hours. When they were done, they got very silly. It started with Julie putting a dab of flour on the end of her mother's nose, which her mother did in turn to her. Then they put a round circle of cinnamon on each other's cheeks. And then they dabbed green food coloring on their eyebrows, and yellow on their lips. They were soon shrieking with laughter, which got Mr. Tyler rushing into the kitchen to find out what further disaster had befallen his "two favorite girls."

    When he saw them in their baking-ingredient "clown" makeup, he solemnly dragged the two of them to the mirror in the hallway bathroom where they could see their silly faces. They all laughed so hard that they had tears running down their cheeks, thereby ruining their "clown" makeup. Tears—Julie thought as she later washed her face clean of the baking ingredients and tears. Curious that it wasn't just sad things, or "mad" things, that got them flowing. Funny things did, too.

    That evening, Christmas Eve, which they usually spent on

their own, the air in the house hung heavily with the "incense" of Christmas—the blending of the aroma of all of the baked goods that now filled tins and plastic containers on the kitchen counters, together with the pungent balsam scent that "blossomed" indoors only ever at this time of year. And weren't they all, naughty children that they were, feeling slightly sick from skipping supper and eating their fill of the banquet of baked goods instead?

CHAPTER 22

A Blue Monday

Christmas, which fell on a Friday that year, and the intervening Saturday and Sunday, were like a golden mirage that just vanished, *swoosh,* come the gray grimness of the Monday morning after Christmas.

Actually, the cheery Christmas trees and gilded and glittering decorations in the new-patient waiting area of the Leverett Sumner Smith Memorial Cancer Center were at odds with their collective gray, cheerless mood. The waiting area, which clearly had been designed with calm and comfort in mind, was also at odds with the anxiety and gloom that hung like mildewed rags from everyone's face.

The flock of new cancer patients, and their families and friends or whoever was with them, were "condemned criminals" waiting for the punishment phase of their trial, while all around them scurried people in white lab coats and scrubs, paper skull caps, face masks, and surgical booties. They looked like the hazmat squads sent out to deal with deadly substances, which, if one thought about it, cancer was. Thus, fear hung heavily in the air.

During the long wait when the only thing to do was "watch" helplessly as evermore anxious thoughts crowded into her brain until there was hardly standing-room for them all, one particularly awful thought sent her spirits spiraling out of control. Every new patient sitting there carried within them some kind of cancer that, even at that moment, while waiting for the new-patient paperwork to be done, was busy, helter-skelter, deviously dividing and dividing again, doubling, quadrupling, double quadrupling, making more cancer cells. Exponentially dividing! That's what they were doing. While the admitting people were obsessing about Social Security numbers, telephone numbers, and insurance card numbers, her mother's breast tumor has gone from 3,761 cells to 5,803 cells in a half hour! Wasn't that the most important number?!

Julie looked about the room at the other people in the waiting area. Were any of them having similarly distressing thoughts? Well, no one looked very happy.

****

An hour later, her mother's new-patient paperwork done, with some small talk with her parents and other minor distractions under her belt, Julie had finally calmed herself down. She didn't communicate her anxiety about what she was to learn was called the doubling rate of cancer cells to her parents. (And, yes, it was something to be concerned about.) They didn't need her fears heaped on them.

They were now waiting for a hospital volunteer to take them to the breast cancer clinic. Smitty's was huge, and it was easy, especially for new patients with lots on their mind, to get lost, so all new patients were sent off with someone to guide them to their first appointment, unlike Hansel and Gretel who were left to fend for themselves and ended up being pushed into a witch's oven. And that wasn't going to happen to them? Maybe getting lost at Smitty's and finding a gingerbread house instead was a better bet?!

Finally they heard "Mona Tyler? Mona Tyler?" being called out over the crowd of new cancer patients. There were a lot of them by now. Some people were having to sit on the arms of chairs, on the tops of coffee tables and end tables, even on the floor. Julie remembered her mother saying that Dr. Chambers had said the cancer center was quiet during the holidays. If this was quiet, what was busy like?

The man who'd called out their name was an older man in a tan jacket.

"Hi, my name is Roger Moulton," the man said in a pleasant voice with a friendly smile as he shook all their hands. "I'm a volunteer here, as if I needed to tell you," he laughed motioning to a huge button pin that said "VOLUNTEER." The Tylers all laughed politely. "I'll warn you," he said as they followed him, "it's very easy to get lost here. Don't be afraid to ask for directions if you think you're lost."

The breast cancer clinic was on the tenth (top) floor of the hospital's main building. Their trip to the tenth floor was infuriatingly interrupted at each floor by more people getting on than off. Julie just wanted to get to the tenth floor and get down to business! They were soon, however, pinned at the back of the elevator.

The doors had only just closed on the fourth floor when Julie felt this panicky feeling surge up in her that she hoped wasn't claustrophobia, because, if it was, she'd be having a full-blown mental meltdown by the time they reached the tenth floor. By then, Julie was pressed up against this Roger in a way that she hadn't anticipated being pressed up against a man until her wedding night. She also had a woman's fanny pressed right up against her groin. It was all too cozy for her taste.

On the next, fifth, floor, a man in a wheelchair pushed by his wife got on, which meant everyone having to squeeze in even more. Julie could feel her knees being bent backward in a not-anatomically-correct mode. The people in the elevator, all those toward the front who were not trapped and having a claustrophobic meltdown at the back like her, insisted, midst all kinds of jollity, on making room for them. "The more the merrier," "you'd better take this elevator; the next one won't be here for another hour," people bantered, which got some chuckles. 'Ha, ha' Julie thought as she felt sweat begin to drip from her armpits.

Just outside the door on the fifth floor, she could see three lab-coated young Asians smiling and waving at the man and woman. When the door closed, the man said to his wife "Marilyn, how could we have gotten so lost?" At that he craned his neck around to explain to all of them that they'd gotten lost in some part of the hospital where laboratories were. "Golly, I don't know who was more surprised, us or the three young people you just saw giving us the *sayonara.*"

Here you could hear the beginning ruffle of laughter. Julie could also feel the butt of the woman in front of her starting to jiggle unpleasantly against her midsection.

"There were more bottles and glassware in the place than a Coca Cola plant," the man continued. "The three people you just saw, when they saw me and the wife comin' in, me in the wheelchair and her with a purse the size of Ohio, they froze up and began to chatter at us like mad squirrels. I think they were mainly afraid we'd break something. After they got us turned around and on our way back here, they were quite pleasant. Well, I say that," the man said after a slight pause.

By then everyone on the elevator was grinning, Julie, too.

"I mean I couldn't understand a word they were saying."

"Darling," his wife now put in, "they were probably saying 'You chowderhead. Didn't your mother tell you not to wander off or the gypsies might get you!'"

Everyone, cancer patients, friends and family members, Roger, Julie, her parents, the woman in front of her with her rear end pressed up against Julie, burst out laughing. It *was* very funny.

The hilarity, however, decreased incrementally as the elevator stopped and let people on and off the remaining five floors. By the time they got to the tenth floor, the Tylers' laughter, Roger's, too, had stilled, as had that of the other people bound for this floor, which also, per a sign just outside the elevator, had the Brain Tumor Clinic on it. No wonder everyone who got off on that floor was so serious.

CHAPTER 23

Hurry Up And Wait

As they made their way to the breast oncology clinic, which did seem labyrinthine with all its lefts and rights and straight-aheads, Roger regaled them with his life story, and he was an older man, so it was a long one. He'd grown up in the city, seen all the industries depart to places "where the labor's cheaper," remembered when the factory district, the haunted ghost-town Julie and her mother had journeyed through the night of the mother–daughter dinner, had hummed with life, "infused a good healthy money stream into the local economy." He'd worked as an accountant all his life. He had five children. He and his wife had been married for 47 years. He'd retired early because he thought he "was tired of numbers and final net worths and reports to shareholders that tried to put a positive spin on the bottom line." That had been 8 years ago. "The week after my retirement party," he said with a sad smile, "I was diagnosed with some very rare kind of leukemia." It had explained the tiredness he thought was due to burnout. The *good* news was that it wouldn't kill him immediately. The *bad* news was that it would kill him eventually, say between 7 and 10 years later.

Julie did the math. This was zero hour for him, and flickering across his face like a home movie were all the things he probably wouldn't live to see—his grandchildren's graduation from college, his granddaughter's marriage and the birth of great grandchildren, his fiftieth wedding anniversary. They were photos—and Julie could somehow see them clearly in her head—that would never be taken. The man was quickly back to his friendly, welcoming self.

"Here we are, folks, your final destination," Roger said as

he extended his right hand toward a very large room full of people. To Julie, his gesture was much like Vanna White gesturing at a curtain that hid yet another wonderful prize from which to choose. In their case, though, it wasn't, Julie knew, anything they'd want. A snowmobile, a set of bowling balls, an above-ground swimming pool, death-dealing breast cancer.... No to all of them.

They settled into three seats in the surprisingly crowded room. From what Dr. Chambers had said, she expected to have the whole place to themselves. Now all they had to do was wait some more.

A half hour went by, then an hour. A woman across from them grumbled to the man who was with her that she would never have expected to be able to crochet an entire afghan while waiting for her appointments at Smitty's. Much to Julie's dismay, there was a long, crocheted strip of an afghan made of variegated yarn in various hues of turquoise that extended from her lap down to her ankles. She had to stand up to turn it around to crochet it from the other direction. When the woman's name was called, it took her a good minute to fold up the afghan strip, with her husband's help, and put it away in a large Christmas shopping bag from Macy's.

Another half hour went by. Finally, Julie got up, said she was going to the bathroom, which she did, but when she was done, she didn't rejoin her parents. Instead she wandered around the waiting area. She needed to work off more of the anxiety that was now torquing all her nerves such that they probably looked like some kind of fencing material that could probably make her a lot of money in Texas.

She went to a window that looked out onto the city she'd grown up in, now fully accoutered in its winter clothing. She was able, from that height, to make out in the distance the fuzzy, gray, wooly knolls of Woodland Hills where Ainsworth was snuggled down into its protected nest. She felt her heart constrict to half its normal size. That's right, the last time she was there, the day she came home to find her mother dug in behind a mountain of tissues, she'd been very happy. It was Christmas break, there were heaps of baked goods to be sampled at home, all was right with the world . . . . She felt that little tickle on her lower lids that presaged tears. She blinked her eyes hard to beat them back. She looked off to her right to distract herself. Wouldn't you know, *there* she could just about make out Symphony Hall where she, her mother, and her Aunt Babs had so enjoyed The Nutcracker *months* ago, it now seemed. Her tears gained the advantage and soon they were gushing over her lids and down her cheeks.

"What are you thinking about, honey?" It was her mother who'd come looking for her, wondered where she'd gone for such a long time.

Her mother only needed to see the tears coating Julie's cheeks to guess the answer to that. Something related to her breast cancer, of course.

"I'm looking at all the places where we were so happy just a little while ago," she explained tearfully.

Her mother smiled softly, didn't tear up though, put her arm around Julie, pulled her close, and the two of them just stood there spotting, pointing out to each other, more familiar landmarks that reminded them of a once-happy time, which, her mother promised, "we'll be happily back to one day not too far off."

`Oh, that she could believe that, Julie thought. When had her mother's promises, like sitting in her lap being rocked in the rocking chair, ceased to be a sure-fire thing?

"What are you two up to??" It was her father standing right behind them who was now wanting to know why they'd gone missing. They'd forgotten all about him. "You had me worried, Mona. I thought maybe you'd fled."

That was a reasonable concern, and Julie could see in her mother's eyes, when she turned and looked at her father, that that thought hadn't occurred to her. This was followed by a look of yearning, wanting to flee, escape from her cancer. Next, however, it was obvious that her mother realized that wherever she went the tumor would go, too, and only get bigger and deadlier. There was no escape. It was another example of the only way to get out of the mud was to go through it.

Julie's father put his arm around her mother's back and guided her gently back to where they'd been sitting. He kept his arm around her, not letting go, held her close, until her name was finally called out. It was an Asian male who called her name. He introduced himself as Wei (as in 'whey' he explained), and explained that he was Dr. Ramachandran's, Dr. R as she was known to all hospital personnel (good thinking!), physician's assistant.

They were also to learn, after lengthy experience, that PAs did all the detailed work that the doctors didn't have time for. The doctors at Smitty's were like Greek gods come down from Mt. Olympus. (She'd be glad when the effects of the Greek mythology she'd studied last fall finally wore off....) The cancer doctors' knowledge was so rarified, so special and precious, that they were left to handle only the most important, crucial, details of their patients' care.

CHAPTER 24

A Family Secret

In the examination room, Wei asked question after question, plowing through all of her mother's personal and family history, carefully entering all the pertinent information her mother dutifully supplied into the computer database for all who treated her mother to see.

Everything was going like clockwork until the questions got snagged on her mother's family history of cancer. Specifically her mother's (Julie's grandmother's) breast cancer in her early 40s.

"What was the outcome of her treatment?" Wei asked.

"I don't know," her mother said mysteriously.

Wei wrinkled his brow and cocked his head. How could she not know the answer to such a question? But he was preparing to just let it go at that, respecting cancer patients' sometimes eccentric behavior, when her mother spoke up.

"It's because my mother was killed in a car crash before her cancer treatment ended," Mrs. Tyler explained.

Wei entered the explanation into the database, maintaining all the while his impassive, professional expression, preparing to get on to the next question. But then her mother veered sharply off in an unexpected direction.

"I say she was killed in a car crash, but the family thinks it might have been suicide. My mother became very depressed during the treatment. The scar from the mastectomy got infected. During the chemotherapy she lost about 50 pounds—she looked like someone from Auschwitz." It seemed to be getting harder and harder for her mother to get the words out, but she had to keep going, vent them, get all the "poison," bitterness, out. "Then her arm on the mastectomy side swelled up to the size of an inner tube. Then came the awful radiation burns from the cobalt 60 treatment."

Wei, Julie, and her father continued to listen, Wei intently and respectfully, though he'd leaned back and stopped entering notes into the computer database. The only thing in "motion" was Mrs. Tyler's voice.

"One night, after everyone had gone to bed," Mrs. Tyler was continuing with her story, seeming to find it easier going now, "my mother let herself out of the house, got into the car, and the next thing anyone knew (I was away at college at the time), two policemen were at the front door telling my father, *insisting*, that it was his wife's body that was in the gray Ford station wagon that had crashed into a concrete abutment on the freeway.

Everyone tried to believe that she was going out for cigarettes, but the problem with that was that a Cumberland Farms was only five blocks down from where they lived." Here, her mother lost it. Her face crumpled, like a deflating foil balloon. "Oh dear Jesus," she whispered, "I can't go through what my mother went through. Just watching what the treatment did to her . . . ." And then her mother stopped talking, squeezed her eyes shut as if to block out both the memory *and* tears, and sat still for a moment. Then she opened her eyes, said "I'm sorry" to Wei in a whisper, adding in only a slightly stronger voice "You'll have to excuse me. I'm not doing too well dealing with all this."

Wei leaned over to her, laid his hand on her arm, and said tenderly, but with all the authority in the world, "Mrs. Tyler, I can't promise that your treatment will be easy. But I can say that the treatment for breast cancer has advanced a lot since your mother's day. We use many of the same tools, but we've gotten much better at preventing the serious side effects your mother had. And you don't have to apologize for anything. Cancer patients have carte blanche permission to feel whatever they feel, and to show it."

Just as Julie was trying to swallow the whole gob of emotion churned up by her mother's verbal "rampage," Dr. Ramachandran, Dr. R, entered the exam room and took charge. (Julie later figured that her name had been shortened to Dr. R because she simply didn't have enough time to hear her multisyllabic name spoken dozens of times each day.)

If the physician had been having a hectic morning, however, she didn't show it. She was the perfect image of serenity, and something else—Confidence? Strength? An ability to gain mastery over any breast tumor? Any and all were welcome.

"Hello, I am Padma Ramachandran," she shook hands first with Julie's mother, then her father, then Julie.

If it hadn't been for her white lab coat that rustled stiffly with starch, she could have been Scheherazade in *A Thousand and One Nights.* She was *that* beautiful, *that* exotic. But plunked down at Smitty's in the U.S. of A., she was all Westerner, all business. Although she smiled warmly when she greeted them, she was professionally serious as Wei reviewed with her the notes he had recorded in the database.

As he scrolled down through the incredible, Julie realized, amount of information he had gotten from her mother, he pointed out various things to Dr. R, who stood behind him scrutinizing the information with her own version of dark Asian eyes. Together they also scrutinized the mammograms and notes from the ultrasound examination her mother had brought with her to Smitty's that day.

The two seemed to be speaking in a foreign language, cancer-speak. Ominous-sounding words, such as 'intranodular primary,' 'microcalcifications,' 'nonsessile,' and 'contralateral breast,' slithered about the room

And then Dr. R got snagged in the same place Wei had gotten stuck—her Grandma Burch, a woman Julie hadn't even known, had hardly ever thought about. She'd died (committed suicide?) when her mother was just a little older than she was, 17 or 18. She'd only seen photographs of her, including one, she thought, in which she'd been leaning back against a gray station wagon. But, of course. That was the car she'd died in.

"You have said that your mother was in her early 40s when she developed breast cancer?" Dr. R said in her lilting half-British, half-Indian–inflected voice.

"Yes," her mother answered uncertainly.

"And you say that she was adopted?"

"Yes," her mother answered with a now puzzled look on her face.

"Do you know anything about your mother's family ethnicity?"

Julie knew that her grandmother had been adopted, but what her mother was about to relate came as complete news to her.

"Yes, I do know," Mrs. Tyler said quietly, seeming to brace herself for more unpleasant revelations. "She was, not surprisingly, illegitimate, but her adopted family, my grandparents, knew the mother's family. The mother was Irish, the father was Jewish. Supposedly they loved each other very much, but her mother's staunchly Catholic family and her father's staunchly Jewish family refused to let them marry— And, likewise, neither family wanted anything to do with their half-blood child, my mother. My grandparents were childless and were just thrilled to get a child. Ancestry didn't matter in the least to them."

It was the stuff of which legends are made (Romeo and Juliet of Verona, Tony and Maria of *West Side Story*, Helen and Paris of Troy . . . .)

"Ah—" Dr. R said, with a momentarily sad expression. The look suggested to Julie that she understood, all too well, how families could thwart love matches.

Then she was back to business and talking about something called a "break-a-gene," as in an Italian gangster threatening to "break-a' someone's knuckles." But whatever this "break-a gene" was (Julie would only later find out that it was how the abbreviation BRCA was said aloud, though she never knew what BRCA stood for), it appeared to be serious, *deadly* serious.

Dr. R explained that an abnormality in the gene was

highly prevalent in Jews from Central Europe. And that women who had the gene were "particularly prone to getting an aggressive form of breast cancer."

Because of Dr. R's Indian accent, the "particularly" danced like a songbird on her lips. But the "aggressive form of breast cancer" sank like a dead weight in the silent room.

Dr. R continued to speak, as kindly and reassuringly as possible as she "broke" the dread news. "You have several things that suggest you have the abnormal gene, Mrs. Tyler. Therefore, I recommend we test you for the gene. It will affect how we plan treatment. Wei, please arrange for this today, if possible, and for a fine-needle breast biopsy tomorrow morning, which I think will be adequate for our purposes."

Then Dr. R dealt Julie an unexpected blow.

Settling her eyes on Julie, she said "If the test is positive for the BRCA abnormality, it will be prudent to test your daughter for the abnormality as well."

Seeing the look of sickened fright on Julie's face, she reached over, clasped Julie's hands, and said, "There, there, little one, *nina baba*," something in Indian that Julie knew had to be some kind of endearment. "Right now, there is nothing to worry about. You are far too young to worry about this right now. This we will test for way, way in the future." And she flung one hand up into the air as if she were telling her, a small frightened child, an ancient Indian fairytale.

"Now, Mrs. Tyler," she said, back to the professional formality of a cancer doctor, "I would like to examine your breasts."

Between watching Dr. R probe and palpate her mother's breasts, then fingering the tumor, and the shock that that could be her on the exam table in a few years, Julie began to feel very woozy. And as Dr. R continued to poke and probe and prod the *tumor*, the *mass*, the *lesion*, in her mother's breast, the room began to spin. And everything began to seem very far away. And before everything went completely black, she caught sight of her father's face. He wasn't looking too good either.

The next thing she knew, she was coming to on a couch in the waiting area. Her father, the stalwart one, the strong one, the ex–star quarterback, was sitting beside her in a wheelchair, his head propped up with a hand. He, too, had fainted, or come close to it.

Dimly it seemed as though they were being ministered to by angels in all the colors of the rainbow. But, then, it turned out that they were just plain ordinary nursing assistants dressed in different-colored scrubs. Once they'd made sure that Julie and her father had returned safely from total unconsciousness, they disappeared—winging their way back to their regular jobs.

And then, out of nowhere, Julie's mother materialized, standing over them, her hands on her hips saying in a very loud, quarter-Jewish, Bette Midler voice.

"A fine lot you are. Here I'm the one who's the patient and you two are dropping like coconuts!"

At this, behind them, they heard many of the nearby people break out laughing.

"Come on you two reprobates," her 'Bette Midler' mother said next, "Let's go get some lunch."

That occasioned *further* hilarity that now seemed to inebriate the whole room. In her not-yet-fully conscious state Julie realized that laughter *was* possible on the tenth floor of Smitty's main clinic building, though mirth was in short supply in her just then.

"Onward Christian soldiers," her father mumbled as they turned down the corridor Roger had led them down *years ago*, it seemed. It wasn't until they got into the elevator that he realized his wife was pushing him in the wheelchair, and only after he noticed that the people getting off the elevator were looking at him with particularly sympathetic eyes, thinking, of course, that he had a brain tumor. After all, that could be the only reason a male patient would be on the tenth floor of the clinic. Needless to say, he jumped out of the chair as the elevator doors closed, and on the next floor he was found to be standing staunchly behind a wheelchair with his wife sitting in it, something he'd insisted on as an appropriate punishment for her quite merrily having enjoyed getting away with her little deceit. Julie, meanwhile, was having this strange craving for gingerbread.

CHAPTER 25

Bad News

The biopsy results weren't good. Julie's mother tested positive for the BRCA1 gene abnormality. (Apparently there was also a BRCA2 gene abnormality. How nice to have a choice . . . .) And Dr. R had some further bad news.

It was on the Thursday of her Christmas vacation. Vacation, yeah, a week from the fateful day she'd arrived home from school to find her mother a bunched-up, tear-soaked person on the couch. Had their lives ever been normal? No, she was getting her life mixed up with some other girl's.

Julie and her father sat silently as Dr. R spoke softly, gently, *directly* to her mother.

They'd been surprised not to see Wei arrive first. Instead, after an increasingly anxious half hour of waiting in the exam room, it was Dr. R who entered first, followed by a silent, serious Wei. Julie knew from that that things had taken a serious turn. Hope? Had she just heard something *whooshing* out under the exam room door?

Dr. R began by telling them all the bad things they'd found in the biopsy of her mother's tumor and other parts of her left breast. It seemed that there were lots. They'd also found cancer cells in a biopsy of her mother's left-armpit lymph nodes, another bad sign. Then Dr. R got a look on her face that made it quite clear that this was one of those times when she hated her job. "Mrs. Tyler, as your treating physician, I must explain to you that more and more women with the mutated BRCA gene, such as what you've got, are electing to have a double mastectomy."

"What?!" her mother, her father, and Julie chorused.

"It isn't because there is cancer in your right breast," the doctor was quick to say, "it is what we refer to as a prophylactic, or preventive, measure. If the tumors that result from the abnormal BRCA gene weren't so aggressive, we would follow you as we do with other women with breast cancer. But BRCA positivity renders a woman at a four times greater risk of breast cancer in the other breast. Women do it mainly for peace of mind, many out of concern for their families, not wanting to put them through a second breast cancer and its treatment."

Julie and her father moved uncomfortably in their seats. Julie could feel sweat beginning to trickle from her armpits. It was the most awful moment in a string of awful moments of late.

"What do you recommend Dr. R?" Julie's mother said quietly after a good half minute. Her face was bleached of all color. It had an almost freezer burn look to it.

"The decision is ultimately yours, Mrs. Tyler," Dr. R answered as gently as she could. "However, I must tell you this. Cancer cells are very smart. They're very good at finding ways of surviving. Some cancer cells become resistant to the chemotherapy. Some cancer cells are from the very beginning hard to eradicate. Some...."

"So you're saying that I should at least have the one mastectomy," her mother cut in, not wanting a lecture on the vagaries of cancer, having had her fill of the topic.

Dr. R didn't say anything, only nodded, almost imperceptibly, with a clear "yes" in her sorrowful dark eyes.

"Dr. R, do I have to make the decision about the double mastectomy today?" her mother said, jockeying for time, for some kind of control over this thing that had gained heartless ascendancy in her life.

"Yes, Mrs. Tyler. I would *want* you to take time to think about this," Dr. R said, reaching over with her delicate hand and grasping her mother's hands, which were now clasped, white-knuckled, in her lap. "If it would help for you to talk with other women who've been faced with the same decision, other women with the BRCA mutation, I can put you in touch with them. We have a group of women who have volunteered, are most glad, to talk with any woman facing the same decision. It is a hard decision," she said, joining her other delicate hand with the one that already held her mother's hands.

Then Dr. R pulled her hands away, sat back, and looked compassionately at her mother, as did Wei standing in the background. Now it all hinged on her mother, and they, Julie, and her father all knew it, they could only be bystanders, at best supporters.

"How long would I have before I need to make the decision, Dr. R," Mrs. Tyler asked in a simple quiet voice.

"I have gone ahead and had Wei schedule an appointment for you with a breast cancer surgeon for this coming Monday morning, but that doesn't mean you have to make your decision by then. Dr. Gardner, one of our best breast cancer surgeons, I should mention, would need to know enough ahead of time so that she could plan your surgery accordingly. You can also postpone making the decision until after your first mastectomy, if you wish."

"Or I can decide to have only the one mastectomy and that's that," her mother added, holding out for the larger patch of blue sky that she *hoped* she'd be getting that day. Everyone knew that Smitty's was tops. Cure was a cinch for them. Apparently not.

"Yes, certainly. You can do that," Dr. R said, though Julie could tell that wasn't *really* what she favored.

"Thank you, Dr. R," her mother said quietly as she rose from her chair, calling a halt to further discussion. In silence Wei, Dr. R, Julie, and her father stood up, too, and in silence they filed out of the room, kind of like you did at church after the Good Friday liturgy.

CHAPTER 26

Monsieur Pierre to the Rescue

So, the old year was ending on a bad note. And the New Year was beginning on a bad note. What was that quotation from Emerson her English teacher two years ago had so loved to quote? Something like "foolish consistency is the hobgoblin of little minds." Right now she couldn't have agreed more.

They went to The Lido for an early supper. The garlic-permeated hubbub reigned supreme as usual. The waiters rushed about carrying trays laden with plates of steaming food and gigantic (mostly Al Capone) pizzas. And the noise in the room was at its usual deafening decibel. Volcanic (Mt. Vesuvius!) eruptions of laughter, loud voices, the shouts of waiters to laggard underlings, Frank Sinatra and Perry Como straining to be heard in the rare ebb in the noise level. It was The Lido at its Italian *dolce vita* best, though that afternoon Julie felt as though she were looking at it through a telescope on Mars.

"Why you not a'smiling?" Giuseppe, one of The Lido's long-time waiters, asked as he cleared away the dirty dishes of the table's previous occupants and wiped it clean of the most conspicuous splotches of food. (The restaurant was too busy for obsessive-compulsive waiters.) "This-a' new year! Everybody happy!" he proclaimed as he handed out the menus and then sped away toward the kitchen. His long acquaintance with them entitled him to chide them amiably. He didn't want, didn't have time, to hear their troubles.

They ordered. They ate. They barely talked. Each was lost in their own world, all of them pretty bleak, pretty Mars-scape-ish....

Of greatest, almost frightening, concern, Julie's mother

was dead silent. The only words she spoke during the whole meal were "spaghetti Bolognese," when Giuseppe took their orders.

Julie and her father exchanged numerous anxious glances. Neither of them could even snag her mother's eyes, which pretty much remained fixed on the pepperoncini jar in the middle of the table. Even when her mother ate, Julie could see that she wasn't paying attention to what she was putting in her mouth. She could have been eating clumps of wet sawdust, and she wouldn't have noticed.

There was so much happy holiday noise in the room that their grim silence could go relatively unnoticed. And, by the time their meals arrived, only the most giddy, slightly insane, or very inebriated, person would have attempted to puncture the din in the room.

But busy and distracted as Giuseppe was, he took note of their mood. When it came time to pay the check, he said, putting one hand heavily on her mother's shoulder: "Whatever make-a' you sad—I hope New Year will fix. I pray for you," a promise that he clearly meant to keep. And then he was gone into the blithering idiocy of The Lido the day before New Year's Eve.

****

If her mother's silence, her disconnectedness, in The Lido was scary; in the car on the way home, it was terrifying.

Julie's father made numerous attempts to make contact with her, but she rebuffed each one.

"Looks like we might get a dusting of snow tonight."
silence.
"I think *Roman Holiday*," her mother's favorite movie, "is on TCM tonight."
"oh."
"Shall I make some popcorn?"
Only Julie said a clear "yes." Her mother's mumble could

be taken either way.

And so it went for pretty much the next 24 hours.

They found her mother asleep on the couch in the morning. She'd gone to bed in her own bed that night but must have gotten up during the night.

Julie hadn't slept all that well herself, and when she did sleep, the dreams were all pretty distressing. They were mostly of the parental-guidance, graphic violence and imagery kind.

Appropriately, she woke up with a horrible taste in her mouth. It was only lethal garlic breath from her meal at The Lido the night before, but it fit her mood to a T.

Strangest, perhaps most disturbing of all, when Julie and her father found her mother curled up asleep on the couch, she was clutching a rosary. Julie knew that it was her Grandma Burch's rosary with its pink quartz beads and cloisonné "Our Father" beads, because her mother had shown it to her on several occasions, as in "Julie, I just want to show this to you so that when I die you'll know it's something special."

First of all, was it "when I die" time? Second, she'd never seen her mother pray the Rosary(??)

That was when Julie's spirits began to assume the same cheerless frosty gray this last day of the year had chosen as its garb.

Her father puttered around, finding *lots* of things to do in the basement and garage. Her mother sat curled up on the couch with the Christmas tree lights on(?!) flipping through back issues of *National Geographic* and *Smithsonian* and *Martha Stewart Living.* Nothing on the glossy pages seemed to get her attention. Every article topic was, like, too "slippery." Her attention just slithered off. But she'd showered, dressed, and made cream of tomato soup and toasted cheese sandwiches for lunch. The soup had globs of unmixed tomato soup in it and the toasted cheese sandwiches were burned on at least one side.

"Boy, these are good," both Julie and her father said, while they crunched away on the burned layer of the bread. In a way, though, they *were* good. They were a tangible sign that her mother wasn't totally gone missing.

"Tweedle?" her father said, as they were cleaning up. "Do you think you want to go to Babs' tonight?"

Julie's Aunt Babs was hosting the family New Year's celebration that night.

Her mother got a stricken look in her eyes, as though she'd forgotten tonight was New Year's Eve and they were expected at Aunt Babs. "Oh, dear—" her mother said. "I don't know if I feel up to it."

"I can call Babs and tell her you're under the weather. She won't mind. In fact, if we didn't show up, she probably wouldn't even notice it, there'll be so many people there. On the other hand, Tweedle," her father said gently, "it would probably be better for you to get out rather than moping around here."

That was the wrong thing to say. "I'm not moping," Julie's mother retorted heatedly. "I'm trying to make an awful decision that I was *totally* unprepared for."

But Julie's father, the prosecutor, was not easily intimidated. "Maybe *moping* isn't the right word, Tweedle, but a few hours in the company of family who know and love you won't do you any harm."

Her mother got a pleading, leave-me-alone look. Seeing it, Mr. Tyler said "Okay, honey. We won't go. I can understand your not wanting to be surrounded by a bunch of partying people. I'll call Babs now."

He'd just reached for the wall-mounted phone when Julie's mother said. "No, Bob, wait. We'll go."

His hand frozen halfway to the phone, he looked quizzically at her mother. Had she really changed her mind and wanted to go? Or was she being something of a spoiled brat, not getting her way, but getting her way nonetheless. . . .

It turned out to be the former. "Really, Tweedle," her mother said, "I would like to go. I really do want to be surrounded by family tonight." She put on the outfit she'd worn to the mother–daughter dinner, complete with the scarf her Aunt Babs' had "lent" her.

"I thought you had to give that scarf back to Aunt Babs?" Julie asked, braving some mischievous chatter, when her mother entered the living room where Julie and her father sat waiting for her.

Mrs. Tyler gave Julie a slight grin and her eyes shone with a slight twinkle. "You're right, little miss sharp eyes," she quipped, "but you'll notice I'm wearing it to her house. My plan is to give it back to her at the end of the evening, and not before."

Actually, at the end of the evening, Babs insisted that she keep it. It became her mother's favorite scarf to wear over her chemo-bald head, but that was some ways down the road as yet.

****

On the way, her mother said "I'm sure that Miss Manners wouldn't approve, but even though it's New Year Eve, I'm going to break my bad news to the gang [i.e., the Tyler family] tonight."

Actually, she didn't need to say a word. Everyone there knew. Did her mother really think the Tyler Telegraph wouldn't have gotten the news out to everyone in the family?

No one was maudlin. No one over-the-top sympathetic. It was as though everyone had practiced what they were going to say to her, and everyone got it just right, from "sorry to hear about it, kid" to "I've asked everyone in my prayer group to pray for you" to "let me know if you need me to take you to any of your appointments," all of them accompanied by warm hugs.

Actually, the last one got a lot of mileage—literally. It was to become known as the Tyler Transport, as family and friends signed up to bring her mother to her various appointments at Smitty's. This included the day-long chemotherapy sessions, the daily radiation treatments, and appointments with various cancer specialists who seemed to have some kind of weird popularity contest going on as to who had the most patients waiting to see him or her at any one time, was Julie's guess. Mrs. Tyler was never to go alone to Smitty's. Like everything in life, though, this wasn't all milk and honey, not when these stalwart family members included the likes of the ever-judgmental Aunt Alice and the ever-talkative cousin Beryl.

After all the hellos, Julie's mother went on to, apparently, have a good time. Her laughter might not have been as golden or bountiful as usual. And, indeed, her face was dead serious under its smiles. But, 'thank God,' Julie thought, her mother's frozen Siberian silence seemed to be thawing a bit. Happy New Year!

The highlight of the evening didn't, however, occur at the stroke of midnight, the ushering in of the New Year. It occurred in the anticlimactic hour after the tumult of hugging and kissing and wishing everyone a hearty, happy, and *healthy* (the latter said with great emphasis to her mother by everyone there) New Year, accompanied by more warm hugs. Even Mrs. Tyler seemed to abandon herself temporarily to the joy of the moment.

At 12:05, when all the well-wishing was over, her mother sat down in an armchair next to the Christmas tree. Julie could see that her mother looked tired, though the cheer and jollity of the evening had put *almost* a glow on her cheeks. Yes, spending the occasion with the Tylers *had* been good for her.

The various members of the Tyler clan began to leave in batches. These consisted of families with young children, many carried out asleep in their parents' arms, and old folks also up way past their bed time, usually in the company of a son or daughter who buttoned up their coats, made their hats snug, made sure they got down steps and into cars without slipping on icy spots.

Even though the number of people had thinned, the hour was late, and everyone had to be tired, not everyone was ready to call the party quits—not ready yet to reenter the dank cold reality of the world outside. These stalwart few gathered in the living room. With the resumption of some peace and quiet in the house, her Aunt Babs's old blond Labrador retriever Dollie wandered wearily out into the living room.

Actually, she wasn't *that* old, because she'd just had another litter of puppies. Her swollen teats wobbled pink and painful looking in two long rows from each side of her chest and belly.

"So how many litters has that poor dog had now?" asked Gordon, one of Mr. Tyler's first cousins.

"Seven," her Aunt Babs said around a mouthful of food. She'd been so busy making sure all of her guests had gotten fed, she'd had no time to feed herself.

"Seven?!" said Louise, who was married to Gordon.

"How many were in the litter," someone else asked.

"Sixteen," her aunt said around another mouthful of food.

"Sixteen!?" everyone chorused in amazement.

Her aunt could only nod her head and roll her eyes as she tried to swallow her last bite-full.

"I thought you weren't going to breed the ole girl anymore," Gordon said as the dog plodded heavily across the room, her engorged teats swaying back and forth. She crossed the room, lay down in front of Julie's mother with something like a groan, eased onto her side, stretched her paws out toward her mother, and fell asleep.

"Well, I didn't plan to breed her again. But tell that to Dollie and the oh-so-buff black standard Poodle named Monsieur Pierre who leaped over the back fence so that he and Dollie could have their little tryst."

As the image of this played out in everyone's mind, everyone began to grin.

"Well, then," said Julie's Aunt Alice, who, to everyone's endless annoyance, knew everything and let everyone know what she knew, "you shouldn't have let Dollie out when she was in heat."

That said, her Aunt Alice sat back and assumed her standard holier-than-thou look. (Julie's Uncle Pete had once said that she should have become a contemplative nun. Then he corrected himself "No, she should have become one of those anchorites, or whatever, who get walled up in a hut and pray for the rest of their lives." Aunt Babs had chided, and corrected, him. "Honey, anchorites disappeared with the Middle Ages," to which he replied "Like I said, she should have been an anchorite —")

"Well, the problem was that Dollie let herself out," Aunt Babs was replying to Aunt Alice's disapproving comment. "She caught one look at Monsieur Pierre, the canine Matt Damon of the neighborhood, in her very own yard, panting wildly and barking 'ooooh, *ma chère, ma chérie*' in his sexy Louis Jourdan dog voice, and she was out the door *tout de suite*."

"Well, then, dear," continued the indefatigable Aunt Alice, "you should have shooed this Monsieur Pierre away."

"Well, yes, I probably should have, but when I looked out the window and saw how deliriously happy Dollie was, I mean, well, it just had it all over artificial insemination—"

At this point, came several tiny shrieks of laughter, and then the whole room was rollicking with laughter, with Aunt Alice the one holdout. The funniest part was that Julie's Aunt Babs hadn't meant it to be funny. She really hadn't been able to interfere with Dollie's and Monsieur Pierre's passionate love making.

Once the laughter died down, about seven minutes later, people began to realize that it really was now time to go.

****

On their way home in the car came the moment that was the *true* highlight of the evening, well, more correctly, of the first day of the New Year. Julie's mother spoke up just as they were heading down the street, the tires of the car crunching on a thin coating of frost on the dark street.

"You know," she said, "I've always thought, and now I know for certain, that God has a sense of humor—"

Given everything that Julie's mother'd been through that week, Julie's first thought was a silent 'oh, oh—where is she going with this?'

"What makes you think that, Tweedle?" her father asked gently.

"Well, here I've been praying for the past 24 hours for God to help me decide whether to have the double mastectomy or not, and I'm expecting some kind of a choir-of-angels-on-high-singing sign. And what does He do? He sends me poor Dollie with her poor swollen teats. Seeing that poor animal lying there, I just suddenly knew I should go through with the double mastectomy. Compared with that poor dog, I count myself lucky to have only two breasts."

That said, Julie's mother fell silent.

"God moves in wondrous ways—" Julie heard her father murmur, at which her mother looked over at him and gave him a twinkling, merry smile.

In the backseat, Julie gave out a soft laugh. The warm puff of air that came with it felt good on her chill cheeks.

CHAPTER 27

Father Desseau to the Rescue

Julie's mother's difficult decision was made, thanks to Dollie, the poor exhausted mother of sixteen puppies who'd, unknowingly, been asked to fulfill an important mission for God that New Year's Eve. The next two days until Mrs. Tyler's Monday morning appointment with the surgeon went by okay. Her mother wasn't the bright and cheerful person she usually was, but she wasn't "moping" either. An odd thing did happen after Mass on Sunday, though.

As they were wishing the very old, very tired-looking Father Desseau a happy New Year, her mother suddenly said, "Father, can I ask you a couple of questions if you have a minute?"

"Yes, my child," the priest said with his usual kind, benevolent expression. Julie could see, however, a momentary look of weariness at the prospect of answering her mother's "couple questions." Holidays like Christmas and Easter might be fun for most people, but for priests, ministers, preachers, and the like, they had to be a lot of work. Father Desseau had probably been a priest for, easily, 50 years, Julie thought. He was probably at that time of life when he wanted to kick up his heels, well, not literally, of course, after holidays were over and celebrate quietude.

Sensing that Mrs. Tyler's questions might require more than just a simple 'yes' or 'no,' he said, "Why don't we go over to the rectory. I'm afraid my old feet are tired of standing."

Julie had never been inside the rectory, to say nothing of the parlor, the name of the living room in church-speak.

The woman who served as the housekeeper looked somewhat dismayed when she saw the priest with the three Tylers in tow.

"Father, your dinner is ready," she heard the woman whisper.

"Yes, yes, Imelda," Father Desseau said, pressing his hands downwards as if to calm her.

Once settled in the parlor, Mrs. Tyler first told the priest of her bad diagnosis and the treatment decision she had made.

"I'm so very sorry to hear that, my child," said the very old priest sorrowfully, truly unhappy that one of his flock was faced with a serious sorrow.

"Father," Mrs. Tyler said next, "I know Smitty's has its own Catholic chaplain, but would you be willing to come to the hospital the day I have my surgery and perform extreme unction?"

'Extreme unction?!,' Julie thought, her heart leaping into her throat. 'They only do that when someone's dying.'

"Of course, Mona. I will be glad to come. I'm sure the Catholic chaplain at Smitty's won't mind my treading on his turf." The priest grinned mischievously.

The three of them, for the first time ever, were seeing a jollier side to Father Desseau than usually made its appearance in the pulpit. Some parishioners even called him Father Scold because he seemed to be taking them to task like bad children much of the time.

"But, of course," Father Desseau said, "we don't call the sacrament of the sick extreme unction much anymore, since it can be performed when anyone is about to undergo surgery or is seriously ill, though not necessarily dying," he reminded Julie's mother.

Julie breathed a sigh of relief. She must have been asleep the day they covered that in catechism class.

"And I believe you have other questions?" the priest said to her mother with a kind and patient smile.

Not so Imelda, the housekeeper, whom Julie could see at the end of the hallway wearing a very impatient grimace, with her hands placed annoyedly on her hips. Father Desseau's meal was getting cold—

"Yes, father, I do—" Julie's mother said, and then looked extremely uncomfortable at having to disclose the next thing that was on her mind.

"Is it something you wish to discuss with me in private?" the priest asked, noting her discomfort.

"Oh no, father. It's just that it has to do with my doctor. Her name is Padma Ramachandran."

She let it go at that—as though Dr. R's name were the question.

Father Desseau blinked. Even after 50-plus years of hearing confessions and listening to parishioners cough up more troubles than Freud could have shaken a stick at, he wasn't getting Mrs. Tyler's point.

Julie's mother was becoming more unglued, Father Desseau was patiently waiting for more details, and Imelda was about to jettison a Spanish curse in the direction of the parlor. Julie and her father? They were just onlookers, sitting there with sappy grins on their faces, much like the smiles on the bad depictions of saints that crowded the walls of the parlor. They had no idea what Mrs. Tyler was driving at either.

Finally, her mother offered more clues. "I think my doctor is some kind of Hindu, father," Mrs. Tyler said in a choked voice, as though the Church might, like, consider her associating with Dr. R, a Hindu, as some kind of venial, maybe even mortal, sin. "I mean, if she's a Hindu, she worships hundreds of gods and she believes in reincarnation."

"Yes, Mona. I don't know a lot about Hinduism, but I believe you have your facts straight. But I'm still not sure, my dear, what your question is."

Julie, at that point, was now worn out by her mother's beating around the bush. As for Imelda, she was now banging and clattering every pot and pan in the kitchen within close reach. She was now communicating her displeasure using a different medium.

"But she's not a Christian!" Her mother finally got to

the point of her concern. "She believes in Shiva or Krishna or Hanuman or whatever. She thinks a cow is sacred. She believes in reincarnation. She believes that 'oh well, today you die.' No problem, you'll be born again tomorrow as a mosquito or a bluejay or, maybe if you're lucky, as a Hollywood movie star—"

Julie almost burst out laughing at her mother's choice of incarnations. But, she silenced her laughter. Her mother was dead serious about her concern.

"Ah—" Father Desseau said, understanding flooding his face. Now he understood what was troubling the little lamb in his flock.

"I'm just a humble diocesan priest," he began in his old voice, "not by any means an expert on comparative religions. But I do know this," he looked straight at Mrs. Tyler and said in a clarion clear voice. "Every faith believes in good and evil and the consequences of good and evil actions. Thus any *true* adherent of any faith is taught that pursuing anything but the good puts the welfare of their soul at risk. Thus, someone like your Dr. Ramachandran"—amazingly he'd gotten Dr. R's name right at the first go—"who has entered the art of healing, would consider it vital to the salvation of her soul, regardless of her belief about the afterlife, to render the very best care at her disposal. And, from what little I know of the doctors at Smitty's, they all put in incredibly long hours for comparatively little pay. They are doctors who take their responsibilities as healers quite seriously. Unlike the many Catholic doctors who fleece insurance companies for all they can. But that's a topic for a later conversation." Here the priest's voice trailed off and ended with a shake of his head at the *not*-model behavior of some Catholic physicians.

"Point well taken, father," her mother said in a contrite voice.

With that, Father Desseau rose stiffly to his feet and the three Tylers rose obediently with him. The Sunday school lesson was over.

At the door, Mrs. Tyler said, in a clearly relieved voice,

"Thank you, father. I feel a lot better after talking to you."

"You are most welcome, my dear child," he smiled kindly and made the sign of the cross expressly over her, "I will pray for you. Just let me know the day of your surgery, and I will give you the sacrament of the sick beforehand," he said as he closed the door and turned his face toward his dinner and the unhappy Imelda. He had yet another dragon to contend with before he could celebrate post-holiday quietude.

CHAPTER 28

Double Mastectomy Monday

Mrs. Tyler had her double mastectomy the Monday after her appointment with her plastic surgeon. Julie wasn't with her either of the two Mondays. School resumed on the 3rd, and she had an algebra test on the day of her mother's surgery. Her father, too, hadn't been present the day of the surgery. He had to be in court, since "crime," like opportunity, waits for no man. Aunt Babs went in both of their steads. It was soon after that that the Tyler Transport went into high gear.

For some out-of-the-blue reason 'Santa' had given Julie a diary for Christmas. She was no Anne Frank hiding in an attic in Holland waiting for the stomp of Gestapo boots searching out yet more Jews to feed the fires of the Holocaust. But she *was* going through her own hellish (small 'h') time. Come to think of it, though, her one-eighth Jewish blood *would* have been enough to have gotten her herded onto a train to Auschwitz. But that was fodder for later musings. She had enough problems right now.

So on January 1 of that year, she began recording each day's happenings. But, first, she set the ground rules.

First, there was to be no crudeness, as in (especially!) no word-turds, as she liked to call them, especially ones referring to sexual acts or the products of biological functions. Her mother was right: if Jane Austin could make Mr. Darcy sexy without a lot of groping and gasping so also could she write her outpourings sans the same.

Second, there was to be no detailed status report of the day's events re: her mother's cancer. A simple numerical rating system would do, starting with 1, for okay, to 10, for there weren't words to adequately express how awful the day had been with regard to her mother's cancer. Thus the 10 also stood for infinity. Why avoid mention of the details of her mother's cancer and all its fall-out? Well, to answer a question with a question: why would a person keep stubbing their toe just to "remember" the pain?

The day of her mother's double mastectomy rated a 10, and that's all she wrote, just the two numerals writ large on the page. When her Aunt Babs picked her up after school and brought her to see her mother in her hospital room, all she could think when she first saw her was: 'How could something that's supposed to *cure* my mother make her look like she's just been in a car wreck?'

Gone was the chipper person of the night before when she'd been settled into her hospital room, preparatory to her 5 a.m. surgery the next morning. Mrs. Tyler had tubes going in, tubes coming out—fluids of one sort or another in constant transit through her body.

Her voice was hoarse because, her Aunt Babs explained, of the breathing tube that had been placed down her throat during the operation. She was so hoarse that she sounded as though she had laryngitis. But, then, when she did speak, the words didn't make much sense. Things like "baking soda, butterflies, and blueberries," which, for some reason, she said over and over. Was her mother, in her drugged state, making blueberry muffins on a long-ago summer day?? Or maybe she was just practicing her alliteration skills?

Julie and her aunt could only look at each other with sad, frightened looks and shrug. Was this normal or something to worry about? Other than that her mother was asleep. Julie and her Aunt Babs were just talking about leaving—it didn't seem as though their presence there mattered—when, suddenly, the door to her mother's room banged open and in charged an Ichabod Crane-like figure in dark rose-pink scrubs. The "Ichabod" person turned out to be a *she* named Faith Gardner. *She* was her mother's surgeon, whom Julie had not met yet. Her Aunt Babs *had*, that morning. Julie could hear her aunt grumble something under her breath that sounded an awful lot like "bitch," and Julie knew she wasn't referring to her dog Dollie.

Taking absolutely no note of Julie or her aunt (like had they turned into hospital furniture?), Dr. Gardner did a quick inspection of her mother's various tubes. Then, she flipped her mother's cover back, whipped up the front of her mother's johnny, and inspected the white bandages that swathed her mother's breasts, make that chest. The breasts were, of course, gone.

"Nurse!" the surgeon shouted.

Julie could hear, like, hundreds of feet running. Every nurse within a five-mile radius was on his or her way to her mother's bedside.

The first nurse to arrive was a very young, small, blond woman (child?) with a white, frightened look on her face. She reminded Julie, for all the world, of one of those teeny, tiny white (Japanese?) mushrooms that no one seemed to buy. She'd seen people in the supermarket pick up the packages, exclaim how cute they were, and then when they saw the price, blink and put the package back.

"Why hasn't this drain been changed?" Dr. Gardner demanded of the frightened-waif nurse.

"I don't know, doctor. She's not one of my patients—" the nurse whispered.

"Well, she is now!"

Just at that moment, Dr. R walked in. She'd been wearing her beautiful, serene Scheherazade smile, until she spotted Dr. Gardner standing there. She didn't change her smile, but Julie could see her eyes become guarded.

"Oh, it's you," Dr. Gardner said, as if she were disappointed it wasn't Zeus entering the room.

"Hello, Dr. Gardner," Dr. R said politely. "How is our patient doing?"

"Mrs. Tyler's surgery went quite well in my hands. I did complete nodectomies in both axillae, and intraop sections of her right breast and nodes," the breast without the tumor, "looked clean."

It seemed to Julie as though this Dr. Gardner was taking full credit for her mother's clean bill of health. Whatever, as long as she was right.

"I am most happy to hear that," said Dr. R. "But, of course, we'll have to wait for the postoperative pathology report before—"

"Well, *of course*, we'll have to wait for that!" Dr. Gardner said in an outraged, what-kind-of-idiot-do-you-take-me-for voice.

Julie and her aunt looked at each other helplessly. Should they just bow out of this scene to avoid embarrassment to all parties?!

At that point, the poor hapless nurse who was assigned to her mother entered the room running, as if her life depended on it, and the white mushroom nurse exited just as speedily . . . Aunt Babs, Julie, and the two physicians left the room while the nurse and a couple of attendants changed the miscreant drain.

In the corridor, Dr. Gardner and Dr. R stood off to one side discussing her mother's case in hushed voices. Dr. Gardner could, apparently, speak in a *humane* manner—just when Julie would have liked to hear what she was saying. . . .

When Julie and her aunt were allowed back into her mother's room, they found her fast asleep, and looking very comfortable, so they tiptoed out, her aunt whispering "I think your mother needs sleep more than company now." She and her Aunt Babs then went to Beijing Noodle, a popular chic Chinese restaurant. The food was great, and her aunt's company was great, but it wasn't the same as the combination of her mother and The Lido. It just wasn't.

Julie's father stopped by to see Mrs. Tyler later that evening, after a long day in court. He likewise found her sound asleep. He sat there stilly for about an hour, just watching her, holding a hand that didn't have an IV stuck in it. Then he got up, gave her a gentle kiss on her forehead, and whispered "I love you," before he crept quietly from the room.

They were to find out later that Dr. Gardner went by various unofficial names, such as Dr. Dragon, the Barracuda, the Valkyrie, and other unprintable names, none of which were preceded by "doctor." So, Dr. R was a Hindu and Faith Gardner, with a name like Faith, must be a Christian or a Christian substitute, kind of like saccharine was to sugar. But Dr. R was ever so much more pleasant that Dr. Dragon, which just went to prove that Father Desseau was right. You couldn't judge a person solely by their faith.

The next day, Julie found out that she'd *flunked* her algebra test. A first! She'd *never* flunked anything ever, never even come close! But when she looked at the test she could see where she'd made some pretty stupid mistakes, ones she wouldn't have made if thoughts of her mother's surgery hadn't been tearing her subconscious mind to shreds. It was just the same ole, same ole angst.

CHAPTER 29

Nemesis

While all this was going on, some really strange, as in inexplicable, things were happening at school. For example, one day she discovered that the lock on her locker had been changed. She hadn't forgotten the combination. She'd had the lock for four years, for goodness sake. Fortunately she'd been early to school that day, which made her only a little less late than she would have been to her civics class the first period that morning. It'd taken the school maintenance man with a hacksaw to "unlock" the combination lock that wasn't even the right make of lock for the school. That didn't mean that she didn't have to pay the school 25 dollars for replacing the lock. Only 10 dollars was for the lock. The remaining 15 dollars was a school-penalty charge for damaging school property, as in reparation for the school-issued lock she'd had for four years that had gone totally missing through absolutely no fault of her own!

Then an essay she'd brought to school on the day it was due mysteriously disappeared from the folder she'd put it in in her backpack. No problem. She must have thought she put it in the folder but didn't. (She was so absentminded these days, she could walk out of the house without shoes and not notice it.) She'd bring in the one she'd left at home. The problem with that was that the essay was due on a Friday, so the teacher, who was new to Ainsworth that year, was concerned Julie would use the missing homework as an excuse to get two more days to polish her prose.

Thus, besides the printed document that she needed to bring in on the following Monday, she also had to bring in a flash drive with the electronic document on it as proof that the essay hadn't been further fiddled with after the day *and* time it had been saved to her hard drive. What bothered her the most was that, one more time, her honesty was called into question. Curiously, she never found the essay at home that she knew she'd printed off the night before it was due. She'd had to print a second one.

Then, at the end of school one day, she opened her locker to find that someone had dumped green food coloring through the vent in the locker, which had stained in an unattractive tie-dye pattern the back of her light gray toggle coat. It wasn't food coloring, though. Whatever it was, it didn't come out at the cleaners, so she had to buy another coat. The problem with that was that it was the end of the season and finding a winter coat that she would want to be seen in public in (*one that wasn't* made of metallic, purple, or orange fabric, trimmed with cheap fur, or so padded and quilted that it made her look like the Michelin man) was like finding a needle in a haystack.

It was her Aunt Babs who came to the rescue. At the local Lord & Taylor, she found a really beautiful Ralph Lauren toggle coat made out of 100 percent camel's hair that was discounted 75 percent because one of the toggle loops had come unstitched. No one wanted to buy such a defective(?) coat. Even though she wasn't really handy with a needle and thread, Julie, with her mother's guidance, sewed the toggle closed and she ended up with a jacket that was three times more expensive than her previous one and twice as attractive! And, if Gloria's grandmother could be recompensed for her dentist's bill, so could she apply for recompense for the jacket ruined on school property. Which she was, and Dr. Drescher was only too glad to okay the insurance claim for it, especially after she learned how the jacket had been damaged. So whoever'd ruined her first coat was the real loser because she was the one with the brand-new RLL camel coat. Just to be on the safe side, though, she'd brought a heavy-duty zippered bag to put the coat in when it was in her locker

Then came something really below the belt, really slimy. Up until this point, Julie knew she was the victim of pranks. She and her mother had talked about it and decided the best thing to do was to ignore them, and they would stop of their own accord. Whoever was doing it, and it didn't take much effort for Julie to know who that was, would get tired of it. Then came the prank that cinched it, that couldn't be ignored for what it was.

It started with an unexpected summons to go and see the school nurse. It turned out that *someone* had told the woman that she'd overheard Julie telling some friends (whose names were not revealed to the woman) that she thought she'd picked up genital herpes from her boyfriend but she was afraid to tell her parents about it because she didn't want them to know that she'd lost her virginity. The nurse was interested only because she was concerned that the venereal disease, which, technically, genital herpes is, the woman explained to Julie in a tone of voice that was about as sympathetic as a horned toad, would get spread to the other girls through contact with toilet seats, gym equipment, even desk chairs the woman had said!

The nurse would not take Julie's fierce, outraged word for the fact that such a confidence could never have been overheard because it had never been uttered because she had no such disease because she was a virgin, for heaven's sake, not that that was any of the woman's business! But the nurse, having "a responsibility to the student body as a whole," as she patiently explained it, insisted that Julie be tested for genital herpes, which necessitated a most discomforting, physically and mentally, vaginal swab. The test result, of course, came back negative. To spare her parents any anguish, which neither needed right then, she was able to get the test done without their knowledge. (But, so why did she need their written consent to go to the local art museum on a class trip?)

But the rumor mill did not keep her totally fabricated case of genital herpes confidential, because one day she arrived at school to find that someone had written "STD gal" (couldn't they come up with something more original?) on her locker in indelible black magic marker. The words couldn't be removed by any means known to man (i.e., any kind of chemical). All the school maintenance man had been able to do was to spray paint over the words in a color of paint that had a lot more red in it than the original paint on the locker, which, of course, gave the distinct impression that her locker had some kind of herpetic rash. Just ducky.

The graffiti on her locker had been the final straw. THAT had been the day she marched over to Dr. Drescher's office and told her about all the nasty tricks that had been played on her, including the ruined winter coat, which the woman was already aware of. Of course, not having any solid clue as to the culprit(s) —though the Cow-turd damsel and her coven of friends seemed shoo-in suspects in Julie's mind, there wasn't much the director could do. She would ask security to be more on the watch for suspicious behavior around Julie's locker, but that was all she could do until someone got caught red (or was it green?)-handed.

But good fortune was on Julie's side that day. She was striding in the door of the classroom building fresh from her visit with Dr. Drescher, full of the satisfaction that she'd set into motion something to foil the perpetrator(s) of the mischief, when she ran into Gloria Jackson.

"Hey, girl," Gloria greeted Julie in her usual glad fashion, "you look like you're loaded for bear."

Julie laughed. "I am of sorts."

"Anything to do with that wicked little comment written on your locker this morning?"

"That and other things." She then listed all of the other annoyances that had been piling up since the confrontation with Alexis in Dr. Drescher's office. "I just came from Dr. Drescher's office. I complained to her about all the nasty tricks that have been played on me," she said in a suddenly loud voice.

Gloria, baffled by the sudden loudness of Julie's voice, turned and looked in the direction Julie's eyes were going in. There, hiding just inside of the door to the library, was Angelina Baker, Alexis's second-in-command. She'd just started to emerge from the library when she'd either spotted or heard Julie. Whether it was to hear what Julie had to say or to just avoid Julie, it mattered not to Julie. She'd come back from Dr. Drescher's office with her spirit encased in Kevlar. She was going on the offensive.

"So Dr. Drescher is having a CCTV camera set up in the hallway focused on my locker to try to catch who's doing this crap," Julie finished exultantly. That wasn't quite true. What the director was going to have the building crew do was install a fake CCTV camera that one could buy at Lowes and was used to get anyone with a criminal mind to maybe take up decoupage instead.

After that, the mischief ceased... mostly.

****

Anyway, the first written entry of note in Julie's diary fell toward the end of January.

Mrs. Tyler had made an excellent recovery from her surgery because of, or in spite of, Dr. Gardner's care. She sure had no bed-side manner. In a matter of a few weeks, the drains had been removed, the bandages had come off, and there were no infections in any of the scars. *And* neither arm had turned into an inner tube. Wei was right so far. Cancer treatment wasn't always a chamber of horrors.

One day after school, before her father'd come home, her mother said quietly to her, "Honey, would you mind coming upstairs to my bedroom with me? I want to show you something."

"Sure, Mom," Julie said, baffled by her mother's request. Her mother'd already shown her her Grandmother Burch's rosary; what more was there to show? Maybe her Grandmother Burch's diamond tiara.... 'Ha ha,' she thought as she followed her mother upstairs.

It turned out to be a surprise of a different order, one not as enticing even as a rosary. When they got to Mrs. Tyler's bedroom, her mother said, "Julie, sit down here on the bed with me. I'd like to show you my chest now that the incisions have healed." At that her mother paused and looked down into her lap, as if showing them was as hard for her as it would probably be for her daughter to see them.

"Sure, Mom," Julie said in a very small, tentative voice, hoping that her mother would hear in them the 'no!' also the 'why?,' that she really wanted to shriek.

Not reading her daughter's mind like a good mother would, she was already reaching up and unsnapping the snaps of the duster she was wearing.

Julie looked down and away. She could see, out of the corner of her eyes, that her mother's shoulders were bared. She wore no bra—didn't need to, of course. And then something lifted her chin and firmly directed it toward her mother, not a human hand, though, and she looked.

What she beheld were two crescent-shaped surgical scars outlining the bottom curve of where her mother's breasts used to fall. She didn't faint or scream or anything. She just beheld a fact of life, her mother's and her father's and her lives. And she was ... okay with it. Some days later, it seemed like she'd grown up in that moment, taken on at least the left sleeve of the mantle of adulthood.

The "viewing" over, her mother put her arms through the sleeves of her duster and began to snap it up. And then Julie, like, for the first time, saw the complete male-like flatness of her mother's chest, the breasts that she had suckled as a child, the ones she'd fallen asleep on, used as pillows, gone. And then, she couldn't help it, tears began to roll down her cheeks.

Then she saw that tears were also rolling down her mother's cheeks. And then her mother started up in a tearful voice "You know I've always thought that grief had to do with people you love dying. But," here she took a deep shuddering breath, "I wouldn't have thought one would grieve over the loss of a part of one's body—"

"Oh, Mom," Julie said. "I'm so sorry." She could have,

maybe should have, gone over to where her mother sat and put her arms around her to comfort her. But it didn't seem as though she could make such an action seem anything but schmaltzy. It didn't suit the ineffable sadness of the moment. So Julie and her mother just sat there, not saying anything, waiting, it seemed, for their respective sadnesses to wear off.

This was on top of a very interesting day at school, as her diary entry described.

> *Today Alexis came up to me after lunch and actually put her arm around my shoulders like the sister I don't (probably fortunately) have. (BTW, when Alexis put her arm around me, I got a strong whiff of new leather. When she turned around, I saw she had a brand new LOUIS VUITTON backpack. She must have gotten it for Christmas. A $3,000 backpack! Well, but, does she have a Ralph Lauren 100% camel hair toggle coat?!) To continue—she told me she'd heard about Mom's having breast cancer and she wanted to know how she was doing. I felt like Howdy Doody with my hinged jaw hanging open. Did she think I'd be stupid enough to believe that she has an organ that does more than just pump blood throughout her body(!) But I played the dunce. It seemed the safest way to go. I told her my mother was doing fine, just fine.*

Her academic life? It was continuing to be battered by the forces let loose by her mother's cancer. After the F on her algebra test, she'd gone on to get a D on an algebra exam. She'd also scored a dismal B+ on a history test (a subject she always aced) and an even more dismal B on an English essay (the one that had gone missing both at school and at home, but some of the grade had been due to its "lateness."). *Surprisingly*, though, she'd gotten an A++ on a biology paper. Surprising because science was *not* her strong suit. But, curious about this BRCA1 gene abnormality that was "break-a-ing" their lives apart, she was curious about *it* and other causes of cancer. And, having spent enough time in Smitty's patient education center poring over scientific articles (supposedly intelligible to someone without five PhDs), textbooks on cancer, and a variety of pamphlets and booklets, and having to produce some kind of 1500-word paper on a scientific topic of her own choosing, she did hers on "Cancer and Its Causes."

One of the really interesting tidbits of information she'd gleaned from her research was that there are genes, mostly screwed-up (mutated) ones like her mother's, that "predispose people to cancer," but the people who have the genes, called "carriers," don't *always* get cancer. It takes something like exposure to certain chemicals, bad nutrition, sunbathing, alcohol intake, and smoking for the gene to get up to its little hijinks. What had triggered her mother's BRCA1 gene, Julie wondered? Her mother neither smoked nor drank to excess, never sunbathed, was obsessive about nutritious food, and, as far as she knew, had not worked on the Manhattan project.

She then made the *big* mistake of showing her paper to her parents, with it's A++ emblazoned on the top and the science teacher's comment "Miss Tyler—this is excellently done. Good research. Very logically presented and organized. And very comprehensive. Perhaps science is your forte!"

Her mother'd been drinking a cup of coffee at the time. It was after supper, and she and Mr. Tyler were sitting there discussing their days.

"Read it to us, Julie," her father had said.

Pride. It was all about pride, wanting to show off her A++ paper! But it was *only* because it'd been her *only* success in a now string of academic mishaps, misfortunes, and misadventures.... Surely she could be forgiven a tad, a small balm, if you will, of pride. Her punishment came swiftly.

Specifically, the moment she read out "one of the suspected causes of cancer, especially bladder cancer, is the caffeine in coffee," her mother slammed her cup of coffee down on the saucer, sloshing coffee all over the place, shouting "oh no—I shouldn't be drinking this," as if it was a ptomaine cocktail she'd been holding to her lips. And it didn't end there.

That night, she threw out all the coffee, tea, caffeine-containing sodas, even the box of instant hot cocoa. Sure, chocolate has caffeine, or something *like* it, in it, but a cup of hot cocoa now and then? Was that like a venial sin in the world of oncology?

And, then, Julie and her father were faced with having herbal teas with various exotic names as their only beverage, besides water. Milk was out, too. Her paper'd also mentioned that estrogen exposure is associated with breast cancer, and, yes, her paper in all its "comprehensive" glory had included the fact that milk often has traces of estrogen in it. They give it to the cows so they make more milk. Estrogen! That much-maligned hormone which it seemed every female attributed all her problems to. But this ban on milk? Come on. This was not her real mother, in her right mind.

The ban on caffeine lasted for about two weeks and ended up being the cause of her parents' first *ever*, in her hearing, argument.

"I don't care what fancy names they give these teas," her father sputtered one night after supper, "they all taste like grass cuttings to me. Can't we have even an eight-ounce jar of instant coffee in the house—but *not* Sanka," he was quick to clarify, knowing his wife's clever legal mind.

"No, Bob," came her mother's practically hysterical retort. "If we have it in the house, I may be tempted to drink it!"

"I'll hide the jar in the garage. I'll take it with me to work. I'll—What are you doing with my bottle of Glenlivet single-malt scotch?!" he shouted.

"I'm getting rid of it. Remember, alcohol is also a cause of cancer. It was also in Julie's A++ paper."

'Why?!' thought Julie, her head in her hands upstairs in her room, '*Why* did I ever write that paper?' '*Why* did I read it to Mom and Dad?'

"Don't pour that down the sink, Mona," she heard her father say next in a very warning voice. "Put that bottle down!" he shouted.

Which her mother dutifully did—on the kitchen floor.

Julie heard first a loud thud, followed by the deep clinks of the heavy glass bottle breaking. This was followed by the sound of yet more breaking glass as her father stormed out the kitchen door and slammed it behind him, in the process breaking one of the small panes of glass. The next sound she heard was her father backing the car out of the driveway and then roaring down the street, tires squealing unhappily, registering their own protest.

She'd been studying her algebra book, trying to get her grade in the course back on track. It was beginning to seem, for all the world, like a drunk person trying to walk a straight line. However, she was finding nothing funny after her father slammed the kitchen door. Fittingly, she slammed her algebra book shut. The heck with x's and y's and all the unknowns in algebra. She had more important unknowns to deal with, and they were proving a lot more distressing than algebra's.

So, she went to bed, but rather than sleeping, she lay there in the dark with silent tears streaming down her cheeks. She didn't know it, but the full moon shining in her window that night made a pretty sight of the silver rivulets that made a delicate lace on her pretty face with its perfect complexion and rosy cheeks. But, then, she wouldn't have cared a fig if she *had* known. She was too aware of her discombobulated life. Her mother acting like a nincompoop. Her father, too, at least tonight. Her school life teetering on the brink of destruction due to forces beyond her control (there were yet more pranks to come). She wanted her real mother, her real father, her regular life back, and that included tea, coffee and Glenlivet scotch for her father.

*****

Her father must have gone to one of those building supply stores that cater to obsessive-compulsive midnight handymen who can't wait until the next day to, like, put different knobs on the kitchen cupboards. Except for the reek of whiskey (from the Glenlivet single-malt scotch), everything in the kitchen was normal in the morning. The broken glass had been cleaned up, the kitchen floor was *especially* shiny (was it the Glenlivit?), and a new pane of glass in the door window with the sun shining through it, preening, it seemed, because it was now the most perfect, most clear glass pane in the 30-year-old door.

CHAPTER 30

All Things Considered

The next day when Julie arrived home from school, she found her mother in the kitchen having a cup of tea while listening to "All Things Considered" on NPR.

"Will you join me in a cup of tea?" her mother asked.

"Sure, Mom."

She headed toward the pantry to get a teabag, her heart sinking at the thought of drinking a cup of tea named Tibetan Nirvana, Jade Delight, or Soothing Slumber. Her father was right. It didn't matter what exotic name they gave these teas, they all tasted like hay—and *not* Heavenly Hay!

"Oh, you don't need to make yourself some tea, honey," her mother called after her. "I've made a pot of it. It's there on the counter."

Then came two surprises.

The first was that the teapot was her mother's treasured Royal Doulton "Real Old Willow" teapot and next to it a cup and saucer in the same pattern. They rarely used any of this, her mother's best, china. It wasn't even brought out for Christmas or Thanksgiving when it was her mother's turn to entertain the family. "There are always too many children running around," her mother'd explained to her time and again when she, a child, had tried to wheedle her into using it for some upcoming family gathering. No, her mother only ever used it for small, adults-only dinner parties. Julie didn't think she'd ever eaten off it, just gazed at the pretty stuff on display in her mother's china cabinet, each year as she grew taller being able to see ever more shelves of it, until one day she made the wondrous discovery that she could see all five shelves' worth of it!

The second surprise was that the teapot was filled with true-blue, standard-variety, caffeine-laden black tea. (There also proved to be *real* coffee for supper. And, a few weeks later, her father was to discover a new, unopened, bottle of Glenlivit single-malt scotch in the liquor cabinet.)

Then there came a third surprise. That night they even ate off the "Real Old Willow" china and were to do so for quite a while thereafter.

Julie's father, if he noticed, didn't say anything about the china. But then, Julie figured, he probably wouldn't notice something like that. He was just glad, gleeful even, to see coffee back on the menu. But he kept silent about that, too, just raised his eyebrows and gave Julie a conspiratorial wink when Mrs. Tyler set the cup of coffee in front of him, and then a wide-eyed, mouthed 'wow' when this was followed by a slice of scrumptious chocolate cake with fudge icing Aunt Babs had baked and brought over that day. (Had she been in cahoots with her father, maybe even her mother, re: the reappearance of things chocolate in their diet?)

After Julie'd gotten her cup of tea that afternoon, she joined her mother at the table. Together they listened to the program. There was a particularly interesting segment about childhood traumas and the lingering effect they have in adulthood. The next program was about global warming, which neither Julie nor her mother could bother worrying about right then, so her mother reached over and switched off the radio.

Musing in the silence that followed, her mother said, "I hope my cancer won't have a traumatic effect on you, Julie."

Julie hadn't told either of her parents anything about the pranks that had been played on her at school or much about the downward drift her academic performance was taking, thanks, yes, to her mother's cancer. She wanted to spare her mother knowledge of that. She was lugging enough angst around these days, what with all her cancer treatment and its side effects. She didn't need Julie's piddling angst, too. So, rather than answer her mother's question, she just shrugged and went on to answer her mother's question with a question, one which, she realized afterwards, there would never be a better time to ask.

"How about you, Mom? How did you handle your mother's cancer and her death?" by suicide ... the words seemed to whisper themselves in the silence that shifted for a moment between them. And, yes, she'd been uneasy about her mother going the same route as her grandmother ever since she'd learned of it.

"Well," her mother said, taking a deep, fortifying, breath, "First of all, I was away at college when she was sick. So I wasn't around for most of the time she was going for her treatments and her doctors' appointments. I was also older—almost an adult, which gave me a different perspective on the situation. I did come home practically every weekend to help out at home. But it wasn't the same for me as it would be for you."

At this she looked over at Julie with a completely neutral look, tacitly giving her a second chance to say something about the adverse effects of her cancer on her daughter's life. Julie just shrugged, as she'd done before. First off, she didn't really want to talk about her problems. Second, she wanted to hear more of what her mother had to say about her experience with *her* mother's cancer, especially the suicide part.

Realizing Julie had nothing she wanted to say, her mother started talking in a strange higher-pitched voice. It took Julie a couple seconds to realize that this was her mother's college girl voice, the one she had when her mother had had cancer. She started off by saying that her mother was a wonderful person and a wonderful mother, the 'wonderful' underscored both times. Then she paused—she needed a moment to collect herself, "When my mother died," she began with difficulty as if she were plowing a field that had never been plowed before. "When she took her own life," she got out, having made it through a particularly hard clod of earth, "I don't know—I don't think I was able to grieve for her like one should for a mother."

Her words were coming more easily now. "It was as though she didn't deserve that kind of grief. I know that's a horrible thing to say about one's mother. But I think that grief is like some kind of currency, treasure maybe. The amount of grief you 'spend' on a person is a measure of their worth. What my mother did was, just, such a selfish act that hurt so many people...." Her mother's words tapered out here and she went silent. Julie kept her mouth shut, just let her mother think through her ambivalent feelings about her mother's death due to the less-lofty cause—suicide.

Julie was also thinking a big "whew." Her mother may have gotten her BRCA1 gene from her mother but not her suicidal tendency. Time for more tea.

But her mother had more to say about childhood traumas. This time she spoke in an even higher-pitched, almost childish, voice. "I had one trauma when I was a child that left me, I'll admit, with a very deep scar."

"What was that, Mom?" Julie asked, feeling her heart speed up much like it had on last year's Christmas tree Saturday when her father'd started telling her about his trauma suffered in youth at the hands of Alexandra Riley-Dolan. But she was older, more mature, now than she had been that day in the Christmas tree lot (was it only three months ago?), and she knew without a shred of doubt that she could take whatever her mother had to tell her without flinching.

"I was only about 5 years old at the time," she began, back to her grownup voice. "The family upstairs had two daughters. One was my age. Trudy was plain like me," she said matter-of-factly, thereby providing Julie with more reassuring proof that she hadn't somehow telepathically communicated her concerns about her looks to her mother in the days leading up to the mother–daughter dinner, now years in her past....

Then followed her mother's story of an awful deed dealt her when she was far too young for the wound to, yes, leave anything but a deep scar.

Her mother's Sunday afternoon had gotten off to a happy enough start. The woman who lived upstairs had invited the 5-year-old Mona to accompany her and her two daughters on visits she was making to her friends.

"The other daughter, Margaret Rose, and woe betide anyone who called her 'Maggie' or 'Margie' or 'Rosie' in her mother's hearing, was a beautiful child. She had curly platinum blond hair, cornflower blue eyes, and porcelain-like skin. She was exquisite—a Shirley Temple kind of child," Julie's mother said sourly.

That would explain why her mother always grumbled when there was a Shirley Temple movie on TCM. Her mother hadn't been the earth-incarnate, beautiful-bauble child that Shirley Temple was.

"To Margaret Rose's credit, though," her mother was now saying, "it was mainly her mother who was deranged about her looks. Margaret Rose hung upside down on the jungle gym, played hopscotch, tag, and skinned her knees along with the rest of us."

But that awful Sunday afternoon that had left a deep scar in her mother's memory of childhood, Trudy and Margaret Rose's mother had gotten it into her Shirley Temple–addled brain to march the three girls from friend's house to friend's house. At each house, she lined the three girls up and asked each of her friends (and from her mother's description, it seemed as though there had to have been a dozen of them) which was the fairest child of them all. Margaret Rose's mother was the neighborhood Snow White wannabe....

And, then, to Julie's further horror, didn't every one of this witch woman's cronies pick, without a moment's hesitation, Margaret Rose as the "fairest of them all."

Julie looked at her mother after she'd finished her telling of that awful long-ago childhood trauma to see the effect it still had on her. She expected tears to be running down her cheeks. The occasion warranted them. Her mother had every right to weep. But instead she had this wry, even wise, smile on her face.

"I happened to run into the once-beautiful Margaret Rose a couple years ago," her mother went on to say. "She recognized me. I didn't recognize her. I say 'once-beautiful' because *Margie*, which she insisted I call her, had become what would be best, *charitably*, described as blowsy. She'd put on *a lot* of weight—at least 50 pounds, I'd say. Her hair was no longer a lustrous platinum blond. It was more the color of rust—a home-done coloring job that had gone very bad. And Margie's once porcelain-like skin was now more like old Etruscan pottery."

So there *was* some justice in the world, thought Julie, subconsciously filing Margaret Rose's devil mother in the same mental folder with the Cowper women. She and her mother didn't exactly laugh at that point. Who could? Her mother's "funny" ending to her story couldn't cancel out one iota of the trauma, the memory of which had to have opened her mother's old wound at least a bit. But she had to give her mother credit. She wasn't sitting there weeping uncontrollably, rending her clothes, relishing the opportunity to indulge in self-pity, expecting Julie to do the same.

"That's awful, Mom," Julie finally said quietly, looking at her mother, *her* eyes now brimming with tears as the awfulness of what the woman had done to her, yes, dearly beloved, mother finally hit home.

Her mother smiled back, looked down in her lap, let a couple seconds go by, and then asked Julie a third time whether her cancer was having a serious effect on her life.

Compared with what her mother had gone through, Margaret Rose's mother's heinous deed, her mother's cancer and suicide, her father's accidental death at a fire a year later, which they hadn't spoken of that day, and now her cancer, *her* problems seemed pretty minor. It did seem a good time, though, to bring up Alexis's mysterious friendliness of late.

"Hmmm—" her mother said wonderingly when she heard about it. "I wouldn't expect someone like that to do such an about face. But, then, knowing that a classmate's mother has cancer might just bring out someone's better nature," she mused.

There was more silence as each of them drifted about in the quiet stream of their own thoughts about the ramifications of trauma in youth. Quiet, nothing. In truth, Julie was trying to drive back into its cage this wild fright she was suddenly experiencing at thoughts of the mysterious motive behind Alexis's "caring" behavior. Her mother only knew Alexis as the girl who'd accused her of lying about her mother bringing the orange dragon bean salad to the mother–daughter dinner. She, of course, knew nothing about the dirty deed the woman had dealt her husband in college, and she certainly didn't need to know about it now, if ever. Besides, that was her father's bailiwick.

Mr. Tyler came home just as Julie was setting the table for supper with the "Real Old Willow" plates. Setting the table with her mother's china brought to mind that other china—the Orange Dragon china bowl that had led to so much strife for so many people (her, Gloria, Mrs. Jackson, Dr. Drescher, for starters). Like a chain reaction, that, plus the sight of her father looking very tired when he first got home, led to an even more horrifying thought, one that she'd had before, but that was before her mother had been whittled down to a person of uncertain sex by the mastectomy and alopecia (the tidy medical term for the *loss of all her body hair* due to the upcoming chemo). Maybe Margaret Rose had lost *her* looks but Alexandra Riley-Dolan Cowper surely hadn't. And, judging by the way the woman had come on to her father in the Christmas tree lot, she also hadn't changed her tune.

CHAPTER 31

Cancer Woes

That night her mother had been her real self, but it wasn't to last. Chemotherapy loomed in the near future.

First had come the hair loss. Clumps of hair on her mother's pillow in the morning and in her comb when she combed her hair after showering. Soon she didn't need a comb. There was no hair *to* comb.

Of all the visible signs of cancer, for Julie that was the hardest to take. Without her hair *and* breasts, her mother became a different person, that stranger of indeterminate sex. Also of indeterminate race when her skin donned a kind of greenish grayness. Was she even of this world? Then, one day, Julie noted something even more odd about her mother's face. It was as though someone had taken an eraser and erased some of her features. Of course! Her mother's eyebrows and eyelashes, the hair all over her body, were gone, too. Duh—

And then, after what they called a couple cycles of the chemo, her mother'd gone on to slow down, not just in her movements, but in her talking and thinking as well. Seeing these changes in her mother was an awful lot like losing her. She wasn't her real mother. She was more like an apparition, the ghost of the person her mother had been *in life*. Even harder, it was something she couldn't talk to her mother about. In fact, she couldn't talk to her mother about any of the things that, on a day-to-day basis, troubled her. Her mother wasn't strong enough, physically or mentally, to shoulder any of her problems. And it wouldn't be fair to expect her to!

One day when she was feeling really sorry for herself on this score, Julie had a sudden insight. She'd just gotten it!

This vacancy in her life meant to be occupied by her mother was God's way of preparing her for her mother's death. How thoughtful of Him! And, yes, she was mostly mad at God these days. Her anger and her angst were the worst they'd ever been.

"I think I have chemo brain," her mother said one day about that time, when she discovered she'd put the ice cream away in the cupboard instead of the freezer. She'd "discovered" her mistake a couple of hours later, so the ice cream wasn't spoiled, just melted. They had, actually, quite yummy vanilla ice cream "drinks," spiked with ginger ale, for several nights in a row thereafter. But they all agreed that the frozen variety of ice cream was preferable. It'd at least given them something to laugh about at the time.

"I feel as though I'm being pickled," her mother said at the end of one very long day of chemo. It'd been especially long because she'd had the chatty Aunt Beryl with her. That night at supper she'd asked Julie and her father not to talk. She was just so tired of hearing human voices.

After watching a program on how archeologists thought the Egyptian pharaohs were mummified, her mother amended her view of chemo. "No, I got that wrong," she'd announced after the show was over. I'm being mummified." She even had a good laugh at that. Thank heavens, Julie thought, her mother's sense of humor hadn't gone the way of her hair.

She was also finding that her mother's cancer was making her think more deeply about things, and her diary became the receptacle for some of these "deeper" thoughts. For one thing, Julie found herself thinking a lot about death, not her mother's, her own. Up until then, death was something that happened to other people, no one she knew. But, because of her mother's serious cancer, death was now camped on their doorstep. She had to "step" over it at least twice a day, going in and out the door to and from school. That, her science paper on the causes of cancer and the things that can go wrong in the molecules, even the atoms, of a person's body, and a program on TV one night on the universe, what is known (not much!) and what is not known (a lot!), caused her to think, and then write.

> *We live on a completely puny planet in a pretty puny solar system inhabited by a lot of puny people, including me. Earth has existed for trillions of years, and people have existed on Earth for only a speck of time. And no human being, no matter how much he or she watches his or her triglycerides, can expect to live much more than a hundred years. In the greater scheme of things, even people like Alexander the Great are just the blink of an eye in history. Still, everyone, even me, is important in their own way—at least per Father Desseau. Take the fact that I contain a world of thoughts and experiences and emotions, most of which not anyone else knows a thing about. And, like, who but me would care about them? But, then, everyone (even members of the Scars and the Black Lilies? . . . maybe not) has a whole world inside of them. So people are whole worlds walking around, and there are whole worlds at the molecular level and beyond the Milky Way. Worlds within worlds within worlds. And worlds beyond worlds beyond worlds.*

Also beyond words. Once again, she found herself reaching for that *thing* on the top shelf of the cupboard of her brain, and the object, the point of her thoughts, just kept, frustratingly, moving beyond reach. She just wasn't tall enough, i.e., old enough, to grasp it yet.

Her mother, too, had said something the night they'd started using the "Real Old Willow" china that made her realize her cancer was causing a shift in her take on life. "If cancer doesn't cause a person to think twice about what is important and what is unimportant in life—my best china, for instance—then their illness, all that they have to go through, is a waste," she'd finished, and by way of saying that she wanted no discussion of what she'd just said, she turned and left the kitchen where Julie was setting the table. Come to think of it, there'd been a lot of hints about her mother's changed take on life. Take the fact that Julie'd come upon her mother praying the Rosary quite a few times, also reading the Bible, especially Psalms and Job, a lot more than she ever used to. Also watching EWTN on cable TV—something she would never have done before. She just didn't have time for "all the holy-rollers on the channel pretending they had some kind of special 'in' with God." She also did not appear to be experiencing Julie's anger with God.

* * * *

So their days, and their lives, like Julie's mother's skin, took on a certain cast.

One of her mother's eventual biggest complaints was that she didn't have the energy to do things, not even things she liked to do. For example, for the first time *ever*, her mother hired someone to come and clean the house. Mrs. Tyler was one of the very rare people (certifiable proof of her "alien" status!) who actually enjoyed housecleaning, though she wasn't a fanatic about it. No matter how much she slept, she felt tired, and it *wasn't* the good kind of tired people are always bragging about. She made that abundantly, angrily even, clear.

Julie was learning from this that, just like Roger Mooney —the man who'd shown them the way to the Breast Oncology Clinic at Smitty's—a place that they could now get to blindfolded—was that everyone with cancer has his or her own story, their own take on the experience. Besides things like praying more and using her best china, her mother's observations sometimes took a humorous turn.

One night at supper her mother confessed that she felt particularly alone with her cancer in the middle of the night when Julie and her father were fast asleep. Of course, that got Julie and her father loudly demanding that she wake them up so as not to be alone, to which she'd put up her hand and told them, in no uncertain terms, to shut up, because she wasn't done telling them what she wanted to tell them. After silencing them, she told them that she'd begun to get comfort from the sound of a life-flight helicopter going over in the wee hours of the morning because it meant she wasn't the only person awake at that moment. The people in the helicopter, and the person they were transporting who also had to be seriously sick, were, too. And, if Julie and her father didn't mind, life-flight was company enough. She also, by the way, said a Hail Mary for the person being transported every time she heard the throb of the helicopter engine.

And, then, there'd been the Saturday afternoon when, Julie in her bedroom and her father doing something in the basement, heard Mrs. Tyler let out a shriek. Both of them came running, only to find a yellow dribble starting about 10 feet away from the downstairs bathroom door, which was now shut. (Of course. That'd been one of the things that her mother blamed on her tiredness. That it made her put off peeing.)

By the time Mrs. Tyler came out of the bathroom, Julie's father had matter-of-factly gone to get the mop and pail and 409 to clean it up. When her mother saw the cleaning stuff, she grabbed them out of Mr. Tyler's hands. "Give those to me!" she growled angrily. "I'll do it." Julie and her father crept off to their respective "hideaways," while her mother went to town cleaning as she had in the days of yore. She slammed the sponge mop around—*bam, bam, bam, bam*—as if she were trying to punish the floor. She was "damned" mad, she'd said under her breath as Julie'd crept away—another sign of the changes in her mother, who'd before never even said shucks. In the end, she only punished herself. She exerted *far too much* effort to mop up a few dribbles of urine.

That night they ordered pizza from The Lido. It was their go-to place for a sure-fire consolatory, even a sort of weird celebratory, meal. They'd made it through another awful experience.

Of course, by this time, her mother had given up cooking entirely—another painful sacrifice for her. Cooking was up there with cleaning in her book of favorite chores. This was where family and friends once again came to the rescue. There was brought to their door a succession of homemade dishes:

chicken pies, turkey fricassee, beef stroganoff, beef stew, and baked chicken with mashed potatoes, gravy, broccoli au gratin, and homemade cranberry sauce, the works. But there were also meals that they, charitably, dubbed "mystery meals." Like everything in life, the food wasn't perfect.

Her grades at school? That was a sore topic. She wasn't failing or D'ing things—yet. But she also wasn't A+-ing things like she always had, and her parents knew it by now because they'd seen her recent report card. She was more just plain ole B–ing things. But neither of her parents gave her a hard time about it. Her father only said in passing as he signed her report card, something her mother usually did, but she'd been lying down all day with a headache so wasn't up to it, "looks like your grades have slipped a bit, sugar." That was also when she got her second summons to Dr. Drescher's office.

CHAPTER 32

A Second Summons to Dr. Drescher's Office

Julie's second summons to Dr. Drescher's office, not including the time she met with the director of her own volition when the pranks being played on her had gotten totally out if hand, bore a very unpleasant resemblance to the one before Christmas. The same snooty page standing sneeringly over her handing her Dr. Drescher's summons. The same location—in the library in the "rocky fastness" of the vertical files. The same heartless winter winds making life hell for anyone outdoors. The same bewilderment over why Dr. Drescher needed to see her. At least her body wasn't racked with menstrual cramps that day. She also had her regulation Ainsworth winter sweater on. Two things to be grateful for.

This time when Dr. Drescher's SS secretary ushered Julie into the director's office, there was no one there except for Dr. Drescher. Was that a third thing to be grateful for?

"Thank you for coming, Julie," Dr. Drescher said with a warm smile that had to mean that she wasn't in some kind of serious trouble. "Please take a seat," she said, indicating a stuffed chair that was conversationally "grouped" with her desk chair, not one of the visitor's chairs across from her where sat delinquents, truants, and others guilty of "moral turpitude," one of her father's favorite names for the category that many of the people he prosecuted fell into.

"I just have a small matter to talk with you about," Dr. Drescher said, once Julie was seated. This she punctuated with a small comma-like flip of her hand, much like the hand motions Dr. R made when she made light of small concerns.

"Mrs. Truitt," Julie's academic advisor, "has brought to

my attention the fact that there has been a rather sudden decline in your grades—*not*," she hastened to say, "that your grades are anything to be ashamed of. In fact," she laughed, "there are students whose families would throw a party in the grand ballroom of The Yorkshire if their daughters got even your current grades—"

Julie smiled at that. It was also a, sort of, compliment, she guessed.

"Mrs. Truitt has told me that she heard your mother has cancer," Dr. Drescher went on to say in a quiet voice. The sentence was spoken as a question.

"Yes, she has," Julie said quietly, looking forthrightly into Dr. Drescher's eyes. And, then tears, which these days seemed to be constantly lurking just below the "horizon" of her eyelids, welled up in her eyes. She looked down into her lap to hide them and her distress, cleared her throat to steady her voice, and continued. "My mother has breast cancer, a pretty serious kind."

There was nothing of the Fuehrer in Dr. Drescher's eyes when Julie lifted her head and looked into them. There was only, what?!, loving compassion(?)

"I'm so sorry to hear that, Julie," Dr. Drescher said. "I had hoped that Mrs. Truitt had heard incorrectly or that it wasn't a serious cancer—" Here her voice drifted out, and they sat in silence for, like, a minute.

But it wasn't an uncomfortable silence. It was a kind of healing—for a minute everything was okay—moment. (It also gave her tears time to evaporate.) Yes, Dr. Drescher, like Dr. R, Father Desseau, and *maybe* Dr. Gardner, had this sort of power about them that enabled them to command the mayhem of life to form into orderly rows and march away, have a smoke in the surrounding woods, for a bit, though Smitty's would discourage the smoking.

"Julie," Dr. Drescher continued, "Given your mother's cancer, I don't want you to worry about your grades right now. You have too many other more important things to be concerned about. Just do the best you can, *liebchen*," The *German* version of "nina baba"? Julie thought. "I'll ask Mrs. Truitt to, at the end of the school year, if your grades continue on their current course, put a note in your file that serious personal problems affected your scholastic performance the second half of the year. And, Julie," Dr. Drescher slowed the flow of her words as if to give Julie more time to ingest them, "if there is anything I can do to help you, please let me know."

"Thank you, Dr. Drescher," Julie said, trying to infuse as much heart into her thank you as she could without breaking down the dam on her emotions she had erected to keep the sobbing kind of tears from getting the best of her. Just a couple more delinquent tears wobbled down her cheeks.

"You can return to your class now. Thank you for coming."

This time, as Julie trooped back to the classroom building through the beastly cold wind that was battering everything outdoors that day, there was a nice warmth in her chest, not the outraged hurt of the previous visit, and no menstrual cramps....

CHAPTER 33

Now What?!

The night that Mr. Tyler discovered the new bottle of Glenlivet single-malt scotch in the liquor cabinet was a night when he'd come home from work in a really bad mood. It wasn't anything to do with her mother (she was "drifting" around the house, but her "ghost" bore a fairly close resemblance to her real self), and it wasn't likely anything to do with his job. If her father let every bad day at work bother him, he'd be coming home in a bad mood every night. Working with criminals, or "cranimals" as he sometimes called the worst of them, no workday was ever a picnic. No, it had to be something else.

This time it was Julie and her mother's turn to eye each other perplexedly as they ate their dinner in the militant silence imposed on them by Mr. Tyler's mood. There was *no* topic that seemed to get his attention, though neither Julie nor her mother ventured to talk about football.

It was a Monday night, and Mr. Tyler did watch Monday Night Football on the TV in the living room, but it could have been *Swan Lake* for all that he appeared to be paying attention to it.

Julie's diary entry that night read:

2.5—School was okay. I didn't get a bad grade on anything, but then I didn't get any tests or homework handed back today, so no reason to celebrate. Mom made yummy corn chowder for supper—the first thing she's actually made in a long time. She didn't make her usual cheese baking powder biscuits to go with it, though. She started to but she just ran out of steam. That explained the lovely cheesy flavor of the corn chowder. She had to put the shredded cheese somewhere. Talk about cholesterol heaven!

Dad was in a really bad mood tonight. Something was really eating away at him, but he didn't talk about it. I feel like my life is a seesaw. I'm the fulcrum, and Mom and Dad are just going up and down, up and down on each side of me, not minding me holding the seesaw up in the middle.

Oh yes, a middling problem. The cleaning woman managed to wash my new bras so that the cups are lavender and the rest is white. That's really going to make a hit in the changing room for P.E. Not a great day—but we did have cheesy corn chowder.

So, all was not lost that day. Julie forgot to note that Alexis had given her a big "HI!" when she passed her in the corridor between classes. But Alexis's behavior had become almost teasingly(?) unpredictable. It was like she, Julie, was the little gray mouse that Alexis, the cat, was batting around, just playing with. One day she'd be almost deliriously, or was that deliciously, deviously even . . . , happy to see her, and then the next day she'd be like a silent iceberg drifting by. So any kind of pleasure Julie'd gotten initially from the girl's friendly overtures had been replaced by wariness. Was Alexis just going to continue to play this game of cat and mouse with her, or was she, like most decent cats would, going to go in for the final kill?

CHAPTER 34

A Wronged Man

About a month later, when Julie came home from school, she discovered both her mother and father sitting at the kitchen table, both having a scotch on the rocks. It was only 3 o'clock on a Wednesday afternoon, and (a) her father was home from work and (b) he and her mother were having a drink?? This indicated that they were either celebrating or *not* celebrating something. The serious expressions on their faces, plus the pile of used tissues in front of her mother, suggested the latter. Julie's brain leapt to the most likely possibility—her mother's cancer had recurred, metastasized, found a new place to take up residence in her body. Location. Location. Location. The same went for cancer. The brain, the liver, the bone, they were prime pieces of property for the upwardly mobile life-style of the more deadly cancers.

"Your mother's fine, Julie," her father said in a serious voice, reading her mind. "Something's happened with me at work that we need to talk about."

"Help yourself to a soft drink, Julie," her mother said in a soft, residually tearful, voice.

As Julie headed toward the refrigerator, she thought 'What, no scotch?' If she was old enough for adult conversations, wasn't she also old enough for an adult drink, which *had* to be more calming than a sugar-laced, caffeine-laden Coke?

When she was settled, with her Coke, into her chair at the kitchen table, her father began to talk. In fact, he did most of the talking.

The whole thing had started the day of the night he'd come home in a very foul mood and had had the atypical drink.

At lunch that day at The Jury Box, where many of the attorneys pleading cases at the courthouse ate and hung out, who came in but Alexandra Cowper. Spotting, with seeming surprise, her old beau, she invited herself to have lunch with him. He hadn't known what to do. He didn't want anything to do with her, but what could he do but reluctantly let her join him. That or risk a scene with the ever-devious Alexandra whose perfidy knew no bounds.

So they'd dined together. Alexandra had drawn him into a conversation about his wife's cancer, feigning, it would seem, enough concern and sympathy that her father talked at some length about his wife's fight with cancer. He'd done it, in part, because he *was* very worried about his wife. But he also thought that maybe Alexandra had changed, could sympathize with him, and could realize that his wife was the most important person in his life.

'In other words, no other woman would be able to replace her,' Julie murmured viciously to herself.

By the time Julie'd gotten home that day, Mr. Tyler had already filled her mother in on his long-ago disastrous involvement with Alexandra Cowper. He'd also told her about the chance meeting with Mrs. Cowper in the Christmas tree lot and of having, in the car afterward, filled Julie in on the cheerleader-from-hell episode of his life.

And now he was repeating for Julie's benefit what had transpired in the four weeks since the day of that fateful lunch.

When he'd gotten back to his office that day, the first person he ran into, of all people, was Brett Bartt (that *couldn't* be his real name), a very pugnacious, tenacious, vexatious investigative reporter for the local paper who shouted in his blunt-weapon voice: "Hey, Bob. Who was the gorgeous dame I saw you with at The Jury Box today? Are you, just *now*, returning from your little audacious assignation? I say any fellow's lucky to have such a specimen of feminine pulchritude in his life." Bartt was also known for his obnoxious use of pretentious prose.

At this point Julie wanted ever so much to call a cab, tear

over to the Cowpers' house, and slug both of them—mother and daughter—in their Princess Grace noses, thereby giving them more of a crone's profile.

Her father had told the "redoubtable Brett Bartt to go pound sand." That the woman he'd seen him with was an old college acquaintance who just happened to come into the restaurant.

"Yeah, right," Bartt had apparently quipped to her father with a sly wink. He'd heard that story before.

Julie was deciding that her next stop in the cab, after having rearranged the two Cowper women's noses would be this Brett Bartt's den or hole or rock he'd crawled out from under.

After that, her father explained, he stopped going to The Jury Box for lunch. He didn't want to chance another surprise encounter with Mrs. Cowper. But the woman was not to be thwarted. She began to call him at work. Each time she called she said she was just wanting an update on how Mrs. Tyler was doing, and Julie's father had given her just vague generalities, not wanting her to know any more details about his life than she already knew.

The truth was, Julie's mother wasn't doing too well. She'd been having problems with this thing called leukopenia. Whatever it was, when it occurred, it meant that Mrs. Tyler's chemo was put on temporary hold or the dose was lowered. It wasn't part of the cancer process, Dr. R had told them; it was a side effect of the cancer treatment. The problem with *that* was that it meant her mother wasn't getting the full force of the treatment needed to rid her body of wandering "hey-ho" cancer cells wanting to journey to other places in her body. The worried looks on Dr. R's and Wei's faces every time it occurred made Julie and her father sick themselves . . . with worry.

Then, besides all the other indignities her mother'd had to endure (two missing breasts, a missing head of hair, missing eyebrows and eyelashes, a total loss of energy), she now, whenever she went out in public, had to wear a facemask. Why? Because the dread leukopenia was a favorite stomping ground for germs. Germs loved an easy victory, were lily-livered when it came to duking it out with a well-mounted white blood cell front. Since it was early March, germs (especially the flu) were running rampant, and her mother needed added "armament" for protection.

Julie'd suggested drawing a Groucho Marx mustache on the mask to cheer her mother up, make her laugh, the first time she had to wear it out in public (just to church for Mass, which was about the only place, besides Smitty's, she went to these days), but her mother didn't find that funny. Well, but who could tell if she'd even smiled with the stupid mask on.

But Julie's father wasn't telling Alexis's mother anything about this. He just always only told her that "my wife is doing okay, all things considered," which was the truth, thank her for calling, and then tell her he had to get back to some briefs he was preparing, or something along those lines, none of which was probably made up. Such was her father's daily diet. Mrs. Tyler had, of course, already heard all these details today, but she was patiently listening to their retelling.

Apparently, Mrs. Cowper had *also* tried repeatedly to get him to meet her for lunch, which he flat out said no to. But she continued to indefatigably call, until one day when she called, Mr. Tyler was in a particularly vulnerable state. Mrs. Tyler was on "hiatus" from chemo, had been for several weeks, because of the dratted leukopenia. He was, as a result, terribly worried, and like a person might do with a total stranger on an elevator, he told her that he was very worried about his wife and why.

This called for words of sympathy, consolation, in return, but for Mrs. Cowper it was the opportunity she'd been waiting (as in lying in wait) for. Per her father, she *gushed* something like: "You know, Bob, I'm here any time you need a good friend. In fact, that's why I moved here after separating from my husband. I just wanted to be near you. Something told me you'd need me close by in the near future. So, if Mona," not "Mrs. Tyler" or "your wife," her father spat out in an angry voice, "doesn't survive her illness, remember I'm waiting here with open arms for you. You'll always be my first and only love,"

(*That*, Julie thought, was probably the only honest thing Mrs. Cowper'd said in her life. Appreciating what a fine and desirable man her father was was also probably the only truly laudable thing she'd done in her life.)

"That was the wrong thing to say to me, especially right then when my nerves were so frayed" her father said angrily. "I told Alexandra that she'd overstepped the bounds of acceptable behavior, as she had once before with me—something I had *not* forgotten—and I would advise her to cease trying to make contact with me or I would be forced to have a restraining order filed against her."

Julie wanted to cheer at that point. Instead she asked her father how the woman had responded.

"She didn't," he barked with a dry laugh. "All I heard was a click. She'd hung up on me."

By now it was supper time, so they ordered yet another pizza from The Lido.

While Julie's father was out picking up the pizza, and his story was on "pause," Julie and her mother had a little time to talk.

For a while, they just sat at the table, hardly saying anything. Her mother was clearly avoiding discussion of what had happened to her father that day at work, and her silence was making Julie very nervous. At least, she reasoned, she knew the bit about Alexandra Riley-Dolan's dirty deed in college. She'd had time to chew and swallow *that* nasty morsel whole. But her mother was hearing *everything* for the first time that day. And now she was having to hear it all for a second time, *and* just when her immune system was at a low ebb again.

It worried Julie that the low white blood cell count would also make her mother far more vulnerable to any personal upheavals in her life having nothing to do with her cancer. And, yes, her A++ paper on the causes of cancer had said that personal problems can up the frequency of genetic breaks that lead to cancer cells forming.

It was Mrs. Tyler who broke the silence. "Honey," she said, smoothing her finger along the edge of a round tray painted yellow with a circlet of black ivy in its center. It was where the salt and pepper shaker and sugar bowl had been kept for as long as she could remember. Funny that she'd never really noticed it before, a funny humdrum thing on this anything but funny humdrum day.

Her mother was talking in a very serious voice. Julie forced her wandering, wayward attention back to what her mother was saying. "I want you to know that I believe your father is a very good man—a truly outstanding individual. And, even minus my hair, and my breasts," she said with a hint of a smile, "I have no doubts about his love for me and you. The problem is . . . ." Here she teared up and her words started coming out in clumps like her hair had two months ago. "I know that I'm supposed to forgive this awful woman for what she's done to me and you and your father *and* his reputation." That was as far as her mother got. The remaining words got clogged in her throat, and she was grabbing tissues out of the tissue box and pressing clumps of them against her face to mop up the tears.

And Julie? All that registered in her brain were her mother's ominous words regarding what Mrs. Cowper had done to her father's reputation. That was the part of the tale she had yet to hear.

But, at this point, what could she say? She *wanted* to say something wise and comforting, something à la Father Desseau. But all that came out of her mouth was "I know, Mom. Let's go toilet paper the Cowpers' house!"

By the time her father got back with the pizza, he walked in, not on two somber females, but two very silly gals who, by then, had expanded beyond all limits the Halloween-type tricks they were going to play on the well-deserving Cowper duo. Nothing was too "good" for them.

CHAPTER 35

Another Shattered Orange Dragon Bowl of Sorts

Their rate of devouring the pizza slowed by the fourth slice of The Lido's "Al Capone" pizza (covered with its usual spent shells, blood, and guts), Mr. Tyler resumed telling more about the latest crisis to deck them.

Julie saw that her mother was very tired. In fact, she looked the same color gray as a mildewed dishcloth. The sight scared her. Her father must have seen the same thing, because he reached over, stroked her mother's gray cheek and said, "Tweedle, why don't you go up to bed. You've heard the whole thing once today. You don't need to hear it again." At that he reached over and placed his hand at the back of her mother's neck so that he could gently draw her head toward him and plant a gentle kiss on her forehead.

Her mother got up from the table, her face made briefly rosy by her husband's sweet attention, and looked most lovingly into his eyes. "Thanks, Tweedledum," she said tenderly, her eyes looking intently into his as if to tell him something that there were no adequate words for. As she headed down the hallway to bed, she called back: "Bob, spare her the X-rated stuff. She's tired, too, and doesn't need to know all the details."

****

With that her father gave her his abridged, or was that expurgated, version of the latest in the unending saga of Alexandra Cowper, nee Riley-Dolan. It might have been her father's sanitized version of the latest in that saga, but, still, by the end of the telling, nothing remained of the happy, secure world of only four months ago. Even her world as of four days ago seemed happy and carefree in comparison. Her life was now proof positive that one does not necessarily have only one serious problem at a time. Her father had been temporarily suspended from his job until he'd been cleared of the charges of attempted rape dating back to his college days.

Brett Bartt had "barfed up" his customary "blather," her father's words. Acting on the proverbial anonymous tip, he'd once again lived up to his proud reputation as "the most ravenous of roving reporters," as he liked to promote himself.

In that morning's edition of the paper, in The Daily Beat section, had appeared the following item, which Julie's father had her read to herself, "because you may have school chums who've read it and come to their own conclusions." That was enough to send her fear into overdrive, and this was before she read Brett Bartt's blather:

> Seems as though the city's Achilles, or is that the Heel, of the DA's office, the city's fabled, famous Bob Tyler, better deserves the appellation the foibled, infamous Bobby the Shmoo Tyler. The city's premier public prosecutor appears to have a skeleton in the closet of his big man on campus—his star quarterback—days. An anonymous tip has brought to light the troubling truism that he was accused of rape, a charge that appears to have been conveniently, and cleverly I might add, covered up. (Had date rape even entered our lexicon then?)
>
> A search of the dean of students' files from that time has revealed nada, zilch, zip re: the incident, which is not surprising, given the tenor of the times.
>
> Acting further on information supplied by the wronged woman, this reporter unearthed the tipster's sorority file, which sheds a very different—in fact, it sheds the *only*—light on the matter.
>
> And what did a pensive perusal of this file disclose? The poor young woman, after receiving no recompense for the double-wrong dealt her—the alleged rape followed by

the total dismissal of charges against this city's famous, now infamous, assistant D.A.—had only the then housemother of her sorority house to turn to. The house mother records in this lone file pertaining to the matter that she urged the young woman to bring her charges to local law enforcement for prosecution, but the wronged young woman, per the housemother, "insisted that she didn't want to do anything that would cause unfavorable publicity, that might bring shame on her family."

So Mr. Public, or is that "Pubic"?, Prosecutor, should it now be your turn in court??? I rest my case.

The D.A. had called her father into his office late that morning, shown him the item in The Daily Beat, and asked for an explanation. He also wanted to know why the matter had never been mentioned, either when he applied to law school, taken his bar examination, or applied for his position in the D.A.'s office. The man he'd "always regarded as my best prosecutor" had "let him down."

That was where her father stopped his recounting of the day's events, in keeping, Julie supposed, with her mother's injunction to keep it brief. But she'd heard enough. Her mother'd been right. She couldn't have handled more.

Julie didn't know what to say to her father after that. Toilet-papering the Cowpers' house wouldn't do in this moment. For one she was too tired to toilet-paper a dog house. For another, she didn't think she could ever laugh or joke again. There were no words, profound or otherwise, that she could come up with to respond to her father's final sizing up of their situation that night. Besides, her father, after he'd finished his up-to-the-latest-millisecond account of the latest crap dished out by the Alexandra Cow-turd fiend, was a million miles away in a state unreachable by words that could retain any warmth for more than a mile.

So, finally, after sitting in silence for several seconds, trying to take in all that she'd just heard, it became too much like trying to save corrupted data to one's hard-drive—something not advisable. "I'm so sorry, Dad," she finally said with as much feeling as she could muster, kissed him goodnight, and headed down the hallway to bed. She felt badly about abandoning him where he sat staring at the too-cheerful yellow tray in the middle—a smiley face tray even. She could have finished with the one-size-fits-all "I'm sure everything will be okay, Dad," except that she was learning that it was a 50/50 chance it wouldn't be okay. Also, somehow it seemed as though the father should say that to the child, not the other way round.

Once in her bedroom with her door closed, though, having been unable to find something heartening to say to her father, she was down to talking to her other Father, the one in Heaven, which she did, on her knees before getting into bed, saying a Hail Mary, a Glory Be, an Our Father, and praying for a quick *and* satisfactory resolution to her father's problem and for her mother's complete recovery from her cancer. She thought she'd better be specific with God about all her needs. He was a busy man, after all. Goodness, considering the state of the world, He must have post-its stuck everywhere on His dais.

* * * *

Despite trying to leave the resolution of all their problems to God, per Father Desseau's instructions practically every Sunday in the pulpit, Julie got no sleep that night. Her pillow might have been a cinder block for all the comfort it gave. She couldn't even close her eyes. She felt like a small, frightened animal who has just beheld the vicious predator (cobra, black widow spider, orange dragon) that means its certain death. Her mother sick with this serious break-a cancer and this equally serious leukopenia, her academic performance cratering (she didn't care what Dr. Drescher had said to her over a month ago, she'd become the Tiger Woods of Ainsworth Country Day School's cadre of honor students). By 2 o'clock, this latest chapter in the Alexandra Riley-Dolan Cowper story began to gather in centrifugal force inside her head. And then flew in a swarm of rapid-fire crazy questions that there were no answers to—because they were so crazy.

Might it have been Mrs. Cowper who had started the ugly rumor at church about her "legitimacy"? *Had* Mrs. Cowper, now that she was divorced, come to live in the same town as her father expressly to win him back or cause him more harm, depending? *Could* it be anyone other than Mrs. Cowper who was the source of the anonymous tip to Brett Bartt? There was always Alexis. She was as capable as her mother when it came to treachery. It *had* to be one of them. *Could* Alexandra Cowper's drive to either recapture her father's affection or, failing that, utterly destroy him been further fueled by the discovery, the night of the mother–daughter dinner, that she'd been passed over for the comparatively plain woman to her left, the real Mrs. Robert Tyler? And then there was the corker. *Could* it have been part of Alexandra Cowper's plan to cause her mother's cancer to make it easier to achieve her wicked ends? Why, it was common knowledge among cancer researchers, of course, that stress upped a person's chances of getting cancer. Mrs. Cowper could have, the night of the mother–daughter dinner, caused her mother enough distress to fire up that ole BRCA1 gene that was wreaking so much havoc in all their lives. And, if you thought about it, it was barely a month later that her mother found the lump in her breast. The timing was perfect.

All these horrifying thoughts circling inside her head, gaining in velocity *and* ferocity, soon had her reeling into the bathroom, where she had just enough time to position her head over the toilet and throw up all of the undigested Al Capone pizza. It was fitting. She was going through her own Valentine's Day Massacre....

Of course her parents heard her vomiting. Soon after the last dry heave, Julie's head resting on the edge of the toilet bowl, the bathroom light went on, and she found herself enwrapped in her mother's and father's arms, and with that came murmurings and croonings of comfort.

None of them moved for several minutes. It was as if they didn't want to let go of each other. On the other hand, Julie thought with what little remnant of her brain wasn't given over entirely to angst, what a place to be drawing comfort from each other, sitting on the floor of the bathroom right next to a toilet bowl full of partially digested Al Capone pizza. Just about then, someone reached up and flushed the toilet, not her, though. Her arms were pinned to her side in her parents' embrace.

Once more, the vision of the shattered Orange Dragon bowl in the pool of bean salad reeled into her head. She was beginning to feel really sorry for that dragon.

CHAPTER 36

A Snowy Haven

The morning found the three of them seated around the kitchen table, which seemed to have become the hub around which their lives were spinning (now, out of control). It was 10 o'clock. Her mother didn't have an appointment at Smitty's that day (a rare event!). Her father didn't have a job to go to. And Julie, for the first time in her four years at Ainsworth, hadn't gone to school that day. First, because she was exhausted from her sleepless night. Second, because she might actually be suffering from a stomach bug.

A third reason, which she kept from her parents, but which explained why she hadn't balked very much at staying home from school, was that she didn't have the heart to go to school. Who knew what Brett Bartt's allegations might stir up at school? Her father'd been right in being concerned about this possibility the night before. And then there was a fourth reason that she also kept from her parents. She didn't know what she might do to Alexis when she crossed her path. There was a real, though slim, chance of her committing a violent act. That she might be driven to such an act scared her.

They were *all* sick at heart that morning. But Julie's mother was soon back in bed with a slight fever. She hadn't felt too good the day before, but with Mr. Tyler's bad news, who knew whether the cause was physical or emotional. A fever indicated a wandering germ had found its prey.

Her father called Wei, who said that as long as her fever didn't go above 100 degrees, she should stay at home. He prescribed plenty of fluids, bed rest, and Tylenol, the usual deal. Her father was to call him if her temperature went above 100.

From there on in, their day turned out to be an almost-cozy one. By then, Julie and her father had ensconced themselves in the identical wingchairs in the bay window of her parents' bedroom, which looked out over their backyard. They were there to keep her mother company and to be nearby in case she needed anything. Mainly Mrs. Tyler just snoozed. It seemed to Julie that she snoozed better with them there than if she were alone in the room, at least judging by what her mother'd told them of her sleeping habits of late. All she knew was that every time her mother woke up and spotted the two of them sitting just across from her, she grinned, said "Hello you two. I hope you're finding my snoozing entertaining," and went right back to sleep with a smile on her face that pretty much stayed there until the next time she woke up.

Julie was taking the opportunity to study algebra, starting with the first chapter and then proceeding chapter by chapter until she caught up with the current chapter they were on. Perhaps she could find the twist or the turn she'd missed, thereby finding herself walking in this wilderness of numbers, unknowns, parentheses, brackets, and function signs. If she'd liked her math teacher, Mr. Hennessey, better, it might have helped. She might have gone to him for some remedial help. But, frankly, he gave her the creepy crawlies. He obviously knew his math. He wouldn't be teaching at Ainsworth if he didn't. But the greasy comb-overs. The fact that he had this habit of leaning back smugly in his chair with his arms behind his head, revealing underarms wet (stained!) with sweat. And the fact that he laughed, usually at some classmate's expense, like a hyena ... (He didn't expel air when in laughed. He sucked it in.) It didn't add up to a charming, approachable person.

That morning, her father started reading a book he'd been wanting to read for a very long time. It was called *Remembrance Rock*, by Carl Sandburg. ("I thought he was just a poet, dad," Julie remarked to her father. Apparently not. He'd also, according to her father, written a series of books about Abraham Lincoln. Eyeing the very thick book, Julie wondered how he'd had time to write anything but *it*.) Her mother, of course, mostly slept.

Midmorning, it began to snow—a lazy kind of snow where the snowflakes just kind of nonchalantly drifted down, as if they were just pretending to snow. But they didn't fool snowstorm buffs like Julie. They meant, at the very least, a serious snowstorm. Actually, by mid-afternoon it had turned into a blizzard.

Just before lunch, when the snow hadn't yet shown its serious side, they got a call from their next door neighbor, Tilda Stein. She wanted to know if they'd like a pot of chicken soup that she'd just made.

Of course!

"I saw you were all home," she said loudly from the kitchen, where Mr. Tyler had gone to let her in. "Herb called to say he's stuck in Baltimore because of the snow—these southerners—a quarter inch of snow, and the world's coming to an end. Anyway, he's my best customer for the soup. Without Herb here, I can have my favorite meal—a chocolate sundae!" she laughed as she turned to go carefully back down the steps. She talked all the way down the steps. She *loved* to talk. There was already enough snow upholstering the outdoors, Julie noted, to make Mrs. Stein's voice sound muffled.

Mrs. Tyler, whom Julie thought asleep, mumbled "A chocolate sundae for supper in a blizzard??"

"You'd better be nice what you say about her, Mom. She might be a cousin," Julie quipped. Mrs. Stein was Jewish.

Her mother gave a little laugh. "Actually, I can't think of anything nicer." Mrs. Stein was a favorite in the neighborhood. She could always be counted on to spearhead some kind of neighborhood activity. And she regularly showed up with food at the houses of neighbors who were going through a difficult stretch, as in them....

Mrs. Stein's chicken soup was Billy Crystal FAB-U-LOUS. They had it for lunch and supper, and there was still some left for the next day. 'Thank you, Tilda! Thank you, God!' Julie thought as she ladled the soup into her mouth, being careful to think "God" rather than "Jesus" since, after all, Tilda Stein was Jewish....

By that night, her mother's temperature was an A+ 98.6 degrees. About 7 o'clock, Wei called to find out how her mother was doing. Julie took the phone. (Her father was downstairs putting the kitchen in order.) Wei explained that he was calling at Dr. R's request to check on her mother and was very happy to find out that her temperature was normal. As she was hanging up the phone, it occurred to her that Wei got in at 7 every morning, the time they most often saw him. It was 7 in the evening now, and who knew what other tasks remained to be done before he headed home. Father Desseau had been right when he'd said he'd heard that Smitty's staff routinely put in long hours.

At bedtime, it was also diary time. She hadn't written anything in the diary the night before. She'd just plain forgotten. And, that night, staring at the blank page for the previous day, she decided not to go back and record anything. She could have just scrawled a big 10 on the page, but the idea struck her as childish and dumb, and so she didn't.

She assigned a 2 to the day re: her mother's condition, given that her fever had gone away, and then she began to write.

Today was like God was wrapping us up in fleece (snow!). It was a cocoon day. The blizzard outside stood for our lives, all swirling around us out of control. Our cozy warm house, Dad and me reading in the bow window, and Mom tucked in bed. We were all safe. It was fun to watch the snow going crazy because it couldn't get at us. It was like being in the snake house at the zoo, and you've got your nose pressed up against the window of the snake tanks, and the cobras and coral snakes and rattlers are going crazy because they can't stick their fangs into you. And then there was Mrs. Stein's chicken soup that thoroughly warmed up our insides. And then there was Wei calling like an angel sent from on high to make sure Mom was okay.

She was tempted to add "but what will tomorrow

bring?," but didn't. Tomorrow was just going to have to cool its heels until she got to it. (What was that thing that Jesus had said about each day having an anxiety sufficient unto itself?) She climbed into bed and got a good night's sleep. She was also encouraged by her chapter-by-chapter plodding through her algebra book. Somehow, seeing it more as a whole, it was making much more sense to her. She didn't think she'd ever be a math whiz. But at least she wouldn't be a math flunkie.

CHAPTER 37

Facing the Music

Julie awoke the next day with a queasy uneasiness, an angst she hadn't yet experienced. Her day-long reprieve from the potential fallout at school over "Brett Bartt's bombast" was 'ovah.' But wait. She sat up and looked out her window. The outdoors was smothered in snow. Surely, school would be cancelled that day. She'd have another day to gird her loins!

But no, the mighty snowplows had labored through the night, and per the local newscaster, "all major arteries are open." The image of puddles of blood (hers, mainly) along the sides of all the main streets in the city came to Julie's mind.

All over the city, the engine of the day was sputtering to life—literally. As she got dressed, she could hear snow blowers going full tilt up and down the street. While the snowplows were busy with the arteries, the snow blowers were busy with the capillaries—the sidewalks, the paths, the driveways, etc.

So, thanks to her father, who drove her to school that day in the indomitable Volvo because the carpool mom had cancelled out, she made it to school, just. Everyone who made it to school that day was late. Maybe the main arteries were open, but the side streets were mostly unplowed Arctic wastes. Half of the students weren't even there, including, thankfully, Alexis Cowper. Maybe she'd been killed by a falling tree limb heavily encrusted with snow, Julie hoped.

She had walked into school that day prepared for the whole gamut of possible reactions to Alexis. Chief among them was puking, but violent acts were not outside the realm of possibility. (It just *had* to be Mrs. Cowper, aka Mrs. Cow-turd, who'd tipped Brett Bartt off.) Actually, there was nothing funny about it. Alexis and her mother scared her. They were evil, but not the Steven King, "entertaining," kind of evil. They were the real thing, the kind that scraped its horny tail over filthy floors, that breathed out the stench of death and decay, and that sent out searching flicks of its forked tongue, seeing who else it could lick and then ensnare.

But there was still her schoolmates' possible, unpredictable, reaction to Brett Bartt's "dirt" to contend with. So, for much of that snowy day, Julie went from class to class with bated breath, expecting at any moment a sudden belt of disgust?, repugnance?, condemnation? from one of her classmates. But nothing. It would appear that no one at school that day had read Brett Bartt's blather of two days before.

One had, though—Gloria Jackson—of course, news hound that she was, especially when it came to the local legal scene.

"Hey, girl." It was Gloria's warm voice coming from behind her. Then she felt Gloria's warm arm encircling, even enfolding, her shoulders as she came up beside her. "Are you doing okay?" she said, looking concernedly into Julie's eyes. "I saw the thing in the paper about your dad," she said softly, her eyes sad because of the sadness she saw in Julie's eyes.

Gloria knew, Julie knew, that the charge of attempted rape was pure hokum. Gloria would *know* that Julie couldn't come from the loins of a man capable of such an abominable act.

"Is there anything I can do?" Gloria asked.

It would have been a suitable occasion for tears, but, quite honestly, she was tired of crying. And, besides, tears didn't seem to be getting her anywhere these days.

"Thanks, Gloria," she said simply. "Do you know a good PR man who can fix my dad's reputation?" she asked with a bleak grin.

"There's *one* person I know of," Gloria said, thoughts of that person seeming to suddenly blossom right behind her brightening eyes.

"Really?" Julie said, surprised that Gloria might know of such a person.

"Yeah," she said, "He died on a cross two thousand years ago."

There was no "smart" answer to that kind of answer. Julie could only shrug, sigh, and nod sadly as she cast her now-tearing eyes to the floor.

And then she saw Gloria mysteriously reaching over and taking the yellow highlighter she was grasping in her hand. Gloria put it to her lips like a pretend mike and, incredibly, began to sing, right there in the hallway semi-swarming with students on that semi-snowy day.

> *Nobody knows the troubles I've seen.*
> *Nobody knows, but Jesus.*

Gloria was Marian Anderson, Aretha Franklin, Ella Fitzgerald, Lena Horne, and Queen Latifah, all rolled into one.

> *Nobody knows the troubles I've seen.*
> *Glory, hallelujah.*

Girls walking by began to stop and listen and then smile. Gloria was good—very good, recording contract good. The larger the audience, the more gloriously Gloria sang. One couldn't not stop and not be "moved" by it. She moved onto the next verse of the Negro spiritual.

> *Sometimes I'm up, sometimes down.*
> *Oh, yes, Lord.*
> *Sometimes I'm almost to the ground.*
> *Oh, yes, Lord.*

It was the day after a blizzard. The number of students in the hallways was fewer by half. The atmosphere was more laid back, helped by the fact that many of the girls had worn jeans and casual tops to school, which the school said was okay on bad-weather days. Gloria sang another verse.

> *Although you see me going long so.*
> *Oh, yes, Lord.*

> *I have trials here below.*
> *Oh, yes, Lord.*

At one point during Gloria's impromptu performance, Julie looked out at the rapt audience of girls who'd stopped to listen to her. All of them were caught up in the "soul" of the spiritual, with two exceptions—Dawn Dawson and, next to her, Angelina Baker, neither of them even close to "rapt." She spotted Dawn, in particular, peering over the outer perimeter of girls clustered in the hallway her eyes searching like a spotlight to identify the person with the voice and talent that threatened to topple her from her Broadway-star-in-residence pedestal at school. And when Dawn saw who it was, it was as if her eyes had suddenly stumbled over a disgusting object (an old dried-up dog turd?) on an otherwise perfectly manicured lawn. That was how disgusted she looked. Then Gloria sang the final verse.

> *If you get there 'fore I do.*
> *Oh, yes, Lord.*
> *Tell all-a my friends I'm coming too.*
> *Oh, yes, Lord.*

Dawn Dawson and Angelina Baker! Alexis Cowper's second and third in command, both of whom could do her as much harm as Alexis. She felt her stomach churn, but that was as far as it went. (Thank you, Lord!) The main attraction remained Gloria, until the bell for the start of class rang, which meant that everyone was late for class.

But none of the teachers that day, everyone knew, would care. Rules were for everyday days, which this wasn't. Most of the girls who'd made it to school through the snowdrifts had done so because they'd rather be there learning something than watching the soaps at home. Today everyone, students *and* teachers, all!, was feeling the camaraderie of the brave, the bright, the elite.

So the day was a good one—until Julie was at her locker fishing out her boots, scarf, hat, and the other *accoutrements* of winter, when she heard this *voice* coming from behind her. It could have been parrot. A witch with laryngitis. A rusty hinge.

"What is this I saw in the newspaper about your father?"

The "voice" was hostile and full of loathing, as Dickens might have put it.

Julie turned and found herself looking into the eyes of someone she hardly knew. Her name was Priscilla Paisley, and all Julie knew about her was that she was the *only* girl in the school with a visible tattoo. It was just a word "NOW!" tattooed onto her throat where a pretty pendant might have hung instead.

It was at that moment that Julie understood what "NOW!" actually stood for. It wasn't a point in time; it stood for the National Organization for Women. Priscilla was an ardent feminist. (And with a name like Priscilla Paisley Julie could understand her need to be constantly, obnoxiously, on the offensive.) And she was clearly NOW out to clear the streets of any male who wasn't castrated, and thus didn't have a testosterone level of 0.

"Excuse me?" said Julie in a calm, controlled voice that, as in Dr. Drescher's office the day Alexis accused her of lying, surprised her.

"Your father—the rapist!"

Julie suddenly knew what the concept of tearing someone limb from limb felt like. But, instead of acting on it, she said. "Don't you mean the *alleged, attempted* rapist?" Julie knew her law. She wasn't her father's daughter for nothing.

"Okay—alleged ... attempted ... " Priscilla conceded in a somewhat smaller voice.

"Also," Julie heard, felt!, herself trumpet in a resoundingly brave voice, "for your information Ms Paisley, in this country all men, and *women*," she added lest Ms Paisley's get her feathers ruffled at the slight sexist slight, "are considered innocent until proven guilty. And that includes my father . . . ." The words, like her words in Dr. Drescher's office the other time she was viciously wronged, mounted similar heights.

She could see Priscilla, in front of her, rummaging around in the attic of her brain, looking for an appropriate comeback, but before she'd managed to even find the little pea of a brain rattling around inside her head, Julie fired the final salvo. "Since when, Ms Paisley, have you become both judge and jury?"

Priscilla didn't seem to remember the exact date when that had happened, though she knew she had the information jotted down somewhere. Her eyes, Julie saw, even shifted around—as if literally looking for something in the empty chamber inside her skull. Finally giving up the search, and her righteous indignation whittled down to pea size, there wasn't anything left for Priscilla Paisley to do but utter a quick, small "okay."

With that, she turned and walked meekly away. As she'd turned, Julie could swear she heard something like a small, hard pea rattling around in a huge echoing chamber. But it *had* to be her imagination.

CHAPTER 38

The Honest Truth

A week later, school had resumed its usual humdrum hum. Alexis Cowper had returned to school, and no, she'd not (darn!) been struck dead by a massive oak tree limb caked with ice and snow and encrusted with jagged misshapen growths of bark. And Julie didn't vomit when she spotted Alexis for the first time, standing amongst her coven of friends excitedly telling them something *very* important and just too, too *wonderful*. Alexis did, however, return to the *non*-notice of Julie she'd shown her before her mother's breast cancer. Somehow Julie wasn't surprised. In fact, she was relieved. She felt more comfortable around the sincerely hostile Alexis than the insincerely friendly one.

A few days later, Alexis's "exciting" news reached Julie's ears. Her mother's divorce from the "wretch" (Alexis's words for her own father, per a reliable source) had been finalized, and in accordance with, and in a devoted daughter show of support for, her mother, she was taking her mother's maiden name—Riley-Dolan. She would now be Alexis Riley-Dolan.

Yes, it was a perfect (i.e., juicy) opportunity to broadcast to the entire student body that Alexis's mother's maiden name came as no surprise to her and why, and that she already knew of the divorce. But several things held her back. First, as she'd already learned at great cost from the bean salad incident, Alexis wasn't about to accept even the honest truth about her mother lying down. (And you had to give her credit for being so loyal to her mother ... sort of.) *And*, if she started to spread the *true* story, would anybody believe her? Would they even listen to her? *Of course*, Julie Tyler would want to defend her father. And, back in her father's college days, didn't every male accused of rape go free? It was always the woman's fault, the slut. No, better to focus on algebra.

Gloria had also, during that time, checked with her regularly to find out how things were going. The latest was that her father had swallowed his pride, and his stubborn prosecutor principles, and hired one of those "scoundrel" defense lawyers he was always complaining about. "Chinese acrobats!" had been one of the nicer names he'd used for them after losing a case to a particularly clever, "agile" one.

But the lawyer he hired, Daniel Friedman, really worked his butt off, to put it nicely, on her father's case. (Julie really liked the lawyer's last name, because when you sliced it into syllables it became 'freed-man.') The lawyer was like a starving dog looking for a buried bone, trying to find someone, something *(ruff, rrruff)* that would clear her father's good name.

Brett Bartt was right. A thorough search of the dusty dean of students' files from that time turned up nothing about the incident. Dean Saunders was now dead, had died of a heart attack soon after the incident, her father had told her that day in the Christmas tree parking lot, so he couldn't be contacted. Using her father's old yearbook, Daniel tracked down various schoolmates of her father's. To a man, and a woman, they now expressed surprise at the accusation of rape that had suddenly surfaced 25 years after the fact. (Did that mean they'd perjured themselves? Maybe they'd all had a come-to-Jesus call in the intervening 25 years that would cancel out the perjury.)

And then Daniel found the "bone" he'd been looking for—Miss Dodge, Dean Saunders' secretary of forty years. She might have been old (97!) and in a nursing home (in New Jersey) because of advanced crippling arthritis, but her mind was as sharp as a tack.

She remembered the incident as if it had happened yesterday. And she was more than glad to give her testimony to a local television crew, who was more than happy to see that it also aired on Julie's city's local television newscasts. Or it might have been Daniel Friedman's idea . . . . It was never quite clear where the idea came from.

Doughty was the best word to describe Miss Dodge. A Hollywood director couldn't have staged it better. Miss Dodge looked like a crumpled up spider in a wheelchair, her arthritis had taken such a toll on her body. But the clear gray eyes that looked out from the corpus of tangled bones were those of a very bright 15 year old—much like Julie's, in fact, which pleased her no end.

Looking straight into the camera, Miss Dodge said "I recall the incident very well, because it was so lamentably wrong." Her voice had not yet been attacked by the arthritis. It came out loud and clear. "Not wrong with regard to the woman," she clarified, "but with regard to the young man involved, this Robert Tyler."

And then she went on to relate a version of the incident that was totally at odds with the PΣΓ sorority version, the sorority Alexandra had belonged to.

The woman, whom she'd named *on TV*, as Alexandra Riley-Dolan, had come to the dean's office early one morning, unannounced and accompanied by a friend. She'd appeared quite upset, and the friend appeared to have come with her for support.

"Dean Saunders was a very good man," Miss Dodge interjected at that point. "No matter how busy he was, he *always* had time for students, especially ones who were in the midst of some kind of difficulty."

So he'd told Miss Dodge to immediately usher this Alexandra Riley-Dolan and her friend into his office. "They were in there quite a while. I couldn't hear what they were saying, but I could tell from the sound of her voice, the *beautiful* one," she said disgustedly, making the "beautiful" sound more like "ugly," "that she was quite upset. Before the two young women came out of the dean's office, I left to go to the ladies' room. While I was sitting on the toilet in the stall doing my business," a somewhat embarrassing admission that didn't seem to faze the ancient Miss Dodge, "two girls entered the ladies' room talking in loud voices. I could hear every word they said. The first one said 'Boy, you've really cooked his goose,' then they giggled like *crazy crows,*" she said disgustedly. "Then I heard the second one, the *beautiful* one, say, and these were her *exact* words, I could never forget them, they were so horrid, so evil, even, 'Bob Tyler's going to find out that you don't just get rid of Alexandra Riley-Dolan like a used tampon.' Such a *crude* thing for any woman to say," Miss Dodge interjected. "And then the two women began to cackle and crow away, like *witches*!" she shouted toward the camera and to whomever out there in TV land needed to be sorted out. (Yes, indeed, Julie thought. In her father's version, Alexandra had said he couldn't just toss her out like a "used tissue." Alexandra's story had gotten cruder with the telling.)

Julie, her father, and her mother saw the first airing of the interview because Daniel Friedman had told them to tune into that evening's news. Good old Miss Dodge, emphasis on the "old" *and* "good." But Miss Dodge wasn't done. She then went on to describe her father's visit to the dean, referring to him as "the terribly wronged young man, Robert Tyler—such a strikingly handsome young man," uttered with a certain passionate longing, which got Julie and her mother laughing oh-so-merrily; her father mainly went red and rolled his eyes. There would be many out there in the law-enforcement community watching the news who knew him and who would most definitely remind him of Miss Dodge's words. Miss Dodge then described how her father had arrived at the dean's office in a "wretched state of mind and, when he learned of the accusation, the first thing he said was: 'it will kill my mother just to hear that I've been accused of rape,' after which he broke down in tears, insisting all the while that he'd done no such thing, that he was, in fact, still a virgin and planned to stay that way until he married."

Julie's father at that point just put his face in his hand, and she couldn't tell whether he was laughing or crying. Then came the clincher. After this young Robert Tyler left the dean's office, she went in and told the dean what she'd overheard in the ladies' room. With that he'd handed her the file on the incident, and told her to destroy it in a manner that suited her, which she did. "He was very disturbed by what this Alexandra Riley-Dolan did, wrongly impugning a young man's reputation for the sake of vengeance."

And what manner of destruction had Miss Dodge selected for getting rid of the file, the eager young reporter asked.

Here Miss Dodge got a look of unalloyed joy in her eyes. "I burned it at home in my woodstove." Once again the doughty Miss Dodge looked right into the camera, her gray eyes for a second holding the attention of maybe a million, maybe more, viewers, sending out a clarion clear warning to all who might be tempted to slander, to bear false witness.

That night, Hank, the DA, called her father at home and told him, in typical locker room fashion, to "get his ass back to work tomorrow morning."

****

Not being totally wily in the ways of the world, it didn't immediately occur to Julie that "Alexandra Riley-Dolan" bore a startling resemblance to "Alexis Riley-Dolan." Now, in point of fact, Alexis's name was "mud." This time, every girl at school must have been tuned into that night's local newscast! The halls at school the next day were literally abuzz with speculation as to the strange resemblance of the two names.

A second dose of justice was served when, the day Julie's father returned to work, who came up to her meekly in the hallway but Priscilla Paisley, with the "NOW!" tattoo almost hidden by her buttoned up blouse. "Julie?" she said in a quavering voice as she approached Julie, who was fishing things out of her locker in preparation for that morning's classes.

"Yes?" Julie answered in an equally quavering voice. Now what did Ms Paisley have in her pea brain?

"I want to apologize for the way I behaved *and* for verbally assaulting you the other day," she said with an apologetic smile. "I had no right. In fact, I was very wrong, to accuse your father the way I did." And then she said the magic, heal-all-ills, words: "Please forgive me."

"I forgive you, Priscilla," Julie responded in true time-honored fashion. "And thanks for the apology," she added, little knowing that she and Priscilla would go on to have a kind of friendship.

For some reason, for little more than a second, Julie felt, inexplicably, 10 feet tall.

And, then, as the school day progressed, Julie was to become increasingly aware that neither Alexis Cowper, Alexis Riley-Dolan, nor Alexis Mud was to be seen anywhere at school. At lunch, Julie caught a glimpse of all her pals, chief among them Dawn Dawson and Angelina Baker, in a tight knot near the door. But when the knot "untied," Alexis wasn't among the girls who sped off in different directions, much like gossip did if you thought about it.

Actually, Julie wasn't to see Alexis again that school year. She just stopped coming to school. Various stories got around about the reason why, but every story was very short on details. It was just a splotchy impressionistic kind of explanation, but not a *valuable* impressionist Renoir or Monet painting. It was purely a hack job.

At first Julie had rejoiced at Alexis's disappearance. It was like she was Miss Muffet and the spider had vanished into thin air. And then, one day, after she'd stopped thinking very much about Alexis, a loud "no" reverberated in her head. It wasn't fair that *she'd* had to go to school every day for the 2+ weeks of her father's period of public humiliation, before the doughty Miss Dodge had set the record straight, while Alexis Cowper Riley-Dolan had just done this disappearing act. To put it bluntly, Alexis obviously couldn't take her own medicine.

And then Julie thought a little more about it. Alexis versus no Alexis? Justice versus injustice? She weighed the alternatives, back and forth, in her head. In the end, the "no Alexis" won out. Justice had been served in its own way. Alexis Mud had been driven away by her own evil mother's trespasses.

CHAPTER 39

Another Scare

The leukopenia continued to be the scourge of her mother's treatment. Her body just couldn't churn out enough white blood cells to keep her immune system primed for an attack of germs of any ilk. The dreaded consequence was an infection—one that took over your whole body and mowed down the puny leukocytes you managed to have in stock. It was biological warfare of the worst kind. And it had the eerie name of *septicemia*. There was that unnerving sibilant, hissing, snakelike sound again.

On March 23, her mother was admitted to Smitty's with a fever of 103 degrees and a diagnosis of septicemia. The night before she'd complained of a headache and chills. Early the next morning, 3:30 A.M. early, she'd shaken Mr. Tyler awake. He immediately knew this was an emergency. He didn't wait to get dressed and drive her to the ER at Smitty's. He called an ambulance. Later, Dr. Barnes, the physician in charge of her mother's care, said her father had made the right call. Mrs. Tyler was seriously ill.

It also happened to be the first day of Julie's spring vacation, which, this time, she considered a good thing, unlike her more selfish self at Christmas who resented vacation time spent at a cancer center. Now she could sit at her mother's bedside round the clock if she wanted to. This way she also didn't have to be at school fumbling with equations when all she could think about was her mother's battle with death.

Mrs. Tyler was in a different part of Smitty's from the one she'd been in before when she'd had her mastectomies. She was now in the MICU, which stood for medical intensive care unit.

And Dr. Barnes was from the internal medicine department whose job, Julie found out, was to treat the side effects of cancer treatment. They were the ones who got cancer patients tottering back on their feet again, enough to continue to march lockstep with their cancer treatment.

Julie also didn't mind the fact that Dr. Barnes was the most handsome man she'd ever seen. Tall, golden blond hair, sapphire blue eyes. What was he doing at Smitty's? Shouldn't he be on the A list in Hollywood? (Actually, Julie was later to discover that the doctor bore a startling resemblance to the statue of St. Michael at church. And his first name, and this couldn't be just a coincidence, was Michael. And, now, after months of living with cancer in their midst, knowing all its wiles and wickednesses, it couldn't be anything other than a tool of the devil that an archangel might be sent to fix. It was also true that she never saw Dr. Barnes again, but Julie decided it best to leave mystical experiences to St. Bernadette of Lourdes and Sts. Lucia, Francisco, and Jacinta of Fatima.)

Most of that Monday, though, she didn't have time for romantic thoughts. She was too absorbed by her mother's labored struggle with death. All of her mother's nourishment was entering through a tube, along with the "powerful antibiotics" (including one very triumphant-sounding one called "vancomycin," as in 'vanquish-mycin') that had been called in as "extra infantry" to help fight this Hitler-like assault of pathogens on her mother's body.

Mrs. Tyler was barely conscious. It was partly because of the infection. They were also giving her sedatives to keep her quiet and comfortable.

There was also a tube coming out from under her mother's covers that was draining urine from her mother's bladder into a clear plastic bag. Oh yes, and they were also giving her mother oxygen via a mask.

Therefore, there wasn't an awful lot left of her mother that was recognizable. Her fuzzy light brown hair, her eyebrows and eyelashes long gone. Her mother's stubby nose hidden by an oxygen mask. Her flat, masculine, chest. The rest of her tangled up in tubing. It occurred to Julie that she *could* be sitting at the wrong person's bedside and not know it, but the humor escaped her.

So, all Julie could do was sit there watching the levels of the fluids in a dozen bags hanging from a rack beside her mother's bed slowly lower and the level of urine slowly rise. The MICU nurse assigned to her mother was constantly showing up, taking her mother's temperature (it was stubbornly staying at a 103 degrees), and emptying, after measuring(?), the urine that had collected in the bag since the last check.

Then Julie noticed that not quite as much urine seemed to be coming out as before. She could understand why. At 103 degrees, the inside of her mother's body would be like a really hot day when you perspired more than peed.

The MICU nurse, however, on her next check gasped when she measured the amount of urine that had collected in the bag. Then, it turned out, her mother's fever had sky-rocketed to 105 degrees. That's when they paged Dr. Barnes and she heard him and the MICU nurse assigned to her mother saying something about septic shock and multisystem failure. There were those hissing snakelike sounds again.

The following hours were a hollow hell. The germs in her mother were winning. There was no arguing the fact. But didn't they realize, Julie thought *heatedly*, that when her mother died they'd die, too? What kind of victory was that?

By then she was sitting in the MICU waiting room where the attendants had sent her so they could bring in the big artillery to fight the septicemia—whatever weapons that included. While sitting there, her head resting against the back of the chair she was sitting in, Julie felt a hand on her shoulder. She looked up into her father's most beloved face. She stood up and threw herself into his arms, sobbing into the lapel of his tweed jacket. He just held her and rocked her back and forth, saying "It's okay, honey. It's okay." Then Julie saw that with her father was the other father in her life, Father Desseau, carrying a small, oblong, zippered bag. He didn't look quite his usual sober, though benign, self. Of course, this time the priest was there to perform extreme unction, done when a person is dying. He was on a very serious mission from God, indeed.

Julie was made to sit in the waiting room while her two fathers rushed in to minister to her dying mother. It didn't bother her to be excluded. She knew the space around her mother was cramped, and the people needed to keep her alive needed space in which to work.

About a half hour later, her father and Father Desseau came out. Her father's expression was etched deep with worry, and also, curiously, baffled.

"Julie," her father said, "do you know how to get in touch with this Martha Jackson?"

Gloria's grandmother? Her father explained that while Father Desseau was performing the rite, her mother'd come to a bit, and all her father could make out of her otherwise incoherent mumble was that she was asking for Martha Jackson. Not once but several times!

Julie knew the two of them had not been able to have their lunch after the holidays because of her mother's cancer treatment. But she knew that Mrs. Jackson and her mother talked frequently on the phone, usually during the day when she was at school. Mainly it was Martha who called her mother during a lull in her work at the mansion in Woodland Hills where she worked as a housekeeper. She called to chat but also to find out how Mrs. Tyler was faring with her cancer.

But Julie had no idea how to get in touch with her. She didn't know the name of the people she worked for or even which of the dozens of mansions in Woodland Hills she worked at. Besides, it was almost 8 o'clock in the evening, so she'd probably be home by now.

"Dad, all I know is that they live at 32 A Street," was the best she could do. (Like she'd *ever* forget that address.)

Her father called directory assistance from his cell phone, but there was no phone number listed for anyone named Jackson at that address. Gloria now had a cell phone; she'd seen her using it, but she had no idea what the number was.

"Dad, maybe we need to just drive over to Mrs. Jackson's home and get her. I pretty much know the way."

Her father blinked, before barking: "To that hellhole part of the city on the first spring night of the year?!" he shouted, his voice escalating in fury, mad at the thought of having to go to such a dangerous place, mad at the germs that were killing his wife, mad at the world.

Of course, Julie realized, the Scars and the Black Lilies, like everyone else, would all be out filling their lungs with the lovely spring air.

"Bob, I think your daughter's right," said Father Desseau at this point. "The best solution is to drive there. Come, let us go —" he urged.

"Father, no—I can't let you go with us. It's too dangerous —I'll drive you back to the rectory, first."

"Nonsense," said the priest. "That will take too long. Besides, I wouldn't mind a little spring night air myself."

As she found herself in the backseat of the car circling the rotary and continuing down MLK Boulevard, the whole experience of the gang fight replayed itself in her brain, even down to feeling as though she couldn't catch her breath, couldn't get enough air into her lungs.

But the Black Lilies and the Scars must have taken the night off. Either that or they were all dead, in jail, on retreat, or —what else?—working late in their labs at Smitty's looking for a cure for cancer? Yes(!), *that* was what they should be doing, rather than looking for ways to kill or be killed. Julie, after all these months, finally hit upon what it was they should be spending, rather than wasting, their lives doing.

As they proceeded through the "valley of the shadow of death" formed by the ugly, cancerous buildings to left and right, Julie heard the priest murmur "God help us." And this from a man who'd spent some years in Rwanda as a chaplain to a teaching order of nuns....

CHAPTER 40

Good Samaritans, Chapter 2

The Little Red Riding Hood house was exactly where the fairy godmother had left it last fall.

Father Desseau said "Good God!" when he saw it. He was as surprised as Julie'd been to happen upon such a treasure of a house in such a grim place.

Julie and her father went to the door, leaving Father Desseau in the car "riding shotgun," he quipped as they were getting out of the car. He didn't, after his initial shock, appear to be particularly fazed by their surroundings. In fact, he seemed quite comfortable, like this was old-home week for him or something.

Both Gloria and her grandmother were at home. Between Julie and her father, the Jacksons were soon filled in on the reason for their surprise visit, their mission, that night.

And, soon, all four of them were hurrying to the car. Under her arm, Mrs. Jackson carried her Bible. Both Father Desseau and Martha Jackson had equipped themselves that night with their black, oblong "weapon of choice" for dealing with her very sick mother. Gloria carried a small overnight bag. She was to spend the night at the Tylers while her grandmother spent the night at her mother's bedside.

All five of them were enveloped in silence on their trip back to Smitty's.

Wedged between Gloria and her grandmother in the backseat, very aware of the closeness of such humane human beings, Julie began to cry. Not loud, racking sobs. Just quiet rivulets of tears streaking her face. And then, simultaneously, she felt a large strong hand take hold of her left hand and a delicate but equally as strong hand take her right hand, like she was a child just learning to walk and she had an adult on either side holding her up, keeping her from falling down.

At the hospital, they just let Mrs. Jackson out at the front door. Julie and her father wanted to go in with her, but the Catholic Father Desseau and the Baptist Mrs. Jackson urged them not to. They both said pretty much the same thing—that everything possible was being done for her mother, and that they needed to let the experts do their job. Although by "experts" they weren't really referring to themselves, the fact that both said the same thing at the same time made all of them laugh, a little. But they *were* experts, Julie thought. They both had God's ear.

They next left Father Desseau off at the church rectory, and then headed home. At home, even though it was late, Gloria insisted on making supper for them. Her father wanted to just call out for a pizza from The Lido, but Gloria wouldn't hear of it, for which Julie was secretly glad. Pizzas from The Lido were ceasing to console.

Julie didn't know how Gloria managed it, but she'd soon whipped a meal up for them using ingredients that, yeah, she knew they had on hand, but who would have thought to put them together as Gloria did?

For the main meal she made "pancakes"—but not the breakfast variety. Hers had chopped ham, chopped onion, and corn in them, with no sugar, just salt and pepper. Splashed on top was maple syrup made savory with the addition of melted butter, paprika, and a touch of cayenne pepper. They were out-of-this-world scrumptious. Julie and her father tore through them. They hadn't realized how hungry they were until their eyes feasted on Gloria's feast! In addition, they had green salads topped with mandarin oranges out of a can, sprinkled with blue cheese and chopped walnuts, and topped with a honey-mustard dressing Gloria had made from scratch. And for dessert they had vanilla ice cream.

All of this took place in the dining room. They ate off the

Real Old Willow china with lit candles in Julie's mother's cut crystal candlesticks providing the only light in the room. Julie had also trotted out her mother's sterling silver flatware. Fortunately the tarnish couldn't be seen in the candlelight. Polishing the silver was ordinarily her job, but when had there been a festive occasion of late? She stopped herself from thinking about the possibility of a reception after her mother's funeral.

Just as Julie and Gloria were about to dig into their ice cream, her father bellowed "Wait!" Their spoons frozen halfway to their ice cream, Mr. Tyler strode over to the liquor cabinet, rummaged among the bottles, and produced a bottle of raspberry liqueur made in France. He poured the liqueur over the ice cream as a syrup. Julie didn't know the name of it—only that it was very expensive, bottled in a roly-poly bottle, and brought out only for special occasions. Was this a special occasion? Yes, it was, Julie realized unhappily. It wasn't every day that one's mother was near death.

The conversation during the meal had drifted from topic to topic, from idea to idea. Gloria was a very comfortable person to be around. She was well informed about current world, national, *and* local, events—better informed than Julie by far, Julie had to admit. She hardly glanced at a newspaper or watched a newscast, unless some kind of mega-event was occurring—hurricanes, royal weddings, presidential inaugurations, *So You Think You Can Dance*, etc.

Gloria seemed to be especially conversant with the local legal and criminal scene. But that stood to reason. She did want, after all, to become a lawyer, specifically a public *defender*, one of that breed of lawyers her father mostly wanted little truck with. Of course, his opinion of them had improved thanks to Daniel Friedman. It made for an interesting, though completely civilized, conversation. Her father, a very experienced assistant DA, who wanted to get all the criminals off the street and in prison, pitted against Gloria, who wanted to stand up and defend people who were too poor and ignorant to stand up for themselves. There were no uncomfortable lulls in the conversation.

For Julie, though, once Gloria and her father got onto the local legal scene, it was like sitting watching a tennis match. She just swiveled her head back and forth between Gloria and her father, watching them "volley the ball" back and forth.

At 1 o'clock in the morning, Gloria and Mr. Tyler laughingly called a truce. Julie'd by then just about fallen asleep with her cheek cupped in the sticky gold-rimmed parfait glasses they'd put the ice cream in—precious and seldom used objects of her mother's mother, her Grandmother Burch.

They just washed the pots and pans and rinsed the dishes. (You couldn't put gold-rimmed china and parfait glasses through the dishwasher, of course.)

Gloria slept in the guestroom, which had its own bathroom. The bed was always made up and the room ready for a guest.

When Gloria saw the pretty room with its ivy print–upholstered stuffed chair and hassock, together with a brass reading lamp, set in a bow window hung with fresh dotted Swiss curtains, the double bed with its matelassé coverlet, the newly refinished, carved chest of drawers that had come out of the loft of some great grandfather's horse barn, it was like she was being ushered into a bedroom fit for a princess.

"What a pretty room," she breathed when Julie flicked on the overhead light.

And then, inexplicably, she rushed over to the bow window and craned her neck about looking at all the dark shapes of trees and shrubs and the roofs of neighboring houses.

But, of course, Julie realized. There weren't any Scars and Black Lily gang members hiding in the hedges. At the very worst there might be a standard Poodle named Monsieur Pierre zealously (amorously!) jumping over the back fence looking for the oh-so-sexy Dollie.

CHAPTER 41

Great Day in the Morning

That morning Julie, and her father, too, as it turned out, were awakened by Gloria singing "Great Day in the Morning" as she washed the dishes from the night before. It was as if they had Marian Anderson singing for their own special benefit.

And it *was* a great day in the morning. (It was also Gloria's way of waking them up, she admitted later.) Her grandmother'd called her on her cell phone at about 7 o'clock that morning to tell her that Mrs. Tyler was "out of danger." Her temperature had dropped to an acceptable 99 degrees. She was being moved to a regular hospital room, and, as Julie was to find out later that morning, all the tubes going in and out of her mother were gone. She was very much alive.

It also "turned out" that Mrs. Jackson had "chided" her mother, she was to laughingly tell Julie later, for having complete mastectomies without breast reconstruction.

Her cheeks red with embarrassment, Mrs. Tyler had confided to Julie that "Martha said I was too young to go around flat-chested. She said I might be Catholic, but I wasn't a nun. She even said something like 'sex was the only entertainment my husband and I could afford.'" Julie and her mother had a good laugh at that. Yessirree—

As far as what had gone on during Martha Jackson's bedside vigil in the MICU, both her mother and Mrs. Jackson were in the dark. Mrs. Tyler didn't remember Father Desseau's performing extreme unction. She had no recollection of asking for Martha Jackson to come to her bedside. And when she'd woken up that morning, feeling 100 percent better, and saw Mrs. Jackson by her bedside, she was surprised, but most pleased, to see Mrs.

Jackson sitting next to her sound asleep and bent over her Bible, which lay open in her lap to the tried-and-true Psalm 23.

Had she experienced *any* kind of angelic presence? Julie asked. "No," her mother said emphatically, shaking her head. Had she seen any visions of Jesus, the Blessed Virgin Mary—even St. Monica, her patron saint? This elicited further emphatic no's from her mother. So her mother'd experienced nothing to attract the attention of either the Pope or the local bishop. But, then, this was the woman whom God had spoken to via an exhausted pooch with sixteen puppies.

And Mrs. Jackson? All she could do was shake her head apologetically and say "I'm afraid I nodded off around 1 o'clock," as if she, like Peter and John and James, had deserted her mother, like Christ, in her hour of great need.

Father Desseau showed up just before lunch and was delighted to see his parishioner vastly improved and "clearly on this side of the sod." He, too, was matter of fact about the "miracle" that had saved her mother's life. "Actually," he said with a certain knowing air, "it's my studied opinion that a man born in a stable, spends most of His life working as a carpenter, and dies on a cross doesn't favor Cecil B. DeMille–type miracles."

"Amen, brother!" Gloria and her grandmother chorused loudly, from on high, behind him.

That *did* surprise him.

"Perhaps I should become a Baptist preacher," he said with a gleaming, mischievous smile to the three Tylers. "I never get that kind of response from *my* parishioners," 'the whole reprehensible lot of them,' Julie figured he probably added in his head. Soon Father Desseau had to head back to church for the noon Mass. The Tylers drove the Jacksons home. Mrs. Tyler was to stay in the hospital for a couple more days.

It was a beautiful spring day, and everything alive seemed to be celebrating the end of winter, as well as her mother's victory over death, or so it seemed to Julie. But, sorry, Julie thought as they made their way down MLK Boulevard, which was now bathed in spring sunshine. Because of, or despite, the glory of the day, the ghetto just looked that much more grim. She was depressed just leaving the Jacksons off at 32 A Street. Their house might be sweet as spun sugar, but it was only a meagre amount of "sugar" next to the mountainous heaps of garbage and trash that constituted their mostly unlivable neighborhood.

CHAPTER 42

More Cancer Fallout

After that, for a while, there weren't many blips on the screen. After that one bad siege of septicemia, her mother's white blood cells got their act together and her cell counts were right where they needed to be for her to continue with *all* subsequent cycles of chemo at the full doses. Then came the radiation therapy, which was no walk in the park either. They'd all thought there'd be nothing to it. There was nothing to getting x-rays in the dentist's office, after all.

But, wrong, it wasn't the same thing. The talk was all about Gray units and how much of the radiation should go to her mother's armpits and the upper, lower, and middle parts of her chest. The treatments were every weekday for a six-week "eternity" of time.

Mrs. Tyler was a trouper during the whole thing. All the staff in the radiotherapy clinic said so. But, aside from the treatments, the special positioning of her body in the radiation therapy machine, and the long waits for therapy, her mother developed very sore, red patches of skin. They were, literally, radiation burns, and there was no ointment or cream that could soothe them. Yes, Julie's mother was a trouper. But she was still human, and she was "damn glad" when the treatment was over.

Nonetheless, Dr. R was very happy with her progress, and she was particularly glad to hear that Mrs. Tyler had decided to undergo breast reconstruction.

She later remarked on Dr. R's enthusiasm over her decision to have breast reconstruction to Julie and her father. Julie could see an amused (gleeful?) expression fanning out over her father's face as he looked over at her mother and said "You're surprised that someone from India, the home of the *Kama Sutra*, would be dismayed about your deciding to get breasts?"

"Oh, Tweedle—" her mother exploded in laughter. And though no more words were exchanged, both her mother and father wore a, for adults only, warm glow on their cheeks for a surprisingly long, silent while.

The breast reconstruction, rather the preliminary steps for it, really took a toll on her mother. After the radiation burns had healed, then the plastic surgeons entered the picture. First, they had to perform an outpatient procedure involving the insertion of what they called expanders. And, yes, as their name implied, they were meant to stretch her mother's skin to accommodate the breast implants. The stretching process was extremely uncomfortable. At one point, after the most recent injection of the salty, saline, solution into the expansion bags on each side of her chest, her mother broke down in tears. Or maybe, Julie thought for a deranged minute, the salty solution was leaking out of her eyes.

"This is silly," Mrs. Tyler said to her silent husband and daughter. "Doing this is all about vanity. I love Martha Jackson, and I know she's well intentioned, but, frankly, I think I should have just settled for a flat chest."

It was entirely her own decision. Julie and her father only made it clear to her that they could live with her looking like Dolly Parton or Olive Oyl, Popeye's flat-chested wife. "As long as you don't punish yourself afterward for not having the reconstruction," Mr. Tyler had said. And there was no mistaking that he was thinking entirely of her needs, not his.

After taking some Tylenol and thinking about it for a couple days, Mrs. Tyler decided to continue with the plan to have a reconstruction. She did, however, decide against the C-cup breasts she had wanted and instead went with the B-cup breasts, which had been her original size, anyway. She wasn't about to go through that much extra pain for the gain of one cup size.

The result, when the reconstruction had been done and

her *breasts* were fully healed, was a Billy Crystal FAB-U-LOUS! This time when her mother summoned her to her bedroom to show her the results, Julie was flabbergasted. Her mother's breasts were beautiful, if it was appropriate for a daughter to say that about her mother's breasts. The plastic surgeons had even created nipples, which they'd appropriately darkened by tattooing her skin. And, her mother explained, by having the double mastectomy, both her breasts were equal in size and shape. If she'd gone with the single mastectomy, they would have had to match her left breast to her, by then, droopy, floppy right breast.

"Good going, Mom," Julie had said at the time with perhaps a tad more feeling than a daughter should use with a mother with new breasts.

* * * *

On the school front, while all of this was going on with her mother, things had settled down academically. She ended the year with a C– in algebra, a B+ in most other subjects, and a most surprising A+ in science. Her interest in science had continued unabated. Now she had an almost insatiable appetite for *all* things scientific. She was now seriously reconsidering whether to go for a liberal arts degree or to instead get a degree in some kind of science, perhaps medicine. She was glad to have the next three years to make up her mind.

There was one real hitch to going into science, and Julie had to admit that it was a pretty corny one. She hated uniforms and yearned for the day when she could wake up and plan what gorgeous outfit she was going to wear that day. The thought of wearing a white lab coat or, worse, scrubs, for her entire working life was, frankly, depressing. But that was not a good (as in *commendable*) reason for pursuing a more fashionista profession. And, no, she wasn't interested in a gray-suit-only law profession either.

* * * *

One Saturday not long after her mother's breast reconstruction when her mother was still recovering from the surgery, she'd taken the bus downtown to buy some underwear at Macy's for her mother, who wasn't up to shopping. Her mother'd gotten it into her head that she wanted some nice underwear for a change, and nothing from Walmart or Target or L.L. Bean would do. She had four criteria: (1) it couldn't be white, (2) it couldn't be cotton, (3) it couldn't be sensible, and (4) it had to be from France. It was something that could have waited until later, but it was *now* that her mother was constantly having to undress for exams and treatments and other procedures.

Julie understood what was behind her mother's request. She'd lost her hair, her breasts, her female identity, and even though her breasts were back, she needed something that made her feel nice. (She also desperately needed new bras. After her double mastectomy she'd thrown all her old ones out. It wasn't her being practical. It was her being angry. Julie remembered the afternoon she'd been in the living room doing homework when suddenly her mother's voice began to ricochet from the upstairs to the downstairs hallway and then back up again. "Well, bras, it looks like the time has come to send you off to the city dump. And just which one of you was I wearing the day my tumor started growing?! Don't think I'm going to give you away, give you another chance to start a damn tumor in some other poor woman," she'd finished furiously as she dumped them into the kitchen garbage can with a loud metallic *bang*. Two things. First of all, her mother never swore. Second when had underwear become people? This was just another example of the way cancer changed people's lives.) Anyway, Julie was more than glad to accommodate her mother's wishes in the lingerie department.

Julie took great delight in purchasing some very alluring, B-cup bras, panties, and slips from France. Then she found some very sheer, alluring nightgowns, also from France. (Would they survive even one wash in the washing machine? *Non!* Labels everywhere on them, in English *and* French, specified that they had to be hand washed.) The nightgowns hadn't been on her mother's shopping list. But they were on sale. They were also, as a result, unreturnable. So, even if her mother didn't like them, she'd have to wear them, put them in the bottom drawer, or give them to St. Vincent de Paul (the thrift store, not the saint). Julie might have had some mischief brewing in her brain when she bought them, but it was also genuinely because she wanted to do something extra nice for her mother, who certainly deserved luxury lingerie if anyone did.

After she'd finished her shopping, she betook herself to the Trade Winds Tearoom for lunch. Macy's had wisely seen fit to retain the restaurant that had been, still was, a major draw for shoppers. It dated back to the 1940s and the department store Macy's had bought out and that Julie didn't even know the name of. With its 12th-floor perch, it had a grand view of the broad river that swept through the city's midst and, in the distance, wavelike bluish hills carpeted with trees just now fitted out with the jazzy green leaves that showed up only in spring. Macy's had carefully preserved the room's art deco decoration, even down to the waitresses' uniforms. Murals on the wall depicted exotic, warm, tropical places, with lots of palm trees, long turquoise sweeps of ocean, and scads of happy sailboats drawn with, like, five quick black brushstrokes.

But what was supposed to be a treat, even down to being seated at a table by a window looking out over the river, turned bitter in the blink of an eye. Julie'd just placed her order for chicken croquettes—her favorite meal at the Trade Winds Tearoom—and hot tea—when a girl her age and a mother her mother's age were seated at the table next to hers. The empty chair across from her that her mother would have sat in was, at the table next to her, occupied by the mother. The two were soon gabbing away, just like Julie and her mother had done *hundreds* of times on a Saturday afternoon after a morning of doing errands.

Suddenly, she was overwhelmed with a sense of loss. Right now, her mother was doing okay. But who was to say that two months from now her mother might be dead of her cancer or its treatment? And then there was the fact that it'd been *months* since Julie and her mother had had such a cozy mother–daughter outing. So excruciating was her sudden sadness that she did something she'd only ever seen done in old movies by, like, Barbara Stanwyck or Bette Davis. She just got up and left. She'd only gotten a glass of water, and thus nothing of what she'd ordered. And she didn't bother to find her waitress to tell her she was leaving. She just left. She had to flee from the anguish, grief, whatever she was feeling. Angst didn't cut it this time.

She managed on the bus ride home to get her emotions sorted out and stuffed in the right boxes in her brain. Thus, when she walked in the door, she was her usual cheery self.

CHAPTER 43

Algebra Again...

It was late June, and it was already hot and muggy. It was the kind of limp weather only a mosquito could love. Julie's mother's double breast reconstruction was well in the past, and, yes, if her mother's hand laundry was any indication, she was wearing the filmy underwear and negligees she'd bought for her at Macy's. At her last visit to see Dr. R, her mother had been declared cancer free—well, at least until her six-month checkup in the fall.

School had ended the week before, and Julie set about doing something she'd been looking forward to—making a pile of her algebra tests and burning them in their rusted, unused-for-20-years hibachi, à la Miss Dodge. It took her awhile to collect them all. She'd just shoved them higgledy-piggledy into her algebra binder. Her gaze had seldom strayed beyond the grade slashed across the top with Mr. Hennessey's sizzling hot pink pen. (Was that choice of colors weird, or what?) Anyway, that morning, she was calm. She'd come to terms with and accepted her failure as a math-lete. It was okay.

But when she calmly looked at the top test, the one she'd failed the day of her mother's mastectomies, something caught her eye. Some of the numbers, especially the ones showing the final results of her calculations, were different from the way she wrote numbers. And then she noticed that the characters not in her hand were always written over erasures. Sure, there should be *some* erasures. But she couldn't have made *that* many erasures —there wouldn't have been time. And the more she looked, the more she realized that, yes, someone *had* to have tampered with her answers. And, yes, as she looked through the pile of algebra quizzes, tests, and homework, she discovered the same sickening curlicue numbers substituted for her forthright, plain-and-simple numbers throughout, up until around the middle of March. About then, her marks had started to improve, but so had the wickedly curlicue numbers begun to disappear. It was also, most curiously, right around the time Alexis had done her disappearing act following the Brett Bartt debacle. But Alexis hadn't been in her algebra class? How could she have gotten to her homework and tests? It didn't matter! *Someone* had scuttled, sabotaged, brought to the brink of destruction her grade in algebra, worked toward ruining her academic standing for the year, even, possibly, for her whole life. (Just as Alexandra Riley-Dolan Cowper's dirty little cute-co-ed deed in college had long-term consequences for her father.) There was only one thing left for her to do, go and find her mother.

She scooped up the algebra papers and brought them downstairs to the screened-in back porch where her mother was sitting reading. Her mother, as soon as she'd looked through them, the furrows in her face deepening as she did so, agreed that there was something very fishy about them, enough to make her very disturbed, too, even angry. She'd never seen her mother's cheeks flush red.

That afternoon Julie and her mother found themselves seated in Dr. Drescher's office. The only sound, as Dr. Drescher examined the algebra papers, was the shuffling of the sheets of paper and the distant drone of a lawnmower, accompanied by the scent of fresh grass cuttings drifting in through Dr. Drescher's open window, the fancy floor-to-ceiling, arched one over the portico. Who knew it swung open on a hinge (like a door) and opened out onto a small balcony built on the roof of the portico? Added to the mix was the sound of her heart beating anxiously for two reasons: (1) what would be the outcome of this meeting and (2) who had done this to her and why? Well, but, it could only be Alexis. It could only be someone with the rare Riley-Dolan mutant gene that put a person at higher risk of committing evil deeds. It was one of those X-linked traits she'd read about. And the culprit gene dwelt on the X chromosome Alexis had inherited from her mother, no doubt about that.

After finishing her close examination of the tests, Dr. Drescher summoned her secretary to get Mr. Hennessey on the phone, which she did. Dr. Drescher said nothing to them, just remained grimly silent, looking at her hands clasped over the pile of algebra tests and homework, as she waited for her secretary to get the teacher on the phone. She was reminded of the scene in the dean of student office when her father had wept in response to Alexandra's accusation. The she-wolf had been right, just wrong about the right person! *She* was the old band-aid that needed to be tossed out. The same for her daughter. They were both biological waste.

Dr. Drescher's conversation with Mr. Hennessey was short and one-sided. That is, she didn't give very much away on her end. As she spoke with him, questioning him about how this could have happened, her voice became more and more terse. Her German accent also became more pronounced, and Julie'd never seen such an expression on anyone's face. Dr. Drescher was actually glowering when she got off the phone, hanging up without even a courteous good bye to Mr. Hennessey . . . . Her usually pale cheeks were also flushed the same color red as her mother's earlier in the day.

After sitting back in her chair and thinking for a bit, Dr. Drescher began to speak in a decidedly strained voice. She was most unhappy, *not* with Julie and her mother, of course. With Mr. Hennessey, who'd admitted that he had allowed one of the students to help him correct tests and homework. The girl wasn't in any of his classes, so it all seemed okay to him. He'd welcomed her help, in fact, thought it very thoughtful of her to offer to help him.

True enough. Grading papers, Julie knew, was the bane of every teacher's existence.

Dr. Drescher further explained that he'd given the girl the sheet of correct answers, and she'd, in his presence *always*, or so he said, corrected many of them. If he'd seen her erasing anything and penciling something in, well, he probably had assumed the girl was fixed something she'd marked incorrectly. (As in he'd seen Alexis doing this but hadn't even thought to ask what she was doing.)

Dr. Drescher went on to say that the student, per Mr. Hennessey, was allowed only to check the answers against the answer key. He did the actual grading. (That would account for the sizzling pink pen that remained the one constant in this whole mess.) "But Mr. Hennessey admits that he could have been distracted by a phone call or some other thing that would have allowed the girl to tamper with test answers without his knowing it," Dr. Drescher said in a voice that descended in weariness. "School policy makes it quite clear that students shouldn't have access to other students' homework and tests, for reasons you yourselves can understand. Mr. Hennessey has therefore committed a serious breach of school policy," she finished in a voice that said she was having second thoughts about working so hard to get her doctorate in education.

She said nothing more about Mr. Hennessey and how he would be dealt with. (Julie wondered if she could make suggestions. Turning his hot pink pen into a dirk and slashing him all over with it was one.)

Dr. Drescher soon directed the conversation to how the situation could be rectified to Julie's and her parents' satisfaction. The three of them discussed various ways in which the wrong done Julie could be righted justly. There was no way of telling what her original answers had been, so the tests and homework were of no help. Dr. Drescher murmured something about retaking the tests, but one look at Julie's horrified face made her realize that that was totally unfair. That would mean Julie studying to relearn everything and maybe ending up with a lower grade.

"Dr. Drescher," Julie said, after a bit, a solution beginning to dawn on her, "I'd just be happy to have a B+ rather than a C-." She was, at first, going to ask for just a B, but someone (Gloria Jackson? Tilda Stein?) whispered in her ear, told her to go for the "plus."

Dr. Drescher pursed her lips, tilted her head to one side, thought about it for a moment, and then said "Considering your grades in other classes, Julie, I think that would be both reasonable and fair. A C- for you isn't your norm. Yes, why don't we do that."

Yes!! She'd won the lottery! She'd gotten a better grade in algebra, gotten more of the "cars" of her academic performance "train" back on track, and was now free to return to the heavenly ease of her summer vacation, all in one fell swoop!

But, in the car and on their way home, Julie remembered something that had first hit her back when Brett Bartt (who, interestingly, had been fired from the local paper) was having his fifteen minutes of fame at her father's expense. Could she even get the words out? *Should* she tell her mother one of the awful thoughts that had sent her, retching, into the bathroom in the early hours of the morning of that snowy day?? Swallowing hard to keep the contents of her stomach where they were, she finally got the question out: "Mom, do you think that Mrs. Cowper might have had something to do with that gossip that was spread about you at church, about you and Dad having to getting married, about me being a bastard?" Julie tried to keep her voice matter-of-fact and neutral. But her mother's reaction was anything but.

With a cry like that of a wounded small animal, she yanked the steering wheel hard to the right. It was a gut reaction. She was only trying to get away from the thing that had just attacked her. The front wheels rammed into the curb, which brought the car to a sudden, jolting stop. But because the rear of the car now stuck out into traffic, cars around them began honking, trying to get around her mother, letting her mother know what they thought of her driving.

Her mother wasn't aware of any of it. She just kept wagging her head from side to side, her eyes shut, her head bent down almost level with the top of the steering wheel, her hands gripping it.

"Oh, Julie . . . " her mother murmured. "Oh, my God," she said in a choked voice, raising her head to look out the window. "It's *all* too possible." (Oh what that windshield had been party to that year . . . .) "Julie, I haven't said anything, because it all seemed too crazy." Here her mother stopped and took a deep breath before continuing. The words seemed to be scraping her throat raw. "The night we sat next to Alexis and her mother, I couldn't convince myself that I didn't know Alexandra from somewhere. But with all that started going wrong so soon after that, I never thought anymore about it. If Alexandra *was* going to our church just to sow that lie, as you're suggesting, she would have had to be very careful not to be seen by your father who would have recognized her instantly. But, otherwise, how do I know her? It's an awful thought, but, yes, like that awful thing our upstairs neighbor did on that Sunday afternoon when I was such a young child, there's nothing to say that Alexandra wouldn't stoop to such a stunt, start that rumor because Bob had jilted her, what?, five years earlier. I suppose all she had to do was find someone who went to our church who could be counted on to spread the rumor. But," here Mrs. Tyler shook her head, her natural legal mind coming to the fore, "that wouldn't explain how I know her. And, one has to hand it to people like this Alexandra, they'll go to great lengths, *and* take great risks, to harm people, even if it's no more than the fact that I was the one who, she probably thinks in her own twisted way, stole Bob Tyler from her. Lord, it beggars the imagination the evil people are capable of. . . ." Here she stopped, just sat looking bleakly out that poor windshield.

In the quiet, Mrs. Tyler suddenly realized the car horns she was hearing had to do with the fact that the rear of her car was sticking out and blocking traffic.

"Oh, my goodness, everyone, just hang on," she said in a hoarse voice, after taking a quick look at all the cars stuck in place by her Volvo. "Gosh, Julie, with my luck, Officer Ward will be on duty. That's all we need."

Julie let out a small laugh.

Her mother then backed up enough so that the front tires could clear the curb when she pulled forward. When her mother turned to look over her shoulder before backing up, Julie could see the tear tracks on her face. Some tears still dribbled down her cheeks. Of all the things that had happened that day, *that* made Julie the maddest. That her mother, who hadn't met her father until long after his undergraduate days, was a victim of this deranged woman's need to hurt everyone in her father's life just because he'd rejected her. That raised the question: How much more stress would it take for there to be enough more chromosome breaks to get another tumor growing in her mother, kill her off so that Alexandra would have a clear playing field again?

****

Later, at home, while her mother was back in the screened-in porch reading more of the book on St. Teresa of Avila she'd been reading that morning, Julie chose to finish up the afternoon curled up in the chair in the guest room looking through a book of photographs (daguerreotypes?) taken by a man called Matthew Brady after the Battle of Gettysburg. It was fitting. As she looked at page upon page of the battlefield carnage, it made her wonder how deep the evil in the world could penetrate before it left you sprawled out dead, your intestines spilling out on the ground.

CHAPTER 44

Birthday Day

That night, the three of them, Julie, her mother, and her father, sat on the back porch as it grew steadily darker, until it was pitch black, not talking about the Cowpers so much as hashing out the nature of evil and its many guises and how one recognizes them and, most importantly, how one keeps evil from bedding down inside one, taking over like cancer, and destroying one's *natural* inclination to do the good. Worse, ruins one's chances of salvation. (It also didn't help the discussion any that they were in the midst of a heavy June bug invasion, and as they talked and the darkness deepened, the bugs bombarded the screens in increasing numbers, kamikaze-like.) Her father, on his end of the discussion, kept stressing "natural law," which he summed up thusly:

"Natural law, the ability to discern between right and wrong, and we're not talking about even the Ten Commandments or the Code of Hammurabi here, is inscribed on man's heart from birth. You can look back to prehistoric times, and you'll find that man has always abided by some code of law, of right and wrong. Murder, theft, rape . . . no civilized society has ever countenanced such acts. Those are the biggies. But then there's character assassination such as we all seem to have experienced at the hands of the Cowpers. *We* know, most everyone knows, that's wrong."

"Except the politicians," Julie had to interject at that point.

"Except the politicians," her father had agreed dryly.

They'd left it at that. Things were revving up for a presidential election that fall, and the usual mudslinging had reached its usual heights, or was that depths?

After that, they'd each had a bowl of milk and Cheerios for their "supper," cheerfully topped with fresh sliced strawberries and granulated sugar, then gone to bed. That day was 'ovah,' finished, kaput.

Julie'd just climbed into bed, turned off the lights, and gotten herself in her favorite sleeping position, when her thought processes, still orbiting around the wrong that had been done to her (algebra fraud?) and the talk they'd had that night, hit on thoughts that had to be set down in her journal, if for no other reason, than they were so toxic, she had to get rid of them—better that they be on paper than close to her heart or brain or some other vital organ. Soon she was sitting cross-legged on her bed with her journal in her lap furiously scribbling down everything that now had her so disturbed.

> *What if I hadn't noticed the suspicious snake-like numbers on my algebra papers? What if, because of Dad's long-ago "sexual misdemeanor," the name Alexandra Riley-Dolan hadn't been emblazoned in the press, which forced Alexis to leave school before the year was over? How much farther might my grade have dropped? What else might she have done? What if Mom and I hadn't happened to sit next to the Cowpers at the mother–daughter dinner, hadn't eaten some of the deadly bean salad, hadn't noticed the Orange Dragon bowl it came in? What if Mom had made her also-popular chocolate mint brownies instead of praline cookies and hadn't scored such a hit with them that she was held up leaving that night, and we hadn't seen the Cowpers leaving with that hideous bowl, I don't care how much it's worth? What if we hadn't picked up the Jacksons that night, brought them home, survived the awful gang fight? And what if Mom hadn't gotten cancer this year, things had just hummed along? What if Mom hadn't gotten septicemia or had died of it? What if Martha Jackson hadn't prayed at Mom's bedside that night in the MICU? And what if Mrs. Cowper had started the rumor at church about my "illegitimacy"?*

That was just a straightforward recounting of the things that had already happened. Then came the corker:

What else might the fiendish Alexandra-Alexis duo have up their sleeves that they're just waiting to spring on us?

After finishing the journal entry, it was a long while before she fell asleep only to dream dreams that were just as disturbing as the thoughts she'd just recorded.

* * * *

The next night, Julie's father walked in the door brandishing some brochures and announcing that he'd booked them for two weeks the beginning of August at a lodge in Glacier National Park in Montana. Julie's spirits were still pretty low from the day before and the night filled with distressing dreams. She was therefore most surprised that her father's news made her spirits rise so rapidly, so gladly.

Okay. Okay. Okay. Things always look better in a brochure than in reality. But there was no way someone handy with Photoshop could improve on the charm of the lodge where they'd be staying (she was to have her very own room!) or the beauty of its setting.

The lodge was turn-of-the-century, Gilded Age, rustic. The lake it looked out on serenely mirrored the blue sky with its playful tufts of white clouds (those might have been Photoshopped in; it would be easy to do). Conifers of various hues wreathed the lake like . . . a virtual Christmas wreath! Yes! And then there was the *pièce de résistance*, the main attraction of the place—the *mountains*. Colossal gray peaks that jetted upward like the spires of Gothic cathedrals, only way higher and way older. And in the various rocky hollows, clefts, and valleys, there were true-blue, actually bluish-greenish, glaciers that, yes, were left over from The Ice Age, *way* longer ago than The Gilded Age. They seemed like huge chunks of some kind of very valuable gemstone, maybe jade, so rare were they.

On her sixteenth birthday, on July 22, Julie and her mother went shopping for clothes for her for their vacation. What did she need besides jeans? Well, besides a few new tops —*not* T-shirts—more fashionable jersey tops with three-quarter-length sleeves and boat necks or ballerina necks, she had to get some dressy clothes. Apparently, lodge guests dressed up for dinner. Julie chose a sea-foam green linen sleeveless sheath dress with a square neck that was just 2 inches shy of her knees.

That night Julie wore the dress to dinner with her mother and father in the formal dining room at The Yorkshire—the same room where they'd been on Nutcracker Sunday, which seemed like a hundred years ago now. For shoes, she wore black patent leather, high-heeled sling-back shoes, which they'd also bought that day. In the store, even in her shorts, she had to admit they looked gorgeous on the beautiful legs she'd inherited from her father, or maybe it was her Aunt Babs.

Julie felt Billy Crystal FAB-U-LOUS. And she looked it, too, she could see for herself when she surveyed her image in the hall mirror. And didn't the glow in her parents' eyes as she descended the stairs and come into their full view where they sat in the living room reassure her that her impression wasn't mistaken?

That night, after finishing their main courses, while they waited for their desserts to arrive, her mother produced from her dressy purse yet another gift. This one was a small, square, robin's egg blue box tied with a delicate white satin ribbon. The box had "Tiffany & Co." printed on it in black lettering.

At first Julie just gazed at the box sitting in the just-cleared space on the brilliant white table cloth before her.

"Open it, sweetheart," her mother said in a soft, but also firm, voice, as if she were urging her to take an important (first?) step (into adulthood?), nudging her little fledgling out of the nest.

Julie untied the bow, lifted the lid off the box, and gasped. It was a not-too-small white pearl, topped by a not-too-small square diamond, suspended from a delicate, glistening, white gold chain. Julie took it from the box and gazed at it in wonderment in the palm of her hand, where it seemed to emit its own special glow.

"Okay, now it's my formal duty, make that pleasure, to put it on you—" Julie's father said next.

Mrs. Tyler smiled a special smile at her that was more woman to woman than mom to kid, as her father stood up and fastened the necklace at the back of her neck. At that Julie experienced, for the first time, the pleasure, no make that the thrill, of receiving the attention of a perfect gentleman, the man, this time, her father. Added to that, her mother said "your father picked it out for you, honey." He had very good taste!

She looked down at the lovely necklace where it lay against the sea-foam green background of her new dress. Even while eating her favorite dessert—bread pudding, and The Yorkshire's was an incredibly rich white chocolate version that just barely met the otherwise staid qualifications of a "bread pudding"—she hardly paid any attention to each delicious mouthful. And then her spoon struck the bottom of the glass goblet, and she honestly couldn't remember eating a dollop of the pudding....

That night in her diary, after describing the *outward* experience of the day, she went on to describe the inner experience.

Tonight seemed more than just a celebration of my 16th birthday. Tonight I think that I got an inkling of what it is to be an adult. I'm sure that dining by candlelight in the formal dining room of The Yorkshire, wearing my new dress and dressy shoes, then getting that beautiful pendant necklace from Tiffany's and having Dad fasten it on me like I was Audrey Hepburn and he was Cary Grant in Charade helped. (Is it okay to have your father be the first real love of your life?) But then, when I saw myself in the mirror, all dressed up, I, for the first time, didn't see a girl, but a woman. And, since this is a journal and I can say whatever I want in it, I can admit that I think

I'm fairly attractive—maybe even beautiful. Not Audrey Hepburn or Grace Kelly beautiful. No one will ever be as beautiful as them. But I'm also a little scared by it all. There's a part of me that doesn't want to grow up, just be a little kid forever. But then who wants to be a Peter Pan and wear that horrible elf outfit for their entire life? Yuck. Yuck. All kidding aside, it's kind of like tonight, and this goes for everyone around my age who really thinks about what it means to be an adult, I started to consciously think and want to act like a responsible adult.

It was another one of those trying-to-reach-something-on-the-top-shelf moments, but this time she had started to get a feel for what it was, started to grasp it even.

CHAPTER 45

Good Samaritans, Chapter 3

A few days before August 3, when they were to leave for Glacier National Park, the phone rang about 9:30 one night. Her father answered it.

Julie didn't know who it was, but from the sound of her father's voice, the person on the other end was in some kind of serious trouble.

All she heard of her father's side of the conversation came just before he hung up: "Gloria, listen close to what I'm going to tell you. I want you and your grandmother to throw some things in a suitcase, enough for several days. I'm going to call some contacts I have at the police department and have them send over a squad car for you." This was all barked like a command to an infantry unit.

Her father explained as soon as he got off the phone. Gloria's mother, Mrs. Jackson's daughter, had broken out of prison. (He didn't say why she was in prison, and neither Julie nor her mother asked.) The woman had been spotted by a police helicopter on the run in a city park that, if you followed it all the way, would deliver her very close to 32 A Street.

That was how Julie and her mother happened to meet Officer Ward again, this time in their bathrobes.

But it was not a joyous reunion. Mrs. Jackson could hardly speak. She just kept casting frightened eyes about as if expecting danger tricked out in any disguise to leap out of every shadow. Gloria had her by the arm, trying to steady her, but looked to be close to collapsing herself.

Mrs. Tyler took charge of Mrs. Jackson, and Julie took charge of Gloria. Mrs. Jackson would stay in the guest bedroom.

Gloria was to have a cot in Julie's room meant for sleepovers. It was now their turn to be Good Samaritans.

As Julie and her mother were rushing around upstairs getting the two women settled, in one transit across the upstairs hallway to get towels and then milk heating for hot milk for all of them, Julie caught sight of her father striding down the downstairs hallway carrying something stiffly in his hand. It was his .38-caliber Smith & Wesson revolver, and from the way he carried it, she knew it was loaded. Would someone's mother, someone's daughter need to be shot?? They only had the gun because, as an assistant DA, he was subject to the occasional death threat, so far, none of them coming true. This was a situation she could never have imagined.

When Julie reentered the bedroom with two mugs of hot milk, she was at first alarmed. Gloria was lying flat on her back on the cot, her eyes clamped shut, the covers pulled up to her chin, completely still, except for tears that straggled down her cheeks from under her black, gathered tulle–like eyelashes.

Julie placed the mug of milk on the bedside table, then sat cross-legged on her bed across from Gloria. She just remained silent. She had no profound words of wisdom for a girl who was scared for her life because of her own mother.

"Gloria?" she finally said in a soft, gentle voice, just to get some kind of ball rolling.

Gloria didn't immediately open her eyes, but she did start talking.

"My grandmother has tried so hard to get me onto a good path in life, one that was a lot better than the one her daughter, my mother, chose. Granny blames herself for the way my mother turned out. But it was 100 percent my mother's fault. She didn't want a path in life. She wanted a fast lane. The faster the better, fueled preferably with speed." Gloria's voice had started out quiet, but here it began to pick up momentum and volume. "And then she diversified, and tried just about any recreational drug she could find to help her escape the hell she'd made for herself. And, of course, she never bothered to think about the hell she was making for all the people who loved her. My granny is strong. Somehow she's gotten through all the arrests, the arraignments, the trials, the convictions for peddling drugs, prostitution, causing public disturbances, and then the crowning glory—her arrest and conviction for murdering someone in a drug deal that went bad. Oh, and then she used a stolen credit card to pay for one of her, I don't know how many, abortions. My mother also virtually murdered her father, my grandfather. He couldn't deal with the fact that the sweet little girl who was his daughter—his only child—could have turned into such a monster. According to Granny, he just got sadder and sadder, and then one day he just died sitting up in the rocker he sat rocking in all day long staring out the window."

Gloria paused and then continued in a softer voice. "I never met him. I was born in prison. It was after my mother'd been sent to prison for second-degree murder, the person she shot in the drug deal."

There was a brief silence. Julie was listening, waiting in the wings with words she thought might be helpful. But Gloria had one final salvo to fire at Julie, anyone listening to the painful narrative of her mother's failed life: "I was *fathered*, for your information, by a prison guard, and I was *born* in the prison infirmary."

By this time Gloria'd opened her eyes and propped herself up on one arm, but it wasn't a friendly, it was a defiant gaze that she leveled on Julie. Julie let Gloria's eyes meet hers, just.

"Does that offend you?" Gloria shot at Julie, mistaking her looking away and her silence for disgust. Gloria was angry and in pain, but Julie knew that it wasn't directed at her.

"No, it doesn't offend me, but it does shock me," Julie said simply, directly, honestly. "And it shocks you, too, it would seem—understandably."

"Yes," Gloria murmured softly, spotted the mug of hot milk, hooked her finger through the handle, and took one small sip, before saying: "It shocks me and sickens me. Every day I wake up like someone with one of those genes that causes you to go crazy when you get older, but you don't know it until one day you wake up and—only in my case I have a sudden lust for purple FMPs, skimpy halter tops, black leather miniskirts, and Black boys wearing do-rags, oversized boxer shorts, and fake diamond earrings the size of *headlights*."

Julie felt an impulse to laugh. FMPs, headlight-sized diamond earrings.... Too funny. But this was a very serious moment. Gloria was being vicious.

"Gloria," she said, after it seemed Gloria was done speaking, embarking bravely on what she'd composed so far in her head. "This probably sounds weird, but, first of all, I'm actually quite honored by the fact that you told me all this. Confiding something like that to a person—I think anyway—is like putting a special seal on a friendship. It's giving me some special privileged part of yourself. In all honesty, I think you're one of the finest people I've ever known."

Gloria cocked her a questioning look.

"Really, Gloria. You just get up every day and say to yourself 'You go, girl!' And you do! And you know what? That's a heck of a lot more than a lot of those dimwit rich girls at school do. You don't sit back and just let daddy pay for everything. And you also don't just sit back and let Uncle Sam pay for everything! You've got pride and guts and intelligence that could deliver you to the moon maybe even Mars if you wanted it. I mean..." here Julie paused and shook her head, "Gloria—you're a walking success story, and you've only just gotten started on your journey."

Here Gloria looked up at Julie, with bright eyes swimming with tears. But Julie wasn't quite done with her "oration." Another thought was blossoming, surging up, in her brain and she had to utter it now, or the right moment in time would be lost forever.

"Gloria, has it never occurred to you that if your mother hadn't gotten pregnant in jail, you probably wouldn't be here now? Either she'd have killed you with heroin or crack or she'd have had an abortion."

The words were harsh, but this wasn't an occasion for niceties.

Gloria's face went blank and nothing registered on it for a moment. No, she hadn't ever had that thought. The room became completely still. Even the night air drifting in through the open window seemed to pause as if to ponder.

"How has that never occurred to me," Gloria breathed with some awe, looking down at the mug of now lukewarm milk. Julie could see the realization sending out ripples in her brain. "Wow," she whispered and looked up at Julie, stumped for words. Julie was silent, too. She'd almost come to the end of her profound thoughts. Actually, she had one more but she kept it to herself. It was the answer to all the questions she'd scribbled, rapid fire, in her diary the night of the day she'd discovered the mysterious snaky, curlicue numbers on her math papers. She'd finally gotten a good grasp on the object on the top shelf. Good *could* come from evil, just like Father Desseau had preached so many times. Heck, that's what the Bible was practically *all* about. But she kept her realization, her profound answer, to herself. It had to do more with *her* personal horrible year than with Gloria's.

After a bit, after the two of them sat thinking their respective profound thoughts, Gloria said "Thanks, Julie. I feel a lot better."

"Really?!" said Julie, totally amazed that her words had worked any kind of cure.

"Really," Gloria said as she drank the last of the now cold hot milk. Julie'd forgotten hers but, with its yucky layer of coagulated milk on top, decided to give it a miss. The two girls nestled under the covers and Julie turned out the light.

A few minutes later, Julie realized she needed to use the bathroom. Drats! As she passed by the guest bedroom to get to the bathroom, she saw that light still shone from under the door. She paused by the door long enough to determine that it was her mother's voice she heard on the other side. This time *she* was reading the Psalms to Mrs. Jackson and wasn't she on

Psalm 23? Like her most favorite line from an old movie, uttered by Barbara Stanwyck in *Christmas in Connecticut:* "How about that!"

The next day Gloria's mother was apprehended, trying to break into 32 A Street, and Gloria and her grandmother returned home. It was now "safe" for them to go home.

CHAPTER 46

Glacier National Park, finally

If the winter and spring had been a waking nightmare, their two weeks in early August at Glacier National Park were a fairytale dream of the purely daytime ilk. In fact, Julie didn't dream any of the nights she was there. She didn't need to. Her days were filled with the stuff *real* dreams are made of. They were visible, tangible, audible, smellable, three-dimensional, *and* memorable.

The brochures her father'd brought home in June hadn't overhyped the place. Just the opposite! You couldn't Photoshop in the clear mountain air, the scent of cedar and pine, the buzzing of bees, the calling of birds, the sound of water—the rushing, rippling, and trickling variety, and the overarching hum of nature at full summer tilt.

The park's three basic colors were blue, gray, and green, with negligible amounts of red and yellow. Blue for sky and water. Gray for the raw, jagged Rocky Mountain peaks that gave a new, or maybe an old, meaning to 'skyscraper.' And then there were the bluish, greenish, whitish jade-like glaciers that wrapped themselves possessively around the shadowed bases of the peaks. They seemed to look down haughtily at the upstart humans for being so uncourageously short-lived.

For the first three days, all they did was sleep. Ten hours at night, an hour after breakfast, two or three hours in the afternoon. Most of these initial days of their vacation were spent on the lodge's ample deck-like porch that overlooked Swiftcurrent Lake, the name of the lake shown in the brochure. It consumed most of the horizontal vista, while the mountains consumed most of the vertical. They sat, and slept, in Adirondack chairs with their collective bare feet perched on a common square Adirondack-style footstool.

They joked, when they were awake, that their feet were getting to know each other. Actually, it was Julie who started it. On the first day, she awoke after a late morning nap to discover that the toes of all their feet were inclined toward each other, like neighbors talking over the back fence. Julie took it upon herself to introduce her right foot to her mother's left foot and then her left foot to her father's right foot, complete with different made-up voices. Her left foot was blunt and roguish, her right, verrrry (très!) romantically French. They got quite silly with their feet chatter, but when Julie's left foot got into a silly squabble with her father's right foot, Mr. Tyler put a temporary halt to their tootsie tête-à-tête. People were looking and laughing.

Actually, it seemed as though the child had come out in everyone staying at the lodge. You could tell the people who'd just arrived from those who'd been there a couple days. The newcomers looked old, even the cranky toddlers. Then, after one night, the child began to peek out in everyone's eyes, and then the child would get more bold, and by the third day—who was minding the store? Merriment was rampant. Silliness was de rigueur and *joie de vivre* was splashed everywhere like the aftermath of a water fight.

During the day, many of the people staying at the lodge went hiking, horseback riding, canoeing on Swiftcurrent Lake (canoes could be rented by the hour), or driving the Going to the Sun Road that cut from east to west through the park.

The first time they drove the road in the rental car with Mr. Tyler at the wheel, yes, the views were beyond the farthest reaches of any superlative. But, except for occasional glances, who dared look? There might be fairly substantial-looking guardrails along the roadsides where there was a sheer thousand foot drop on the other side. But none of them was fooled.

"Who are they kidding?" her father mumbled at one particularly precipitous cliff edge at a sharp bend in the road he was guiding the car around. "Those guardrails have got to be about as good as life vests on airplanes—"

No one laughed. It wasn't funny.

They expressed appropriate amazement at all the breathless vistas, as in Julie had to keep reminding herself to breathe between stabs of panic. She also found herself automatically leaning away from each terrifying plunge, depending on which side of the car it was on.

Once returned to Many Glacier Lodge for lunch, the three of them stumbled across the parking lot and into the lodge like people just arrived from a hundred-mile march fraught with dangers at every turn (and they hadn't?).

They drove the Going to the Sun Road quite a few times after that, each time enjoying more and more of the spectacular scenery, and minding less and less the precipitous plunges alongside the road. They began to stop at various places along the way where a short hike through the woods would deliver them to some hidden paradise—a still lake fringed with mountain flowers, gorges where the water roared through with a Godlike ferocity, waterfalls that rippled and rushed, and trails that wandered through the woods along a sweet meandering stream.

There was one particular natural attraction that they stopped at repeatedly. It was called the Weeping Wall because of the water that poured from hundreds of openings, vents, in the craggy rock face and wept in a steady mourning stream down its sorrowing side. It created its own current of cool air that played with stray tendrils of hair and coated their faces with its icy breath. They must have stayed for close to an hour on their first visit. Hey, there was no place they *had* to be, except where they were. The Weeping Wall never lost its attraction, maybe because, after the year they'd just had, they knew exactly how it felt. They could look it squarely in the face.

Nights at the lodge were special, too, but the complete opposite of days. Days were all about the vast outdoors and the infinitude of space. Nights were all about cozy comfort, turning inward, reentering the womb. There was always a delicious meal to be had in the lodge's dining room, its walls fitted out with moose heads, displays of grizzly bear teeth and arrowheads, Indian blankets, deer antlers, and other Rocky Mountain paraphernalia. A fire built of huge logs always raged in an open fireplace in the great room (nights were always chilly).

After dark, everyone congregated in the great room, nestling into chairs reading, mingling and laughing in groups, writing postcards, or pursuing whatever pastimes pleased. Did just gazing into the fire count? Few people returned to their rooms until bedtime. They were, strictly speaking, it occurred to Julie, only the most recent generation of man to seek company and security in numbers around a campfire during the edgy darkness of night. TVs were banned at the lodge. Not so cell phones, laptops, blackberries, iPods, and other black plastic things that connected one with the outside world. Still such devices were not in much evidence. The *present* wasn't welcome. It could just wait outside the stockade of wilderness and sit on its haunches, waiting to pounce on lodge guests when they willingly, on their own terms, emerged from the park's confines.

Julie's mother had gotten it wrong. People didn't dress for dinner. Guests at the lodge hadn't done that since the 1960s, since hippie-dom had put the kibosh on formality. But people did seem to spruce up a little, especially those who'd spent the day hiking trails, canoeing, or engaging in some other sweaty pursuit. Julie's mother was definitely not up for rigorous exercise. She was still technically recovering from her cancer and its treatment. Julie had, at least temporarily, found that the high altitude had sapped her energy for activities she might otherwise have enjoyed. It took her several days to stop feeling dizzy and nauseous every time she moved.

Mr. Tyler, one day, decided to go along on one of the all-day hikes led by one of the lodge's trained mountain guides. He set off in high spirits but returned a humbled man. He was covered with scrapes. (And why hadn't he worn trousers and a long-sleeved shirt as her mother had suggested?) The insect community seemed to have found him a particularly delectable treat. He was covered with insect bites representing the whole gamut of the local mountain insect community. (And why hadn't he taken insect repellant with him, as Mrs. Tyler had suggested? He had, but it must have fallen out of his pocket on the first tough ascent of the hike.) He'd also lost his hat. (It'd fallen off and tumbled into some deep place reachable only by "winged animals, mountain goats, or men with ropes," he explained in a disgusted voice.) So, his forehead and the top of his scalp where the hair was thinning were painfully sunburned and pimpled with insect bites. He was a mess.

The absolutely worst part for him, however, had been the need for him to wear a "stupid bell on a stupid cord" around his neck for the entire hike—to "shoo bears with bad attitudes away," he grumbled. He hadn't worn a bell since he was a toddler learning how to walk. "It was mortifying." That was his final pronouncement on the whole experience.

If he'd seen anything wondrous beyond all telling, he wasn't talking. He'd apparently been too busy crawling up and down steep inclines and declines and swatting insects. Julie and her mother didn't drill him for details. Perhaps they would dribble out of their own accord over time.

At supper that night he ordered a double scotch, straight up. And then Julie started to laugh—she couldn't help it—her father was such a sight. The top of his head and face were raspberry red. Her mother'd put some kind of ointment on the worst scrapes, giving them an oozing look. And then there were the painful red weals of the insect bites. She couldn't help it. Her father's face reminded her of Oscar-winning makeup for a movie about some world-ending pandemic.

Her father wasn't amused, and Julie could understand that, but he also wasn't annoyed. He could take a joke, just not right now. Mrs. Tyler, too, was struggling to keep a straight face, as a loyal wife should. Treasonous tears of mirth rolled down her cheeks, however. And, then, just as her father was taking his first deep quaff of scotch, he was jolted by a slap on his back, and a strong, young male voice saying "You did pretty good out there, Mr. Tyler."

At which Julie's mother could no longer contain her laughter. "You could've fooled me—" was all she could get out before she went into gales of laughter at the young man's comment. At this Mr. Tyler did smile a reluctant smile. You had to see the humor in it. It was funny.

The young man who'd administered the purely congratulatory slap was, apparently, the guide who'd led the hike. One look at the young man and Julie was in love. Her dad had mentioned his name—Richard—a nice strong name, as in Richard the Lionheart. He was medium height, tanned, and well-muscled. His tanned forearms, visible beyond the rolled up sleeves of his white Oxford shirt, were a testament to his strength. His hair was a dark blond and bleached in places by the sun. (It was now slicked back. He must have just climbed out of the shower, Julie thought, allowing an image of his naked body emerging from the shower stall to slide sleekly through her brain....) He had blue-gray eyes that smiled, a straight nose, lips that said he had a sensitive nature, and a chin that said he had a sensible nature. It was a face that, to Julie, combined all the best human qualities a girl (woman?) would want.

And then his eyes met hers. Time stopped for a second, while her mother went on with her merriment. The small smile he gave her was meant solely for her, as was hers for him. The moment was soon over, and he was gone, over to a table where sat other college students who worked summers at the park. Included among them were some very attractive co-eds, and they all seemed to be enlivened by his appearance at the table. That was the first time Julie's heart had been broken. "And so soon?!" as their neighbor Tilda Stein would have said.

CHAPTER 47

Enter Richard the Lionheart

That night Julie awoke in the deep silence of the darkness that enveloped the lodge and its sleeping inhabitants. Every room had its own balcony, so each room had its own private "passageway" to the outdoors. Julie's room was on the first floor and opened out onto the broad deck and, beyond that, Swiftcurrent Lake. Suddenly, she had this irresistible urge to put on her bathrobe and slippers and go out onto the deck. Something had bidden her to do so, as though to have done otherwise would have given offense.

With no large cities or even large towns for miles in any direction, the stars had the sky to themselves. There was no moon, either, to steal the show. By day things terrestrial held sway. By night even the towering mountain peaks, whose dark profiles Julie could just make out against the star-lit background, seemed apologetically small. Julie could feel the immensity of what she beheld in her chest, of all places. It was probably because, by comparison, it was the only cavity in her body where she could "feel" the immensity of the universe. And by extension, she in her pink bathrobe and fuzzy pink slippers felt puny, like an ant, maybe even a paramecium, in the presence of the celestial display.

Remembering her thoughts of the night of the mother-daughter dinner, she wondered what distant star had been added to the firmament that night. And then there had to be a star for Nutcracker Sunday and her birthday at The Yorkshire and even a whole constellation forming during their two weeks at Glacier National Park.

But what about gangs and gangfights? The treachery of schoolmates? Cancer? Escaped, drug-dealing murderess mothers? Septic shock? Wrongful accusations of rape? Oh, but of course, Julie thought, that was what the black holes were for. They were the toilets of the universe down which the "feces" of life were flushed.

And then her thoughts turned back to the sublime. What about the silence of the heavens? What could she say, even think, about it that wouldn't be a rude noise. It was the hushed, immense silence of the divine.

Just at this point in her musings, she heard a low rumbling growl. It could have been God, or it could have been a grizzly bear. Either was a warning to leave the night and its mysteries to itself. Had she, maybe, like Moses, strayed onto holy ground?

She was speedily indoors and back in bed with a beating heart, her bedroom door firmly shut. It would be a good story to tell her children some day. And this Richard? Wouldn't he make a nice father for her one-day children? Oh, but he was off limits. She'd found out later that night, by pure stealth, that staff were not supposed to fraternize with guests. Nonetheless, Julie fell asleep wearing the silly grin of foolish young love. Or was it so silly and foolish and young?

Two days later, she was to have her first chance to find out. Maybe there was a strict rule about staff not mingling with guests, but it was not breaking the rules for this Richard, in the line of duty as one of the lodge's wilderness guides, to take her out in a canoe and teach her the correct way to paddle a canoe.

Actually, the way it happened was too funny. It was midmorning and she and her parents were lazing away on the deck reading, with their three feet forming their convivial triangle on the wooden footstool. Julie had started reading *Crime and Punishment,* an ambitious undertaking for a 16-year-old, but the story had nonetheless totally swallowed up her attention. Suddenly she heard this loud "Hi!" She was just at the part of the book where Raskolnikov has just killed the landlady and stolen her money, and someone has just entered the hallway, and his perfectly planned, awful, crime is, maybe, about to be discovered.

Nabbed! She'd been caught by the tsar's police, and she'd soon be on her way to Siberia, or worse. She shrieked. It took her parents by surprise, but not the calm, controlled Richard who looked down upon them, and on her, with a soft, though puzzled, smile on his face.

"What are you reading?" he asked "'The Fall of the House of Usher'?"

"Well, actually," she explained, "I'm reading *Crime and Punishment* and I was just at the part where...."

"Raskolnikov has just killed the landlady, and...." He paused and changed direction in his thinking, "you shouldn't be reading such a serious book on such a beautiful day." He said the last in an almost tender voice.

With that, he reached over, gently pulled the book from her hands, and said "Have you ever been in a canoe?"

"No," she said simply. "The most I've done with boats is to float paper ones down the gutter after a thunderstorm." It was the complete truth.

Richard grinned at her response. "Would you like to learn how to float in a *real* boat?" he asked teasingly, invitingly.

"Anything to escape the tsar's police," she said, pleased that she'd come up with such a good quip on such short notice. Her parents were smiling, too, though for a slightly different reason. And Julie, she was suddenly feeling like a carbonated drink, all the way down to her toes.

The next thing Julie knew, as if conveyed by angels (her feet were surely not up to the task), she found herself skimming along the still surface of Swiftcurrent Lake. The surface was so smooth that it perfectly mirrored the surrounding landscape. It made her laugh, and she called back to Richard, who felt like this "presence" behind her, "I think this is the best way of climbing the mountains."

"You mean you're not going to come on the hike I'm leading tomorrow?" he called back, sounding genuinely disappointed.

"And come back looking like my father?" She had to challenge him on that score.

"Well, hey, it's got to be better than *Crime and Punishment* and being sent to Siberia."

"Hmmm, maybe," she said. Her reply wasn't meant to be teasing. She really wasn't sure she had it in her to undertake a strenuous hike. She'd also done few serious wilderness-type activities. And she'd never done so in the company of someone she thought she might be feeling the stirrings of love for.

"Do I have to wear a bell?" she asked next, still bartering for time while she deliberated more about her answer.

"No," Richard responded simply. "But you will have to, the whole time, sing 'row, row, row your boat merrily down the stream!'"

With that he began to paddle like mad, splashing and thrashing the water with his paddle, and driving the canoe in a rather frenzied zigzag course. Fortunately, they were in pretty shallow water. Julie joined in. She paddled hard, and picked up in the right place in the song to create the perfect round of happy children. They competed over who could paddle the fastest and splashiest and who could sing the loudest. Richard won in the first two categories, but Julie surprised even herself with her clear, strong soprano voice.

"Julie," he said in a wondrous voice after they'd tired of the contest, "you have a beautiful voice. Are you in your college glee club?"

College? A little 'oh, oh' sounded in her head. "Well, to be honest," she said, "neither—"

She peered back at him and was met by an appropriately puzzled look. "I'm not in college yet. I'm just starting my sophomore year in high school," she said in a quiet, but *not* timid, voice. Was there something she should have said (signed?) before they stepped into the canoe together?

If there was a flicker of uncertainty in Richard's eyes, she couldn't see it. And she knew for certain there was no flicker of uncertainty in hers.

They'd stopped paddling at this point, and the canoe drifted in the lake's cold currents, as if wondering why all the fun had stopped.

Richard only said sweetly "and your other reason?"

For a moment Julie was confused. What other reason was she giving him about what? "Oh—" she said, a little flustered, finally getting her bedizened thoughts back on solid ground. "Because choir practice is at the same time as field hockey practice." It was true.

"Well, then," Richard got a beaming smile on his face. "If you play field hockey, then you've got enough strength in your legs to also come on my beginner's rock climbing hike the day after tomorrow." He finished his words with a triumphant grin, as though he'd just won a gold medal in the smart aleck event.

Julie didn't know whether her heart was beating faster with love or fear, at the real possibility of falling off a cliff, or at the already-real possibility of falling *hard* in love, only to have her heart broken at the bottom of the chasm.

Richard resumed his paddling with a deep, forceful thrust of his paddle into the lake, which Julie felt solidly in the small of her back. It felt nice.

CHAPTER 48

Another Great Day to be Alive

They continued to explore the nooks and crannies of the shoreline for another half hour or so. Even though this was the first time they'd been together, it didn't seem necessary to fill in all the silences, to jabber away continuously. Besides, it was hard to converse in a canoe. The seating arrangement wasn't conducive to talk.

"It's a great day to be alive," Julie heard Richard say over the background din of birds and insects going about their late-summer tasks on shore.

"Yes, it is," Julie agreed. And then suddenly, unexpectedly, she found herself swallowed up in a vortex of memories of the preceding winter and spring. She'd gone from paradise to hell in a heartbeat. Her throat clogged up with emotion, and she couldn't talk.

There in the sunlight on the satiny sheen of water surrounded by all the mini-miracles of high-mountain wilderness, she was mired in the stinking filth of all the wrongs life had recently dealt out. She wasn't on Swiftcurrent Lake. She was in some kind of pit—cesspool—that she couldn't get out of.

And then she felt a hand on her back and a voice from right behind her. She started. It was Richard, who'd crept forward very carefully, and expertly, so as not to capsize the canoe.

"Julie, what's wrong?" Concern was in every line of his face and in his beautiful blue-gray eyes when she turned to look back at him.

Then Julie remembered where she was and who she was with. And the touch of his hand on her back? It was just enough to trigger a deluge of tears that she couldn't stanch, try as she might. They just kept flowing and flowing. She hung her head in her lap. She felt such a fool. And here she was with this lovely young man whom she was just getting to know, whom she wanted to impress. And, instead, she'd become another watery attraction at Glacier National Park.

Finally, with a mighty effort, she stopped her tears. She still couldn't talk yet, but she could swallow and keep more emotion from welling up in her chest. Richard handed her a clean white handkerchief. She'd begun to sniff and her face was wet with tears.

"Here," he said softly. "This might help."

"Thanks," Julie said, and as she used it to wipe away the tears on her face, and those still clinging to her eyelashes, she tried to crack a joke to make light of her tears. "This will help keep us from having to bail out the boat."

Richard smiled but he didn't laugh. "What about my saying this is a beautiful day to be alive made you cry?" he asked, then waited for an answer.

"Oh, goodness," Julie said. "It really is too beautiful a day to mess it up with my stupid story."

"Julie," Richard replied, "you just wept an inordinate amount of tears for some kind of stupid sorrow." Now he waited, right behind her back, for her story. She could even feel his warm breath on the nape of her neck. There was no escape, and, honestly, right now she didn't know if she wanted one.

And so Julie was "forced" to tell him the story of her horrible year. She left out many of the details. It really was too beautiful a day to dwell on all the nooks and crannies of the dark days of her year that, she'd thought, anyway, were far to the rear of the present moment.

Richard listened patiently, not interrupting, just let her empty herself of her story.

"So," Julie said, to wrap up the abbreviated version of her tale "You can see why today is a good day to be alive. It's an especially good day because my mother is still alive."

This pronouncement, as she turned to look at the young

man, was met by a look of sorrow in the guide's eyes. He looked down as if to hide it from Julie. He, quite clearly, had a sad story, too.

Julie said "Okay, I've told you my sad story, now it's your turn to tell me yours."

"What makes you think I have a story to tell?" He looked up with a small grin.

"Because I can see chapter 1 in your left eye and chapter 42 in your right. So there are 40 chapters in between." She touched the bridge of his nose with her index finger to show him where those chapters were probably filed. The bone beneath was like lovely hard marble, and he didn't flinch in the least.

Richard grinned again. "Tell you what," he said. "Since it's late, and we need to get back, I'll tell you my sad story tomorrow on the trail."

"That's blackmail!" Julie protested.

"No, it's just, as they say in Hollywood, a cliffhanger," he replied as he made his way carefully back to his end of the canoe.

"It's extortion! A criminal offense—a federal crime with a minimum 10-year prison sentence!" Julie continued to shout at Richard's retreating, laughing form.

Totally ignoring her protests, he began, once again, to sing at the top of his voice "row, row, row your boat merrily down the stream!"

That left Julie no choice but to join in on the round. And it was thus that they returned to the dock at Many Glaciers Lodge, two little kids having a merrily happy time.

That night Richard was to show the true measure of his worth.

It was after dinner and a lovely mild evening. Twilight was bestowing its lavender blue mantle over the landscape. It was also a wonderful *evening* to be alive, when suddenly there were shouts and screams coming from out in the middle of the lake.

Julie, leaning against the railing of the deck and looking

out across the lake, had seen three of the college student staff, two girls and a fellow, go out in a canoe. It was too late for guests to rent a canoe, but apparently it was okay for staff to go out onto the large lake off hours.

Julie was alone. Her parents were off, she didn't know where. She was, no surprise, thinking about Richard and feeling sad, for now one extra reason, that their vacation would be over in three days. Shouts interrupted her reverie.

The canoe the three staff members were in had capsized way out in the middle of the lake. Foolishly, Julie had noticed dimly beyond the curtain of her thoughts, one of the two girls had stood up in the canoe and started to do a silly (make that stupid) dance, which was promptly ended with the girl falling into the lake and upturning the canoe in the process.

The problem was that the guests couldn't come to their aid. They were helpless. The canoe paddles were locked in a large wooden locker. Julie'd noticed the three unlock the padlock and collect two paddles—no lifejackets—and then lock it before setting out in the canoe. Julie knew, because Richard had told her, that the lake was especially deep where they were and that he was avoiding it that day because there were a lot of crazy currents—as in swift currents, thus the name of the lake—there that he felt might be too much for her to handle. Julie also knew, because she'd swept her hand in it several times while they were canoeing, that the lake water was icy cold. The three college students were in serious trouble.

Someone must have gone and gotten lodge staff because all of a sudden four people emerged on the run from a door that led from the undercroft of the lodge. One of the four was Richard. But they, too, were helpless when they got to the dock and found the locker locked. Apparently the only person with a key to the padlock was one of the students who were now shrieking for help in the middle of the lake.

It was Richard who took charge of the situation. He grabbed the edge of the locker lid and gave it a mighty pull. He yanked and yanked on it, until in the anxious silence the guests on the deck had fallen into, they could hear the glorious sound of splintering wood. He'd managed to splinter the wood of the locker's lid. Everyone sent up a cheer. The four soon had paddles and life jackets and set out in two canoes. They paddled furiously, no funny game about this. And they soon returned with three wet, shivering, frightened, and very sorry young people.

Richard became the man of the hour. Everyone cheered and clapped as he strode manfully along the dock and back through the door that led to the undercroft of the lodge. He was clearly discomfited by all the attention. He didn't look at the crowd. Just shrugged his shoulders and waved his hand as if to say his heroic actions were nothing.

Julie was very proud of him. He was a hero. But she was also proud that he showed not a bit of pride, which meant that she would have to carefully select the right moment to praise him for his deed. He was definitely her kind of man.

On a less commendable note, was it wrong to be not just a little glad that the two rescued girls were the ones whom, she'd noticed, were the most conspicuously flirtatious with him?

That night she slept with his handkerchief, which she'd forgotten to give back to him, under her pillow. In fact, she never remembered to give it back to him.

CHAPTER 49

Climb Every Mountain

Julie's parents also witnessed the rescue and Richard's role in it. "He seems a fine young man," her father commented later on that evening. That was very high praise from a father who would only surrender his daughter from his protection to a white knight, preferably a crown prince, on a white charger.

The next day was the hike, and Julie didn't come back looking like her father. Anything but. She found she was quite nimble and sure-footed and in her element on the hike. And, yes, field hockey had made her legs strong. Unlike the five other lodge guests along on the hike, she hadn't needed a hand up on any of the difficult stretches. In fact, she found herself helping some of the less able hikers at these places—though she was a little sorry to miss out on an occasional assist from Richard.

"Are you sure you've never done any hiking like this?" he kept asking her.

"Well, there are five years in my life that are unaccounted for. And when I returned from wherever I'd been, all I wanted to do was yodel," she responded to one such query.

Richard laughed. "That explains why you're 16 going on 21 in the maturity category."

"Should I take that as a compliment?" Julie asked seriously.

"Yes," he answered.

'Whew' Julie thought. She'd had a gnawing concern about the age difference.

"Sorrows do that to people," Richard said even more seriously, obviously thinking of *his* sorrows that awaited telling. But there was no good time to talk, not with five other people who were continuously asking how much longer the hike would be, when could they have lunch, when would they start climbing down rather than up, etc. One woman even asked, seriously, if there was a helicopter service she could contact on her cell phone to come and pick her up.

"Richard," (Was that the very first time she'd spoken his name out loud?) "Don't forget you owe me your sad story," she reminded him once when they were relatively alone on the trail.

He looked around at their five charges, and then mumbled "not until the children are in bed."

"Don't worry. I'm a patient person," she quipped. Five children?? Hmmm.

He turned and gave her a soft smile. "That sets my mind at rest. I'll sleep better tonight knowing that," he finished with a grin.

'What?!' Julie thought but fortunately didn't say. 'You're not going to be lying awake thinking of me all night long like I'm going to be doing thinking of you?'

Soon the trail leveled off at a place level with the tops of many of the surrounding peaks.

"They look like islands in an immense blue sea," Julie breathed to no one in particular, as she beheld the magnificent view. It was true. The valley floors were either lost in a blue mist or had an aquamarine lake at their bottom.

At one point their hike took them near one of the glaciers that swept like a frozen torrent down the mountain, but then that's exactly what it was!

One place was known for its echoes. Everyone tried it and was met with a rapid-fire repetition of their calls that dwindled out in the far distance, as in maybe Chicago.

"Sing, Julie," Richard called out.

Sing? What could she sing? What song did she know all the words to. Well, there was one, but was this the right time and place for it? She started it on one note, but found it was too low a key, so she started it again in a more comfortable soprano range. She sang it from beginning to end, every verse of it. She'd never actually sung it. Gloria had that day after the blizzard in the hallway at school, and she'd later asked her for the words.

Nobody knows the troubles I've seen.
Nobody knows but Jesus.
Nobody knows the troubles I've seen.
Glory, hallelujah.

Nobody knows....

After she was done, after the final echo had reached Chicago, there was only silence, and there were tears in everyone's eyes, including Richard's. It would appear that all seven of them had had a rotten year.

They had their lunch and then began the long hike back down. Everyone was glad to finally reach the lodge, including Julie. It'd been quite a workout. Surprisingly, despite all their complaining en route, all five whining hikers seemed quite pleased with themselves for what they'd accomplished that day. A couple, who hadn't known each other at the beginning of the trek, even laughingly patted each other on the back.

Julie couldn't wait to shower and get into clean clothes. She had to rush. Her parents were waiting for her in the great room of the lodge. She opened her closet to look for something clean, not too wrinkled, and attractive.... The only item of clothing that met all three criteria was the seafoam green linen dress she'd worn the night of her birthday dinner at The Yorkshire. She put it and the patent leather heels on. The pearl pendant, too.

When Richard walked by their table at dinner that night, all he did was gape at the lovely creature sitting with Maw and Paw Tyler. He grinned foolishly from ear to ear as he turned to look back at her with admiring eyes, in the process almost knocking over a waiter carrying a tray loaded with dishes heaped with food.

Julie really hadn't worn the dress as a feminine ploy. It *was* the only decent thing she had to wear that night. She'd probably have worn the dress even if Richard had been a pimply-faced jerk—maybe not.

That night Julie wrote the following entry in her diary, which she'd been faithfully keeping.

> *I don't know what to write tonight. Make that I'm <u>afraid</u> to describe my day and my feelings. Like I'd ever forget them anyway! I guess it's enough to say that I know what I feel is the real thing, but I'm also afraid of what I feel. Richard is in college in California, 3,000 miles away from where I live. And he wants to go to medical school and become a trauma surgeon. And I've only just started high school and I have no idea what I want to study in college. Medicine? And I still have to hear his sad story. I wonder what it is? Maybe I'll find out tomorrow, since it'll only be the two of us. How nice that no one else has signed up for the "climb," as Richard calls it.*

With that she went to bed and fell soundly asleep. (She didn't stay awake all night thinking of Richard as she'd expected.) Her alarm went off at 7 o'clock. She was to meet Richard by the registration desk at 8, and then they were to set off for the rock faces. (He was going to bring some kind of breakfasty food, plus lunch.) She was not a little terrified of hanging from a rope with thousands of feet of nothingness to potentially fall through. But there was something about the way Richard handled himself that told her she had nothing to fear.

As she climbed out of bed, she saw that a white envelope had been stuck under her door. It was a note from Richard saying that his twin sister Becka had died after a long battle with leukemia. He had to go home to Philadelphia for her funeral and wouldn't be coming back to the park. He needed to spend some time with his family after the funeral. He was very sorry to have to cancel the climb. Also, he hoped she didn't mind, but he'd gotten her address and phone number from the registration desk, and he'd be in touch once things settled down. No return address, telephone number, cell phone number, or e-mail address. He was just Richard Egan somewhere in Philadelphia. Sure she could have probably easily tracked him down via the Internet. Just Googled the obituary for Becka (Rebecca?) Egan, aged 20, in Philadelphia. But that didn't seem the right thing to do. It seemed kind of underhanded—too much like an Alexandra Riley-Dolan ploy.

Richard had his very justifiable grief, but Julie had hers as well. The sun had now gone out of her day, and her heart. So she crept back into bed, pulled the covers up over her head, and went back to sleep.

The rock climbing would have been cancelled anyway. It was a cold rainy morning. Good. It matched Julie's mood.

She explained to her parents, who were surprised to see her come drooping to their table at breakfast, what had happened. Her mother was mostly silently sympathetic. Her father? He was a babbling brook of platitudes.

"You and Richard are just kids. You both need time to grow up and find out who you are first."

'I know who I am, and so does Richard,' Julie thought back.

"You only spent, what, 8 hours with the young man. That's not enough time on which to base much of a relationship."

'Yes it is,' she thought back hotly to her father. And since when had he become a marriage counselor?

And then there'd been the real corker.

"I don't know about a good-looking young fellow like that. Good looks aren't everything. It's probably all for the best that things didn't work out. It seemed to me that he had every co-ed in the lodge after him."

'True,' Julie thought, 'but he hadn't gone after them. And who was her father to talk about the dangers of good-looking men??'

And, then, dah, Julie figured out what her father was trying to do. It was his way of consoling her. He was giving Richard a bad rap, deploying ways to lessen her feelings of hurt and disappointment.

And then her mother spoke. It seemed to her from Richard's note (written in a very masculine bold and angular script, she had to say), and, yes, Julie had let both her parents read it, that his promise to get in touch with her wasn't as vague as Julie was making it out to be. It seemed to voice a clear intention of contacting her. Also, here was a young man whose twin sister has just died. And whose grief, therefore, must be particularly deep. However, despite that, he had made the effort to get Julie's contact information, which probably was somewhat against the rules, something such a person of seemingly good character wouldn't do unless his feelings for her were "ardent."

Mrs. Tyler's choice of the word "ardent" gave Julie's spirit a lift.

They fell silent for a spell, and then her father slapped his thighs, stood up, and said "Who's up for another spin on the Going to the Sun Road?"

The sun had come out and the day was now fine. They were all up for the ride!

CHAPTER 50

Condolences and Consolations

Julie did, with her mother's decided approval, get Richard's address in Philadelphia at the manager's office so that she could send him a sympathy card. But a sympathy card was not to be had in Glacier National Park where postcards were the order of the day. Julie decided on a blank note card with a photo of the weeping wall on it. But, drats, now she had to come up with something appropriately consoling. After many rough drafts she finally sent him the following note, feeling totally insecure about every word she wrote, feeling as though any future with him depended, like a climbing rope, on every word she wrote.

Dear Richard,

I was so sorry to hear of your twin sister's death. I imagine a twin is more than just a sibling. They're more like an alter self, and that must double the sorrow you feel. I wish I had words that could heal your grief, but since I don't, I'm hoping that the echoes of the song I sang yesterday on the mountain will reach you in Philadelphia. The spiritual consoled me during a particularly difficult time last winter. I hope it will console you, too. You and your family are in my and my parents' prayers. Of course, my parents send their condolences as well.

Most sincerely,

Julie Tyler

P.S. I hope that you don't mind that I got your address from the manager's office.

P.P.S. I was also sorry to miss the rock climbing, especially after I'd spent two hours on the Internet last night looking for the nearest helicopter rescue service. (Just kidding.)

Why did she feel, when she dropped the note into the mailbox, as if she'd dropped her heart in instead?

*****

Two months went by, and she heard nothing from Richard. Her heart got out of the habit of leaping out of her throat every time the phone rang and sinking into her stomach when the mail arrived with no letter from him. School started. She once again was the top scorer on the field hockey team. It was good to have daily contact with Gloria, Jane, and her other friends. Friendship was a good salve to her sorry heart, although she hadn't given up hoping to hear from Richard.

There was only one particularly momentous event during that time. One night her father came home ashen faced. He had terrible news. A man by the name of Cowper had shot himself in the head during an arraignment in federal court in a nearby city where he was facing a charge for income tax evasion. He owed *thousands* of dollars to the IRS. It was, had to be, Alexis's father. He was the right age, and Cowper was not a common name. Would either Alexis or her mother care? Could they muster up any kind of sorrow except for being thwarted in carrying out evil deeds?

About the same time, word filtered around the school that Alexis's mother had married a multimillionaire, and she was now living in a huge mansion overlooking the ocean in Palm Beach, Florida. (Julie guessed that it'd been a very short period of mourning for both mother and daughter.) Alexis'd told her old "buddies" that she called her new father grandpa, because he was so much older than her mother. Fifty years older. His children were not happy about the marriage, but "oh well." Best of all, "grandpa" was paying for *all* of her friends to come and spend their winter vacation with her in Florida. The best part of the story, from Julie's point of view, was that Alexis's new, adopted, name was Bilbenbergerstein. Alexis Bilbenbergerstein. It had a nice ring to it. And, no, she was not able *not* to tell her parents the latest in the ongoing saga of Alexandra Riley-Dolan Cowper Bilbenbergerstein. And, yes, they had a good chuckle over her new surname, too.

"It couldn't happen to a better person," her father observed dryly.

"Well, but just like all good cats, that woman surely always lands on her feet," her mother commented.

Julie ended the discussion with "Snakes don't have feet, Mom."

Oh, and Mr. Hennessey had not returned to Ainsworth as a teacher that year. No one knew why, though Julie had her satisfied suspicions.

****

The first Saturday in November the phone rang about 10 o'clock in the evening. Her father answered it as he did all late-night calls.

"Julie, it's for you," he called softly up the stairs. Expecting it to be one of her knuckleheaded friends who hadn't yet learned how to tell time, she picked up the phone in her bedroom and said "'ello" in her best Cockney-ish accent. "What the blarney are ye' callin' me at this hour fer?" It wasn't a friend. It was Richard.

At first she didn't know who it was. All she could hear was this person laughing.

"Curlytop, are you ever serious?"

There was only one person who could call her Curlytop and live. Richard, once, on the hike at Glacier National Park.

An hour later, when she got off the phone, she couldn't honestly remember most of what they'd talked about. But she knew they'd talked about a lot of things. He, about the card she'd sent and how much her words had meant to him. Also a lot about his sister, his only sibling—what she was like, what it was like growing up a twin, and, yes, this was the sad story he "owed" her. He was back at Stanford in Los Angeles, had started school on time, "but I wasn't too focused on my studies for the first month." Julie could identify with that. She could also reassure him that it would only be temporary.

Julie? She knew she'd talked a lot, about school and such. Richard asked her how field hockey was going, and she just said "I'm expecting them to retire my number when I graduate." He laughed. (She loved his laugh.) He knew from that that his Curlytop was beating the pants off every opposing team. They also exchanged e-mail addresses, and promised to correspond on a regular basis.

And then it became a custom (tradition!) that he called her every Saturday night at exactly 10 o'clock, her time. It was her mother who explained the significance of that. "This is his way of telling *you* that he's not out on a date, and of ascertaining that you're not out on a date, either."

"Oh—" Julie had responded. She could tell from the glow on her mother's face that she was happy for her only daughter. In fact, her mother'd had a special glow about her since their vacation in Glacier National Park. And then Julie found out that it was more than the healthy effects of the clean mountain air. Her mother was four months' pregnant! That would mean that she had conceived during their two weeks in the mountains....

Mrs. Tyler, who'd just told Julie her news as the two were cleaning up in the kitchen after supper, knew her daughter too well not to know that she was doing some quick calculations in her head. "Well, Julie, *you* were the one who bought me those filmy nightgowns, when I only asked for underwear," at which she went beet red.

"Mom, you told me to bring my *flannel* pajamas," Julie pointed out to her. It was true, and her mother'd been quite insistent about it.

Her mother's only response was "I had an alternative heat source."

At that, they heard her father let out a loud bark of laughter in the living room, where he was reading the newspaper.

They looked at each other and burst out laughing. It was

too funny.

So, Julie was going to have a sibling. So, was that a good thing or a bad thing?

She told Richard the good news by e-mail that night.

He responded that pregnancies were known to occur quite frequently after stays at the lodges in the park. Indeed, many of the women had had problems with infertility prior to their visit. There was even a name for it—Glacier Gravida, but she'd have to look *gravida* up. He wasn't going to give her the definition. According to *Webster's*, it meant 'a pregnant woman.'

Poor Mona, Julie's mother. Didn't Julie tell just about everyone in the family the correct name for her mother's condition? Her father thought it was tremendously funny. Her mother only found it politely amusing, but she was a good sport about the ribbing she got. Last year it'd been poor Dollie; this year it was her.

CHAPTER 51

The Second Annual Mother–Daughter Dinner

Despite the fact that she was going on five months' pregnant, Mrs. Tyler was still able to wear the silver-gray jersey dress she'd worn for last year's mother–daughter dinner, *sans* the belt . . . (Like she was going to buy two new dresses in one year?)

It was a joyous evening (a celebration!) from beginning to end. No misgivings about her mother's plainness to disturb her peace of mind. No near traffic ticket from Officer Ward. No Alexis and Alexandra Cowper, and *no* unpitted black olive–mined bean salad!! The Orange Dragon bowl, of course, was history. No entertainment compliments of the Dawsons. Instead Gloria gloriously sang a selection of Negro spirituals, with her grandmother accompanying her on the piano! (Dawn Dawson and her mother *were* there, with their perfect rhinoplastied noses out of joint . . .) Her mother made a quadruple batch of praline cookies, so there was no mad scramble for cookies this year, although that had been fun last year. The Tylers, the Jacksons, and the Webbs sat at the same table, like last year, except that now they were all old friends. And this year the Jacksons spent the night with the Tylers. Night-time journeys into their part of town would always be dangerous. And, oh yes, Mrs. Tyler had just gotten a clean bill of health from Smitty's, and no, Julie didn't have the screwed up BRCA gene. And the *pièce de résistance* of the evening? Her mother's announcement that there was to be another Tyler daughter. She'd just found out the sex that day. Joy (the name her mother and father had already decided on) would be making her grand entrance in early May. Julie couldn't wait. They'd be Joy and Julie

She also couldn't wait for Christmas. Richard would be

spending it with her and her family. His parents were still grieving over the death of his sister and had decided to spend the holiday in Rome, more specifically in the precincts of St. Peter's. (Richard was also conveniently Catholic.) Would he still like (love?) her after he'd met her entire family? "What's not to like?" as their neighbor Tilda Stein would say.

Watch for the sequel to ***The Orange Dragon Bowl***, titled ***Labors of Love (and hate)***, which will be out within the year.

Made in the USA
Monee, IL
23 July 2021